ACROSS THE WALL

ALSO BY GARTH NIX

Sabriel

Lirael

Abhorsen

Shade's Children

The Ragwitch

GARTH NIX

ACROSS THE WALL

A TALE OF THE ABHORSEN AND OTHER STORIES

An Imprint of HarperCollins*Publishers*

Across the Wall: A Tale of the Abhorsen and other stories
Copyright © 2005 by Garth Nix

"Nicholas Sayre and the Creature in the Case": Copyright © 2005 by Garth Nix. First published for World Book Day 2005 by HarperCollins Publishers, UK.
"Under the Lake": Copyright © 2001 by Garth Nix. First published in *The Magazine of Fantasy & Science Fiction* (USA), February 2001, USA.
"Charlie Rabbit": Copyright © 2005 by Garth Nix. First published in *Kids' Night In*, collected for War Child, HarperCollins Publishers, UK and Australia.
"From the Lighthouse": Copyright © 1996 by Garth Nix. First published in *Fantastic Worlds*, edited by Paul Collins, HarperCollins Publishers, Australia, 1998.
"The Hill": Copyright © 2001 by Garth Nix. First published in *X-Changes: Stories for a New Century*, Allen & Unwin, Australia.
"Lightning Bringer": Copyright © 2001 by Garth Nix. First published in *Love & Sex*, edited by Michael Cart, Simon & Schuster, USA, and on Salon.com.
"Down to the Scum Quarter": Copyright © 1987 by Garth Nix. First published in the magazines *Myths and Legends* (1987) and *Breakout!* (1988).
"Heart's Desire": Copyright © 2002 by Garth Nix. First published in *The Road to Camelot*, edited by Sophie Masson, Random House, Australia, and *The Magazine of Fantasy & Science Fiction*, January 2004, USA.
"Hansel's Eyes": Copyright © 2000 by Garth Nix. First published in *A Wolf at the Door*, edited by Ellen Datlow and Terri Windling, Simon & Schuster, 2000, USA.
"Hope Chest": Copyright © 2003 by Garth Nix. First published in *Firebirds*, edited by Sharyn November, Penguin 2003, USA.
"My New Really Epic Fantasy Series": Copyright © 1999 by Garth Nix.
"Three Roses": Copyright © 2000 by Garth Nix. First published in *Eidolon*, Autumn 2000, Australia.
"Endings": Copyright © 2004 by Garth Nix. First published in *Gothic! Ten Original Dark Tales*, edited by Deborah Noyes, Candlewick Press, USA.

All rights reserved. No part of this book may be used or reproduced in any manner whatsoever without written permission except in the case of brief quotations embodied in critical articles and reviews. Printed in the United States of America. For information address HarperCollins Children's Books, a division of HarperCollins Publishers, 1350 Avenue of the Americas, New York, NY 10019.
www.harperchildrens.com

Library of Congress Cataloging-in-Publication Data
Nix, Garth.
Across the Wall: A tale of the Abhorsen and other stories / Garth Nix. — 1st ed.
p. cm.
Summary: A collection of fantasy short stories plus a novella that is set in the world of the Abhorsen trilogy.
ISBN-10: 0-06-074715-3 (pbk.) — ISBN-13: 978-0-06-074715-2 (pbk.)
[1. Fantasy.] I. Title.
PZ7.N647 Ac 2005 2004028086
[Fic]—dc22 CIP
AC

Typography by Robert Hult
❖
First Eos paperback edition

To Anna, Thomas, and Edward
and
all my family and friends

CONTENTS

PREFACE

FOUR YEARS AGO, after a Christmas lunch, my younger brother passed around a very small "book" of four stapled-together pages that he said he'd found while helping my mother clean out a storage area under the family home. The book contained four stories written in shaky capital letters, with a couple of half-hearted illustrations done with colored pencils. On the front, it had "Stories" and "Garth Nix" in the handwriting one would expect from someone aged around six.

The stories included such gems as "The Coin Shower," which was very short and went something like:

a boy went outside
it started raining coins
he picked them up

I had no memory of this story or the little booklet, and at first I thought it had been fabricated by my brother as a joke, but my parents remembered me writing the stories and engaging in this bit of self-publishing at an early age.

I wrote "The Coin Shower" and the other stories in that collection about thirty-five years ago, and I've been writing ever since. Not always fiction, though. In my varied writing career I've written all kinds of things, from speeches for CEOs to brochures about brickworks to briefing papers on new Internet technologies.

I first got into print writing articles and scenarios for the role-playing games "Dungeons and Dragons" and "Traveler" when I was sixteen or seventeen. I wrote for magazines like *Multiverse* and *Breakout!* in Australia and *White Dwarf* in the United Kingdom. I tried to crack *Dragon* magazine in the United States, but never quite managed to sell them anything.

This minor success in getting role-playing game articles or scenarios into print led me to try my hand at getting some of my fiction published. I'd written quite a few stories here and there without success, but when I was nineteen years old, I wrote a whole lot more while I was traveling around the U.K. and Europe, broadening my horizons. I drove all over the place in a beat-up Austin 1600 with a small metal Silver-Reed typewriter in the backseat, a couple of notebooks, and lots of other people's books. Every day I'd write something in longhand in my notebook, and then that night or perhaps the next morning I'd type up what I'd written. (That established a writing practice that has continued for more than twenty years: I write most of my novels in longhand, typing up each chapter on the computer after I've got the first draft done in the latest black-and-red notebook. I now have more than twenty of these notebooks, plus one very out-of-place blue-and-white-striped notebook that I turned to during the stationery drought of 1996.)

I don't write everything in longhand first, though; sometimes I just take to the keyboard. Most of my short fiction begins with handwritten notes, and perhaps a few key sentences put down with my trusty Waterman fountain pen, but then I start typing. The pen comes into its own again later, when I print out the story, make my changes and corrections, and then go back to the computer. This process often occurs when I have only part of the story written. I quite often revise the first third or some small part of a story six or seven times before I've written the rest of it. Often the revision occurs because I have left the story incomplete for a long time, and I need to revisit the existing part in order to feel my way into the story again.

Both my short and long fiction works usually begin with a thinly sketched scene, character, situation, or some combination of all three, which just appears in my head. For example, I might suddenly visualize a huge old mill by a broad river, the wheel slowly turning, with the sound of the grinding stones underlaid by the burble of the river. Or I might think of a character, say a middle-aged man who has turned away from the sorcery of his youth because he is afraid of it, but who will be forced to embrace it again. Or a situation might emerge from my subconscious, in which a man, or something that was once a man, is looking down on a group of travelers from a rocky perch, wondering whether he/it should rob them.

All these beginnings might come together into the story of a miller, once a sorcerer, who is transformed into a creature as the result of a magical compact he thought he had evaded. So he must leave his settled life and become a brigand, in the hope of finding, on one of the magicians or priests he robs on the road, the one item of magical apparatus that can return his human shape.

Or they might not come together. I have numerous notes for stories, and many partly begun stories, that have progressed no further. Some of these fragments might be used in my novels, or at least be the seeds of some elements in one. A few ideas will progress and grow and become stories, complete in themselves. The great majority of my jotted-down ideas, images, and scraps of writing will never become anything more than a few lines in a black-and-red notebook.

The stories in this collection are the ones that got past the notes stage, that became a few paragraphs, then a few pages, and somehow charged on downhill to become complete. They represent a kind of core sample taken through more than fifteen years of writing, from the callow author of twenty-five who wrote "Down to the Scum Quarter" to the possibly more polished forty-one-year-old writer of "Nicholas Sayre and the Creature in the Case."

Fortunately, you have been spared some even earlier efforts, including the heavily T. H. White–influenced short story I published in my school magazine at fifteen, and even my very first professional short story sale, which felt like a great triumph for me at nineteen years old but now looks rather out of place with my later works.

I hope you find some stories here that you will enjoy, or wonder about, or that linger uncomfortably in the mind when you wish they didn't. But if your favorite story is "The Coin Shower," please do not write and tell me that my writing has been going downhill ever since I was six.

GARTH NIX
December 1, 2004
Sydney, Australia

ACROSS THE WALL

INTRODUCTION TO NICHOLAS SAYRE AND THE CREATURE IN THE CASE

I have explored Ancelstierre and the Old Kingdom a little in my novels *Sabriel*, *Lirael*, and *Abhorsen*, and in the process I have found out (for that's often what it feels like, even though I'm the one making it up) quite a lot about these lands, the people and creatures that inhabit them, and their stories.

But there is much, much more that I don't know about, and will never know about unless I need it for a story. Unlike many fantasy writers, I don't spend a lot of time working out and recording tons of background detail about the worlds that I make up. What I do is write the story, pausing every now and then to puzzle out the details or information that I need to know to make the story work. Some of that background material will end up in the story, though it might be veiled, mysterious, or tangential. Much more will sit in my head or roughly jotted down in my notebooks, until I need it next time or until I connect it with something else.

Every time I reenter the world of the Old Kingdom and Ancelstierre, I find myself stitching together leftover bits and pieces that I already knew about, as well as inventing some more that seem to go with what is already there.

"Nicholas Sayre and the Creature in the Case" was particularly interesting for me to write, because in it I connect various bits and pieces of information about Ancelstierre, rather than the Old Kingdom. As always, the story is the most important thing to me, but this novella also gives a glimpse of the people, customs, government, technology, and landscape of Ancelstierre.

Like nearly everything I write, this is a fantasy adventure story, this time with a dash of country-house mystery, a twist of 1920s-style espionage, and a humorous little umbrella on the side that may be safely ignored by those who don't like it (or don't get it). Some readers may detect the influence of some of the authors outside the fantasy genre (as it is usually defined today) whom I admire, including Dorothy Sayers and P. G. Wodehouse.

Planned to be a longish short story, "Nicholas Sayre and the Creature in the Case" grew and grew till it became a novella and ended up taking many more months to write than I had anticipated. It started with these notes:

Nicholas and Uncle to country house
Full of debs and stupid young men
Thing in the Case, eyes follow Nick
Autumn haymaking
thing gets some of Nick's blood?
refuge in river, thing closes sluice
hay fires in a circle
it is powerful, but poisoned
how far are we from the Wall?

That was the kernel, from which a novella grew over about ten months. I don't know why I wrote it rather than something else. It wasn't sold to a publisher, I didn't have a deadline for it, and I had plenty of other things to do. But only a week or so after writing those notes, I sat down and wrote the first three or four pages in one sitting. I kept coming back to it thereafter, caught up (as I often am as both writer and reader) simply by the desire to see what happened next.

NICHOLAS SAYRE AND THE CREATURE IN THE CASE

"I AM GOING BACK to the Old Kingdom, Uncle," said Nicholas Sayre. "Whatever Father may have told you. So there is no point in your trying to fix me up with a suitable Sayre job or a suitable Sayre marriage. I am coming with you to what will undoubtedly be a horrendous house party only because it will get me a few hundred miles closer to the Wall."

Nicholas's uncle Edward, more generally known as The Most Honorable Edward Sayre, Chief Minister of Ancelstierre, shut the red-bound letter book he was reading with more emphasis than he intended, as their heavily armored car lurched over a hump in the road. The sudden clap of the book made the bodyguard in front look around, but the driver kept his eyes on the narrow country lane.

"Have I said anything about a job or a

marriage?" Edward enquired, gazing down his long, patrician nose at his nineteen-year-old nephew. "Besides, you won't even get within a mile of the Perimeter without a pass signed by me, let alone across the Wall."

"I could get a pass from Lewis," said Nicholas moodily, referring to the newly anointed Hereditary Arbiter. The previous Arbiter, Lewis's grandfather, had died of a heart attack during Corolini's attempted coup d'état half a year before.

"No, you couldn't, and you know it," said Edward. "Lewis has more sense than to involve himself in any aspect of government other than the ceremonial."

"Then I'll have to cross over without a pass," declared Nicholas angrily, not even trying to hide the frustration that had built up in him over the past six months, during which he'd been forced to stay in Ancelstierre. Most of that time spent wishing he'd left with Lirael and Sam in the immediate aftermath of the Destroyer's defeat, instead of deciding to recuperate in Ancelstierre. It had been weakness and fear that had driven his decision, combined with a desire to put the terrible past behind him. But he now knew that was impossible. He could not ignore the legacy of his involvement with Hedge and the Destroyer, nor his return to Life at the hands—or paws—of the Disreputable Dog. He had become someone else, and he could only find out who that was in the Old Kingdom.

"You would almost certainly be shot if you try to cross illegally," said Edward. "A fate you would richly deserve. Particularly since you are not giving me the opportunity to help you. I do not know why you or anyone else would want to go to the Old Kingdom—my year on the Perimeter as General Hort's ADC certainly taught me the place is best avoided. Nor do I wish to annoy your father and hurt your mother, but there *are* certain circumstances in which I might grant you permission to cross the Perimeter."

"What! Really?"

"Yes, really. Have I ever taken you or any other of my nephews or nieces to a house party before?"

"Not that I know—"

"Do I usually make a habit of attending parties given by someone like Alastor Dorrance in the middle of nowhere?"

"I suppose not. . . ."

"Then you might exercise your intelligence to

wonder why you are here with me now."

"Gatehouse ahead, sir," interrupted the bodyguard as the car rounded a sweeping corner and slowed down. "Recognition signal is correct."

Edward and Nicholas leaned forward to look through the open partition and the windscreen beyond. A few hundred yards in front, a squat stone gatehouse lurked just off the road, with its two wooden gates swung back. Two slate gray Heddon-Hare roadsters were parked, one on either side of the gate, with several mackintosh-clad, weapon-toting men standing around them. One of the men waved a yellow flag in a series of complicated movements that Edward clearly understood and Nicholas presumed meant all was well.

"Proceed!" snapped the Chief Minister. Their car slowed more, the driver shifting down through the gears with practiced double-clutching. The mackintosh-clad men saluted as the car swung off the road and through the gate, dropping their salute as the rest of the motorcade followed. Six motorcycle policemen were immediately behind, then another two cars identical to the one that carried Nicholas and his uncle, then another half dozen police motorcyclists, and finally four trucks that were carrying a company of fully armed soldiery. Corolini's attempted putsch had failed, and there had surprisingly been no further trouble from the Our Country Party since, but the government continued to be nervous about the safety of the nation's Chief Minister.

"So, what is going on?" asked Nicholas. "Why are you here? And why am I here? Is there something you want me to do?"

"At last, a glimmer of thought. Have you ever wondered what Alastor Dorrance actually does, other than come to Corvere three or four times a year and exercise his eccentricities in public?"

"Isn't that enough?" asked Nick with a shudder. He remembered the newspaper stories from the last time Dorrance had been in the city, only a few weeks before. He'd hosted a picnic on Holyoak Hill for every apprentice in Corvere and supplied them with fatty roast beef, copious amounts of beer, and a particularly cheap and nasty red wine, with predictable results.

"Dorrance's eccentricities are all show," said Edward. "Misdirection. He is in fact the head of Department Thirteen. Dorrance Hall is the Department's main research facility."

"But Department Thirteen is just a made-up

thing, for the moving pictures. It doesn't really exist . . . um . . . does it?"

"Officially, no. In actuality, yes. Every state has need of spies. Department Thirteen trains and manages ours, and carries out various tasks ill suited to the more regular branches of government. It is watched over quite carefully, I assure you."

"But what has that got to do with me?"

"Department Thirteen observes all our neighbors very successfully, and has detailed files on everyone and everything important within those countries. With one notable exception. The Old Kingdom."

"I'm not going to spy on my friends!"

Edward sighed and looked out the window. The drive beyond the gatehouse curved through freshly mown fields, the hay already gathered into hillocks ready to be pitchforked into carts and taken to the stacks. Past the fields, the chimneys of a large country house peered above the fringe of old oaks that lined the drive.

"I'm not going to be a spy, Uncle," repeated Nicholas.

"I haven't asked you to be one," said Edward as he looked back at his nephew. Nicholas's face had paled, and he was clutching his chest. Whatever had happened to him in the Old Kingdom had left him in a very run-down state, and he was still recovering. Though the Ancelstierran doctors had found no external signs of significant injury, his X-rays had come out strangely fogged and all the medical reports said Nick was in the same sort of shape as a man who had suffered serious wounds in battle.

"All I want you to do is to spend the weekend here with some of the Department's technical people," continued Edward. "Answer their questions about your experiences in the Old Kingdom, that sort of thing. I doubt anything will come of it, and as you know, I strictly adhere to the wisdom of my predecessors, which is to leave the place alone. But that said, they haven't exactly left us alone over the past twenty years. Dorrance has always had a bit of a bee in his bonnet about the Old Kingdom, greatly exacerbated by the . . . mmm . . . event at Forwin Mill. It is possible that he might discover something useful from talking to you. So if you answer his questions, you shall have your Perimeter pass on Monday morning. If you're still set on going, that is."

"I'll cross the Wall," said Nick forcefully.

"One way or another."

"Then I suggest it be my way. You know, your father wanted to be a painter when he was your age. He had talent too, according to old Menree. But our parents wouldn't hear of it. A grave error, I think. Not that he hasn't been a useful politician, and a great help to me. But his heart is elsewhere, and it is not possible to achieve greatness without a whole heart."

"So all I have to do is answer questions?"

Edward sighed the sigh of an older and wiser man talking to a younger, inattentive, and impatient relative.

"Well, you will have to appear a little bit at the party. Dinner and so forth. Croquet perhaps, or a row on the lake. Misdirection, as I said."

Nicholas took Edward's hand and shook it firmly.

"You are a splendid uncle, Uncle."

"Good. I'm glad that's settled," said Edward. He glanced out the window. They were past the oak trees now, gravel crunching beneath the wheels as the car rolled up the drive to the front steps of the six-columned entrance. "We'll drop you off, then, and I'll see you Monday."

"Aren't you staying here? For the house party?"

"Don't be silly! I can't abide house parties of any kind. I'm staying at the Golden Sheaf. Excellent hotel, not too far away. I often go there to get through some serious confidential reading. Place has got its own golf course, too. Thought I might go round tomorrow. Enjoy yourself!"

Nicholas hardly caught the last two words as his door was flung open and he was assisted out by Edward's personal bodyguard. He blinked in the afternoon sunlight, no longer filtered through the smoked glass of the car's windows. A few seconds later, his bags were deposited at his feet; then the Chief Minister's cavalcade started up again and rolled out the drive as quickly as it had arrived, the Army trucks leaving considerable ruts in the gravel.

"Mr. Sayre?"

Nicholas looked around. A top-hatted footman was picking up his bags, but it was another man who had spoken. A balding, burly individual in a dark blue suit, his hair cut so short it was practically a monkish tonsure. Everything about him said policeman, either active or recently retired.

"Yes, I'm Nicholas Sayre."

"Welcome to Dorrance Hall, sir. My name is Hedge—"

Nicholas recoiled from the offered hand and nearly fell over the footman. Even as he regained his balance, he realized that the man had said *Hodge* and then followed it up with a second syllable.

Hodgeman. Not *Hedge.*

Hedge the necromancer was finally, completely, and utterly dead. Lirael and the Disreputable Dog had defeated him, and Hedge had gone beyond the Ninth Gate. He couldn't come back. Nick knew he was safe from him, but that knowledge was purely intellectual. Deep inside him, the name of Hedge was linked irrevocably with an almost primal fear.

"Sorry," gasped Nick. He straightened up and shook the man's hand. "Ankle gave way on me. You were saying?"

"Hodgeman is my name. I am an assistant to Mr. Dorrance. The other guests do not arrive till later, so Mr. Dorrance thought you might like a tour of the grounds."

"Um, certainly," replied Nick. He fought back a sudden urge to look around to see who might be listening and, as he started up the steps, resisted the temptation to slink from shadow to shadow just like a spy in a moving picture.

"The house was originally built in the time of the last Trouin-Durville Pretender, about four hundred years ago, but little of the original structure remains. Most of the current house was built by Mr. Dorrance's grandfather. The best feature is the library, which was the great hall of the old house. Shall we start there?"

"Thank you," replied Nicholas. Mr. Hodgeman's turn as a tour guide was quite convincing. Nicholas wondered if the man had to do it often for casual visitors, as part of what Uncle Edward would call "misdirection."

The library was very impressive. Hodgeman closed the double doors behind them as Nick stared up at the high dome of the ceiling, which was painted to create the illusion of a storm at sea. It was quite disconcerting to look up at the waves and the tossing ships and the low scudding clouds. Below the dome, every wall was covered by tiers of shelves stretching up twenty or even twenty-five feet from the floor. Ladders ran on rails around the library, but no one was using them. The library was silent; two crescent-shaped couches in the center were empty. The windows were heavily curtained with velvet drapes, but the gas lanterns above the shelves burned very brightly. The place looked like there should be people reading in it, or sorting books, or something. It did not have the dark, dusty air of a disused library.

"This way, sir," said Hodgeman. He crossed to one of the shelves and reached up above his head to pull out an unobtrusive, dun-colored tome, adorned only with the Dorrance coat of arms, a chain argent issuant from a chevron argent upon a field azure.

The book slid out halfway, then came no farther.

Hodgeman looked up at it. Nick looked too.

"Is something supposed to happen?"

"It gets a bit stuck sometimes," replied Hodgeman. He tugged on the book again. This time it came completely out. Hodgeman opened it, took a key from its hollowed-out pages, pushed two books apart on the shelf below to reveal a keyhole, inserted the key, and turned it. There was a soft click, but nothing more dramatic. Hodgeman put the key back in the book and returned the volume to the shelf.

"Now, if you wouldn't mind stepping this way," Hodgeman said, leading Nick back to the center of the library. The couches had moved aside on silent gears, and two steel-encased segments of the floor had slid open, revealing a circular stone staircase leading down. Unlike the library's brilliant white gaslights, it was lit by dull electric bulbs.

"This is all rather cloak-and-dagger," remarked Nick as he headed down the steps with Hodgeman close behind him.

Hodgeman didn't answer, but Nick was sure a disapproving glance had fallen on his back. The steps went down quite a long way, equivalent to at least three or four floors. They ended in front of a steel door with a covered spy hole. Hodgeman pressed a tarnished bronze bell button next to the door, and a few seconds later, the spy hole slid open.

"Sergeant Hodgeman with Mr. Nicholas Sayre," said Hodgeman.

The door swung open. There was no sign of a person behind it. Just a long, dismal, white-painted concrete corridor stretching off some thirty or forty yards to another steel door. Nick stepped through the doorway, and some slight movement to his right made him look. There was an alcove there, with a desk, a red telephone on it, a chair, and a guard—another plainclothes policeman type like Hodgeman, this time in shirtsleeves, with a revolver worn openly in a shoulder holster. He nodded at Nick but didn't smile or speak.

"On to the next door, please," said Hodgeman.

Nick nodded back at the guard and continued down the concrete corridor, his footsteps echoing just out of time with Hodgeman's. He heard behind him the faint ting of a telephone being taken off its cradle and then the low voice of the guard, his words indistinguishable.

The procedure with the spy hole was repeated at the next door. There were two policemen behind this one, in a larger and better-appointed alcove. They had upholstered chairs and a leather-topped desk, though it had clearly seen better days.

Hodgeman nodded at the guards, who nodded back with slow deliberation. Nick smiled but got no smile in return.

"Through the left door, please," said Hodgeman, pointing. There were two doors to choose from, both of unappealing, unmarked steel bordered with lines of knuckle-size rivets.

Hodgeman departed through the right-hand door as Nick pushed the left, but it swung open before he exerted any pressure. There was a much more cheerful room beyond, very much like Nick's tutor's study at Sunbere, with four big leather club chairs facing a desk, and off to one side a liquor cabinet with a large, black-enameled radio sitting on top of it. There were three men standing around the cabinet.

The closest was a tall, expensively dressed, vacant-looking man with ridiculous sideburns whom Nick recognized as Dorrance. The second-closest was a fiftyish man in a hearty tweed coat with leather elbow patches. The skin of his thick neck hung over his collar, and his fat face was much too big for the half-moon glasses that perched on his nose. Lurking behind these two was a nondescript, vaguely unhealthy-looking shorter man who wore exactly the same kind of suit as Hodgeman but in a much more untidy way, so he looked nothing like a policeman, serving or otherwise.

"Ah, here is Mr. Nicholas Sayre," said Dorrance. He stepped forward, shook Nick's hand, and ushered him to the center of the room. "I'm Dorrance. Good of you to help us out. This is Professor Lackridge, who looks after all our scientific research."

The fat-faced man extended his hand and

shook Nick's with little enthusiasm but a crushing grip. Somewhere in the very distant past, Nick surmised, Professor Lackridge must have been a rugby enthusiast. Or perhaps a boxer. Now, sadly, run to fat, but the muscle was still there underneath.

"And this is Mr. Malthan, who is . . . an independent adviser on Old Kingdom matters."

Malthan inclined his head and made a faint, repressed gesture with his hands, turning them toward his forehead as if to brush his almost nonexistent hair away. There was something about the action that triggered recognition in Nick.

"You're from the Old Kingdom, aren't you?" he asked. It was unusual for anyone from the Old Kingdom to be encountered this far south. Very few travelers could get authorization from both King Touchstone and the Ancelstierran government to cross the Wall and the Perimeter. Even fewer would come any farther south than Bain, which was at least a hundred and eighty miles north. They didn't like it, as a rule. It didn't feel right, Sam had always said.

But then, this little man didn't have the Charter Mark on his forehead, which might make it more bearable for him to be on this side of the

Wall. Nick instinctively brushed his dark forelock aside to show his Charter Mark, his fingers running across it. The Mark was quiescent under his touch, showing no sign of its connection to the magical powers of the Old Kingdom.

Malthan clearly saw the Mark, even if the others didn't. He stepped a little closer to Nick and spoke in a breathy half whine.

"I'm a trader, out of Belisaere," he said. "I've always done a bit of business with some folks in Bain, as my father did before me, and his father before him. We've a Permission from the King, and a Permit from your government. I only come down here every now and then, when I've got something special-like that I know Mr. Dorrance's lot will be interested in, same as my old dad did for Mr. Dorrance's granddad—"

"And we pay very well for what we're interested in, Mr. Malthan," Dorrance interrupted him. "Don't we?"

"Yes, sir, you do. Only I don't—"

"Malthan has been very useful," interjected Professor Lackridge. "Though we must discount many of his, ahem, traveler's tales. Fortunately he tends to bring us interesting artifacts in addition to his more colorful observations."

"I've always spoken true," said Malthan. "As this young man can tell you. He has the Mark and all. He knows."

"Yes, the forehead brand of that cult," remarked Lackridge, with an uninterested glance at Nick's forehead, the Mark mostly concealed once more under his floppy forelock. "Sociologically interesting, of course. Particularly its regrettable prevalence among our Northern Perimeter Reconnaissance Unit. I trust it is only an affectation in your case, young man? You haven't gone native on us?"

"It isn't just a religious thing," Nick said carefully. "The Mark is more of a . . . a connection with . . . how can I explain . . . unseen powers. Magic—"

"Yes, yes. I am sure it seems like magic to you," said Lackridge. "But the great majority of it is easily explained as mass hallucination, the influence of drugs, hysteria, and so forth. It is the minority of events that defy explanation but leave clear physical effects that we are interested in—such as the explosion at Forwin Mill." He looked over his half-moon glasses at Nicholas.

Dorrance looked at him as well, his stare suddenly intense.

"Our studies there indicate that the blast was roughly equivalent to the detonation of twenty thousand tons of nitrocellulose," continued Lackridge. He rapped his knuckles on the desk as he exclaimed, "Twenty thousand tons! We know of nothing capable of delivering such explosive force, particularly as the bomb itself was reported to be two metallic hemispheres, each no more than ten feet in diameter. Is that right, Mr. Sayre?"

Nick swallowed, his throat moving in a dry gulp. He could feel sweat forming on his forehead and a familiar jangling pain in his right arm and chest.

"I . . . I don't really know," he said after several long seconds. "I was very ill. Feverish. But it wasn't a bomb. It was the Destroyer. Not something our science can explain. That was my mistake. I thought I could explain everything under our natural laws, our science. I was wrong."

"You're tired, and clearly still somewhat unwell," said Dorrance. His tone was kindly, but the warmth did not reach his eyes. "We have many more questions, of course, but they can wait until the morning. Professor, why don't you show Nicholas around the establishment. Let him get his bearings. Then go back upstairs, and we can all resume life as normal, what? Which reminds me, Nicholas—everything discussed down here is absolutely confidential. Even the existence of this facility must not be mentioned once you return to the main house. Naturally you will see me, Professor Lackridge, and the others at dinner, but in our public roles. Most of the guests have no idea that Department Thirteen lurks beneath their feet, and we want it to remain that way. I trust you won't have a problem keeping our existence all to yourself?"

"No, not at all," muttered Nick. Inside he was wondering how he could avoid answering questions but still get his pass to cross the Perimeter. Lackridge obviously didn't believe in Old Kingdom magic, which was no great surprise. After all, Nick had been like that himself. But Dorrance had voiced no such skepticism, nor had he shown it by his body language. Nick definitely did not want to discuss the Destroyer and its nature with anyone who might seriously look into what it was or what had happened at Forwin Mill.

He didn't want to dabble in anything to do with Old Kingdom magic, especially without proper instruction, even two hundred miles south of the Wall.

"Follow me, Nicholas," said Lackridge. "You, too, Malthan. I want to show you something related to those photographic plates you found for us."

"I need to catch my train," muttered Malthan. "My horses . . . stabled near Bain . . . the expense . . . I'm eager to return home."

"We'll pay you a little extra," said Dorrance, the tone of his voice making it clear Malthan had no choice. "I want Lackridge to see your reaction to one of the artifacts we've picked up. I'll see you at dinner, Nicholas."

Dorrance shook Nick's hand in parting, gave a dismissive wave to Lackridge, and ignored Malthan completely. As Dorrance turned back to his desk, Nick noticed a paperweight sitting on top of the wooden in-box. A lump of broken stone, etched with intricate symbols. They did not shine or move about, not so far from the Old Kingdom; but Nick recognized their nature, though he did not know their dormant power or meaning. They were Charter Marks. The stone itself looked as if it had been broken from a greater whole.

Nick looked at Dorrance again and decided that even if it meant having to work out some other way to get across the Perimeter, he was not going to answer any of Dorrance's questions. Or rather, he would answer them vaguely and badly, and generally behave like a well-meaning fool.

Hedge had been an Ancelstierran originally, Nick remembered as he followed Malthan and the professor out. Dorrance struck him as someone who might be tempted to walk a path similar to Hedge's.

They left through the door Nick had come in by, out through the opposite door, and then rapidly through a confusing maze of short corridors and identical riveted metal doors.

"Bit confusing down here, what?" remarked Lackridge. "Takes a while to get your bearings. Dorrance's father built the original tunnels for his underground electric railway. Modeled on the Corvere Metro. But the tunnels have been extended even farther since then. We're just going to take a look in our holding area for objects brought in from north of the Wall or found on our side, near it."

"You mentioned photographic plates," said Nick. "Surely no photographic equipment works over the Wall?"

"That has yet to be properly tested," said

Lackridge dismissively. "In any case, these are prints from negative glass plates taken in Bain of a book that was brought across the Wall."

"What kind of book?" Nick asked Malthan.

Malthan looked at Nick, but his eyes failed to meet the younger man's gaze. "The photographs were taken by a former associate of mine. I didn't know she had this book. It burned of its own accord only minutes after the photographs were captured. Half the plates also melted before I could get them far enough south."

"What was the title of the book?" asked Nick. "And why 'former' associate?"

"She burned with the b-b-book," whispered Malthan with a shiver. "I do not know its name. I do not know where Raliese might have got it."

"You see the problems we have to deal with," said Lackridge with a sneer at Malthan. "He probably bought the plates at a school fete in Bain. But they are interesting. The book was some kind of bestiary. We can't read the text as yet, but there are very fine etchings—illustrations of the beasts."

The professor stopped to unlock the next door with a large brass key, but he opened it only a fraction. He turned to Malthan and Nick and said, "The photographs are important, as we already had independent evidence that at least one of the beasts depicted in that book really does exist—or existed at one time—in the Old Kingdom."

"Independent evidence of one of those things?" squeaked Malthan. "What kind of—"

"This," declared Lackridge, opening the door wide. "A mummified specimen!"

The storeroom beyond was cluttered with boxes, chests, and paraphernalia. For a second, Nick's eye was drawn to two very large blowups of photographs of Forwin Loch, which were leaning on the wall near the door. One showed a scene of industry from the last century, and the other showed the destruction wrought by Orannis—the Destroyer.

But the big photographs held his attention for no more than a moment. There could be no question what Lackridge was referring to. In the middle of the room there was a glass cylinder about nine feet high and five feet in diameter. Inside the case, propped up against a steel frame, was a nightmare.

It looked vaguely human, in the sense that it had a head, a torso, two arms, and two legs. But its skin or hide was of a strange violet hue, cross-hatched with lines like a crocodile's, and looked very rough. Its legs were jointed backward and ended in hooked hooves. The arms stretched down almost to the floor of the case, and ended not in hands but in clublike appendages that were covered in inch-long barbs. Its torso was thin and cylindrical, rather like that of a wasp. Its head was the most human part, save that it sat on a neck that was twice as long; it had narrow slits instead of ears, and its black, violet-pupiled eyes—presumably glass made by a skillful taxidermist—were pear-shaped and took up half its face. Its mouth, twice the width of any human's, was almost closed, but Nick could see teeth gleaming there.

Black teeth that shone like polished jet.

"No!" screamed Malthan. He ran back down the corridor as far as the previous door, which was locked. He beat on the metal with his fists, the drumming echoing down the corridor.

Nick pushed Lackridge gently aside with a quiet "Excuse me." He could feel his heart pounding in his chest, but it was not from fear. It was excitement. The excitement of discovery, of learning something new. A feeling he had always enjoyed, but it had been lost to him ever since he'd dug up the metal spheres of the Destroyer.

He leaned forward to touch the case and felt a strange, electric thrill run through his fingers and out along his thumbs. At the same time, there was a stabbing pain in his forehead, strong enough to make him step back and press two fingers hard between his eyes.

"Not a bad specimen," said Lackridge. He spoke conversationally, but he had come very close to Nick and was watching him intently. "Its history is a little murky, but it's been in the country for at least three hundred years and in the Corvere Bibliomanse for the past thirty-five. One of the things my staff has been doing here at Department Thirteen is cross-indexing all the various institutional records, looking for artifacts and information about our northern neighbors. When we got Malthan's photographs, Dorrance happened to remember he'd seen an actual specimen of one of the creatures somewhere before, as a child. I cross-checked the records at the Bibliomanse and found the thing, and we had it brought up here."

Nick nodded absently. The pain in his head was receding. It appeared to emanate from his Charter Mark, though that should be totally quiescent this far from the Wall. Unless there was a roaring gale blowing down from the north, which he supposed might have happened since he came down into Department Thirteen's subterranean lair. It was impossible to tell what was going on in the world above them.

"Apparently the thing was found about ten miles in on our side of the Wall, wrapped in three chains," continued Lackridge. "One of silver, one of lead, and one made from braided daisies. That's what the notes say, though of course we don't have the chains to prove it. If there was a silver one, it must have been worth a pretty penny. Long before the Perimeter, of course, so it was some time before the authorities got hold of it. According to the records, the local folk wanted to drag it back to the Wall, but fortunately there was a visiting Captain-Inquirer who had it shipped south. Should never have gotten rid of the Captain-Inquirers. Wouldn't have minded being one myself. Don't suppose anyone would bring them back now. Lily-livered lot, the present government . . . excepting your uncle, of course. . . ."

"My father also sits in the Moot," said Nick. "On the government benches."

"Well, of course, everyone says my politics are to the right of old Arbiter Werris Blue-Nose, so don't mind me," said Lackridge. He stepped back into the corridor and shouted, "Come back here, Mr. Malthan. It won't bite you!"

As Lackridge spoke, Nick thought he saw the creature's eyes move. Just a fraction, but there was a definite sense of movement. With it, all his sense of excitement was banished in a second, to be replaced by a growing fear.

It's alive, thought Nick.

He stepped back to the door, almost knocking over Lackridge, his mind working furiously.

The thing is alive. Quiescent. Conserving its energies, so far from the Old Kingdom. It must be some Free Magic creature, and it's just waiting for a chance—

"Thank you, Professor Lackridge, but I find myself suddenly rather keen on a cup of tea," blurted Nick. "Do you think we might come back and look at this specimen tomorrow?"

"I'm supposed to make Malthan touch the case," said Lackridge. "Dorrance was most insistent upon it. Wants to see his reaction."

Nick edged back and looked down the corridor. Malthan was crouched by the door.

"I think you've seen his reaction," he said. "Anything more would simply be cruel, and hardly scientific."

"He's only an Old Kingdom trader," said Lackridge. "He's not even strictly legal. Conditional visa. We can do whatever we like with him."

"What!" exclaimed Nick.

"Within reason," Lackridge added hastily. "I mean, nothing too drastic. Do him good."

"I think he needs to get on a train north and go back to the Old Kingdom," said Nick firmly. He liked Lackridge less and less with every passing minute, and the whole Department Thirteen setup seemed very dubious. It was all very well for his uncle Edward to talk about having extralegal entities to do things the government could not, but the line had to be drawn somewhere, and Nick didn't think Dorrance or Lackridge knew where to draw it—or if they did, when not to step over it.

"I'll just see how he is," added Nick. An idea started to rise from the recesses of his mind as he walked down the corridor toward the crouched and shivering man pressed against the door. "Perhaps we can walk out together."

"Mr. Dorrance was most insistent—"

"I'm sure he won't mind if you tell him that I insisted on escorting Malthan on his way."

"But—"

"I am insisting, you know," Nick cut in forcefully. "As it is, I shall have a few words to say about this place to my uncle."

"If you're going to be like that, I don't think I have any choice," said Lackridge petulantly. "We were assured that you would cooperate fully with our research."

"*I* will cooperate, but I don't think Malthan needs to do any more for Department Thirteen," said Nick. He bent down and helped the Old Kingdom trader up. He was surprised by how much the smaller man was shaking. He seemed totally in the grip of panic, though he calmed a little when Nick took his arm above the elbow. "Now, please show us out. And you can organize someone to take Malthan to the railway station."

"You don't understand the importance of our work," said Lackridge. "Or our methods. Observing the superstitious reactions of northerners and our own people delivers legitimate and potentially useful information."

This was clearly only a pro forma protest, because as Lackridge spoke, he unlocked the door and led them quickly through the corridors. After a few minutes, Nick found that he didn't need to half carry Malthan anymore, but could just point him in the right direction.

Eventually, after numerous turns and more doors that required laborious unlocking, they came to a double-width steel door with two spy holes. Lackridge knocked, and after a brief inspection, they were admitted to a guardroom inhabited by five policeman types. Four were sitting around a linoleum-topped table under a single suspended lightbulb, drinking tea and eating doorstop-size sandwiches. Hodgeman was the fifth, and clearly still on duty, as unlike the others he had not removed his coat.

"Sergeant Hodgeman," Lackridge called out rather too loudly. "Please escort Mr. Sayre upstairs and have one of your other officers take Malthan to Dorrance Halt and see he gets on the next northbound train."

"Very good, sir," replied Hodgeman. He hesitated for a moment, then with a curiously unpleasant emphasis, which Nick would have missed if he hadn't been paying careful attention, he said, "Constable Ripton, you see to Malthan."

"Just a moment," said Nick. "I've had a thought. Malthan can take a message from me over to my uncle, the Chief Minister, at the Golden

Sheaf. Then someone from his staff can take Malthan to the nearest station."

"One of my men would happily take a message for you, sir," said Sergeant Hodgeman. "And Dorrance Halt is much closer than the Golden Sheaf. That's all of twenty miles away."

"Thank you," said Nick. "But I want the Chief Minister to hear Malthan directly about some matters relating to the Old Kingdom. That won't be a problem, will it? Malthan, I'll just write something out for you to take to Garran, my uncle's principal secretary."

Nick took out his notebook and gold propelling pencil and casually leaned against the wall. They all watched him, the five policeman with studied disinterest masking hostility, Lackridge with more open aggression, and Malthan with the sad eyes of the doomed.

Nick began to whistle tunelessly through his teeth, pretending to be oblivious to the pent-up institutional aggression focused upon him. He wrote quickly, sighed and pretended to cross out what he'd written, then ripped out the page, palmed it, and started to write again.

"Very hard to concentrate the mind in these

underground chambers of yours," Nick said to Lackridge. "I don't know how you get anything done. Expect you've got cockroaches too . . . maybe rats . . . I mean, what's that?"

He pointed with the pencil. Only Malthan and Lackridge turned to look. The policemen kept up their steady stare. Nick stared back, but he felt a slight fear begin to swim about his stomach. Surely they wouldn't risk doing anything to *Edward Sayre*'s nephew? And yet . . . they were clearly planning to imprison Malthan at the least, or perhaps something worse. Nick wasn't going to let that happen.

"Only a shadow, but I bet you do have rats. Stands to reason. Underground. Tea and biscuits about," Nick said as he ripped out the second page. He folded it, wrote "Mr. Thomas Garran" on the outside, and handed it to Malthan, at the same time stepping across to shield his next action from everyone except Lackridge, whom he stumbled against.

"Oh, sorry!" he exclaimed, and in that moment of apparently lost balance, he slid the palmed first note into Malthan's still-open hand.

"I . . . ah . . . still not quite recovered from the

events at Forwin Mill," Nick mumbled, as Lackridge suppressed an oath and jumped back.

The policemen had stepped forward, apparently only to catch him if he fell. Sergeant Hodgeman had seen him stumble before. They were clearly suspicious but didn't know what he had done. He hoped.

"Bit unsteady on my pins," continued Nick. "Nothing to do with drink, unfortunately. That might make it seem worthwhile. Now I must get on upstairs and dress for dinner. Who's taking Malthan over to the Golden Sheaf?"

"I am, sir. Constable Ripton."

"Very good, Constable. I trust you'll have a pleasant evening drive. I'll telephone ahead to make sure that my uncle's staff are expecting you and have dinner laid on."

"Thank you, sir," said Ripton woodenly. Again, if Nick hadn't been paying careful attention, he might have missed the young constable flicking his eyes up and down and then twice toward Sergeant Hodgeman—a twitch Nick interpreted as a call for help from the junior police officer, looking for Hodgeman to tell him how to satisfy his immediate masters as well as insure himself against the interference of any greater authority.

"Get on with it then, Constable," said Hodgeman, his words as ambiguous as his expression.

"Let's all get upstairs," Nick said with false cheer he dredged up from somewhere. "After you, Sergeant. Malthan, if you wouldn't mind walking with me, I'll see you to your car. Got a couple of questions about the Old Kingdom I'm sure you can answer."

"Anything, anything," babbled Malthan. He came so close, Nick thought the little trader was going to hug him. "Let us get out from under the earth. With that—"

"Yes, I agree," interrupted Nick. He gestured toward the door and met Sergeant Hodgeman's stare. All the policemen moved closer. Casual steps. A foot slid forward here, a diagonal pace toward Nick.

Lackridge coughed something that might have been "Dorrance," scuttled to the door leading back to the tunnels, opened it just wide enough to admit his bulk, and squeezed through. Nick thought about calling him back but instantly dismissed the idea. He didn't want to show any weakness.

But with Lackridge gone, there was no longer a witness. Nick knew Malthan didn't count, not to anyone in Department Thirteen.

Sergeant Hodgeman pushed one heavy-booted foot forward and advanced on Nick and Malthan till his face was inches away from Nick's. It was an intimidating posture, long beloved of sergeants, and Nick knew it well from his days in the school cadets.

Hodgeman didn't say anything. He just stared, a fierce stare that Nick realized hid a mind calculating how far he could go to keep Malthan captive, and what he might be able to do to Nicholas Sayre without causing trouble.

"My uncle is the Chief Minister," Nick whispered very softly. "My father a member of the Moot. Marshal Harngorm is my mother's uncle. My second cousin is the Hereditary Arbiter himself."

"As you say, sir," said Hodgeman loudly. He stepped back, the sound of his heel on the concrete snapping through the tension that had risen in the room. "I'm sure you know what you're doing."

That was a warning of consequences to

come, Nick knew. But he didn't care. He wanted to save Malthan, but most of all at that moment he wanted to get out under the sun again. He wanted to stand aboveground and put as much earth and concrete and as many locked doors as possible between himself and the creature in the case.

Yet even when the afternoon sunlight was softly warming his face, Nick wasn't much comforted. He watched Constable Ripton and Malthan leave in a small green van that looked exactly like the sort of vehicle that would be used to dispose of a body in a moving picture about the fictional Department Thirteen. Then, while lurking near the footmen's side door, he saw several gleaming, expensive cars drive up to disgorge their gleaming, expensive passengers. He recognized most of the guests. None were friends. They were all people he would formerly have described as frivolous and now just didn't care about at all. Even the beautiful young women failed to make more than a momentary impact. His mind was elsewhere.

Nick was thinking about Malthan and the two messages he carried. One, the obvious one, was addressed to Thomas Garran, Uncle Edward's principal private secretary. It said:

Garran

Uncle will want to talk to the bearer (Malthan, an Old Kingdom trader) for five minutes or so. Please ensure he is then escorted to the Perimeter by Foxe's people or Captain Sverenson's, not D13. Ask Uncle to call me urgently. Word of a Sayre.

Nicholas.

The other, more hastily scrawled, said:

Send telegram TO MAGISTRIX WYVERLEY COLLEGE NICK FOUND BAD KINGDOM CREATURE DORRANCE HALL TELL ABHORSEN HELP.

There was every possibility neither message would get through, Nick thought. It would all depend on what Dorrance and his minions thought they could get away with. And that depended on what they thought they could do to one Nicholas Sayre before he caused them too much trouble.

Nick shivered and went back inside. As he expected, when he asked to use a telephone, the footman referred him to the butler, who was very apologetic and bowed several times while regretting that the line was down and probably would not be fixed for several days, the telegraph company being notoriously slow in the country.

With that avenue cut off, Nick retreated to his room, ostensibly to dress for dinner. In practice he spent most of the time writing a report to his uncle and another telegram to the Magistrix at Wyverley College. He hid the report in the lining of his suitcase and went in search of a particular valet who he knew would be accompanying one of the guests he had seen arrive, the aging dandy Hericourt Danjers. The permanent staff of Dorrance Hall would all really be Department Thirteen agents, or informants at the least, but it was much less likely the guests' servants would be.

Danjers's valet was famous among servants for his ability with shoe polish, champagne, and a secret oil. So neither he nor anyone else in the belowstairs parlor was much surprised when the Chief Minister's nephew sought him out with a pair of shoes in hand. The valet was a little more surprised to find a note inside the shoes asking him to go out to the village and secretly send a telegram, but as the note was wrapped around four double-guinea pieces, he was happy to do so. When he'd finished his duties, of course.

Back in his room, Nick dressed hastily. As he tied his bow tie, his hands moved automatically while he wondered what else he should be doing. All kinds of plans raced through his head, only to be abandoned as impractical, or foolish, or likely to make matters worse.

With his tie finally done, Nick went to his case and took out a large leather wallet. There were three things inside. Two were letters, both written neatly on thick, linen-rich handmade paper, but in markedly different hands.

The first letter was from Nick's old friend Prince Sameth. It was concerned primarily with Sam's current projects and was illustrated in the margins with small diagrams. Judging from the letter, Sam's time was being spent almost entirely on the fabrication and enchantment of a replacement hand for Lirael, and the planning and design of a fishing hut on an island in the Ratterlin Delta. Sam did not explain why he wanted to build a fishing hut, and Nick had not had a reply to his most recent letter seeking enlightenment. This was not unusual. Sam was an infrequent correspondent, and there was no regular mail service of any kind between Ancelstierre and the Old Kingdom.

Nick didn't bother to read Sam's letter again. He put it aside, carefully unfolded the second letter, and read it for the hundredth or two hundredth time, hoping that this time he would uncover some hidden meaning in the innocuous words.

This letter was from Lirael, and it was quite short. The writing was so regular, so perfectly spaced, and so free of ink splotches that Nick wondered if it had been copied from a rough version. If it had, what did that mean? Did Lirael always make fine copies of her letters? Or had she done it just for him?

Dear Nick,

I trust you are recovering well. I am much better, and Sam says my new hand will be ready soon. Ellimere has been teaching me to play tennis, a game from your country, but I really do need two hands. I have also started to work with the Abhorsen. Sabriel, I mean, though I still find it hard to call her that. I still laugh when I remember you calling her "Mrs.

Abhorsen, Ma'am Sir." I was surprised by that laugh, amidst such sorrow and pain. It was a strange day, wasn't it? Waiting for everything to be discussed and sorted and explained just enough so we could all go home, with the two of us lying side by side on our stretchers with so much going on all around. You made it better for me, telling me about my friend the Disreputable Dog. I am very grateful for that. That is why I'm writing, really, and Sam said he was sending something so this could go in with it.

Be well.

Lirael, Abhorsen-in-Waiting and Remembrancer

Nick stared at the letter for several minutes after he finished reading it, then gently folded it and returned it to the wallet. He drew out the third thing, which had come in a package with the letters three weeks ago, though it had apparently left the Old Kingdom at least a month before that. It was a small, very plain dagger, the blade and hilt blued steel, with brass wire wound around the grip, the pommel just a big teardrop of metal.

Nick held it up to the light. He could see faint etched symbols upon the blade, but that was all they were. Faint etched symbols. Not living, moving Charter Marks, bright and flowing, all gold and sunshine. That's what Charter-spelled swords normally looked like, Nick knew, the marks leaping and splashing across the metal.

Nick knew he ought to be comforted. If the Charter Marks on his dagger were still and dead, then the thing beneath the house should be as well. But he knew it wasn't. He'd seen its eyes flicker.

There was a knock on the door. Nick hastily put the dagger back in its sheath.

"Yes!" he called. The sheathed dagger was still in his hand. For a moment he considered exchanging it for the slim .32 automatic pistol in his suitcase's outer pocket. But he decided against it when the person at the door called out to him.

"Nicholas Sayre?"

It was a woman's voice. A young woman's voice, with the hint of a laugh in it. Not a servant. Perhaps one of the beautiful young women he'd seen arrive. Probably a not very successful actor or singer, the usual adornments of typical country house parties.

"Yes. Who is it?"

"Tesrya. Don't say you don't remember me. Perhaps a glimpse will remind you. Let me in. I've got a bottle of champagne. I thought we might have a drink before dinner."

Nick didn't remember her, but that didn't mean anything. He knew she would have singled him out from the seating plan for dinner, homing in on the surname Sayre. He supposed he should at least tell her to go away to her face. Courtesy to women, even fortune hunters, had been drummed into him all his life.

"Just one drink?"

Nick hesitated, then tucked the sheathed dagger down the inside of his trousers, at the hip. He held his foot against the door in case he needed to shut it in a hurry; then he turned the key and opened it a fraction.

He had the promised glimpse. Pale, melancholy eyes in a very white face, a forced smile from too-red lips. But there were also two hooded men there. One threw his shoulder against the door to keep it open. The other grabbed Nick by the hair and pushed a pad the size of a small pillow against his face.

Nick tried not to breathe as he threw himself

backward, losing some hair in the process, but the sickly-sweet smell of chloroform was already in his mouth and nose. The two men gave him no time to recover his balance. One pushed him back to the foot of the bed, while the other got his right arm in a wrestling hold. Nick struck out with his left, but his fist wouldn't go where he wanted it to. His arm felt like a rubbery length of pipe, the elbow gone soft.

Nick kept flailing, but the pad was back on his mouth and nose, and all his senses started to shatter into little pieces like a broken mosaic. He couldn't make sense of what he saw and heard and felt, and all he could smell was a sickly scent like a cheap perfume badly imitating the scent of flowers.

In another few seconds, he was unconscious.

Nicholas Sayre returned to his senses very slowly. It was like waking up drunk after a party, his mind still clouded and a hangover building in his head and stomach. It was dark, and he was disoriented. He tried to move and for a frightened instant thought he was paralyzed. Then he felt restraints at his wrists and thighs and ankles and a hard surface under his head and back. He was tied to a table, or perhaps a hard bench.

"Ah, the mind wakes," said a voice in the darkness. Nick thought for a second, his clouded mind slowly processing the sound. He knew that voice. Dorrance.

"Would you like to see what is happening?" asked Dorrance. Nick heard him take a few steps, heard the click of a rotary electric switch. Harsh light came with the click, so bright that Nick had to screw his eyes shut, tears instantly welling up in the corners.

"Look, Mr. Sayre. Look at your most useful work."

Nick slowly opened his eyes. At first all he could see was a naked, very bright electric globe swinging directly above his head. Blinking to clear the tears, he looked to one side. Dorrance was there, leaning against a concrete wall. He smiled and pointed to the other side, his hand held close against his chest, fist clenched, index finger extended.

Nick rolled his head and then recoiled, straining against the ropes that bound his ankles, thighs, and wrists to a steel operating table with raised rails.

The creature from the case was right next to him. No longer in the case, but stretched out on an adjacent table ten inches lower than Nick's. It was not tied up. There was a red rubber tube running from one of Nick's wrists to a metal stand next to the creature's head. The tube ended an inch above the monster's slightly open mouth. Blood was dripping from the tube, small dark blobs falling in between its jet black teeth.

Nick's blood.

Nick struggled furiously for another second, panic building in every muscle. The ropes did not give at all, and the tube was not dislodged. Then, his strength exhausted, he stopped.

"You need not be concerned, Mr. Nicholas Sayre," said Dorrance. He moved around to look at the creature, gently tapping Nick's slippered feet as he passed. "I am taking only a pint. This will all just be a nightmare in the morning, half remembered, with a dozen men swearing to your conspicuous consumption of brandy."

As he spoke, the light above him suddenly flared into white-hot brilliance. Then, with a bang, the bulb exploded into powder and the room went dark. Nick blinked, the afterimage of the filament burning a white line across the room. But even with that, he could see another light. Two violet sparks that were faint at first but became brighter and more intense.

Nick recognized them instantly as the creature's eyes. At the same time, he smelled a sudden, acrid odor, which got stronger and stronger, coating the back of his mouth and making his nostrils burn. A metallic stench that he knew only too well.

The smell of Free Magic.

The violet eyes moved suddenly, jerking up. Nick felt the rubber hose suddenly pulled from his wrist and the wet sensation of blood dripping down his hand.

He still couldn't see anything save the creature's eyes. They moved again, very quickly, as the thing stood up and crossed the room. It ignored Nick, though he struggled violently against his bonds as it went past. He couldn't see what happened next, but something . . . or someone . . . was hurled against his table, the impact rocking it almost to the point of toppling over.

"No!" shouted Dorrance. "Don't go out! I'll bring you blood! Whatever kind you need—"

There was a tearing sound, and flickering light suddenly filled the room. Nick saw the creature silhouetted in the doorway, holding the heavy door it had just ripped from its steel hinges. It threw this aside and strode out into the corridor, lifting its head back to emit a hissing shriek that was so high-pitched, it made Nick's ears ring.

Dorrance staggered after it for a moment, then returned and flung open a cabinet on the wall. As he picked up the telephone handset inside, the lights in the corridor fizzed and went out.

Nick heard the dial spin three times. Then Dorrance swore and tapped the receiver before dialing again. This time the phone worked, and he spoke very quickly.

"Hello? Lackridge? Can you hear me? Yes . . . ignore the crackle. Is Hodgeman there? Tell him 'Situation Dora.' All the fire doors must be barred and the exit grilles activated. No, tell him now. . . . 'Dora' . . .Yes, yes. It worked, all too well. She's completely active, and I heard Her clearly for the first time, speaking directly into my head, not as a dreaming voice. Sayre's blood was too rich, and there's something wrong with it. She needs to dilute it with normal blood. . . . What? Active! Running around! Of course you're in danger! She doesn't care whose blood. . . . We need to keep Her in the tunnels; then I'll find someone . . . one of the servants. Just get on with it!"

Nick kept silent, but he remembered the

dagger at his hip. If he could bend his hand back and reach it, he might be able to unsheath it enough to work the rope against the blade. If he didn't bleed to death first.

"So, Mr. Sayre," said Dorrance in the darkness. "Why would your blood be different from that of any other bearer of the Charter Mark? It causes me some distress to think I have given Her the wrong sort. Not to mention the difficulty that now arises from Her desire to wash Her drink down."

"I don't know," Nick whispered after a moment's hesitation. He'd thought of pretending to be unconscious, but Dorrance would certainly test that.

In the distance, electric bells began a harsh, insistent clangor. At first none sounded in the corridor outside, then one stuttered into life. At the same time, the light beyond the door flickered on, off, and on again, before giving up in a shower of sparks that plunged the room back into total darkness.

Something touched Nick's feet. He flinched, taking off some skin against the ropes. A few seconds later there was a click near his head, a whiff of kerosene; and a four-inch flame suddenly shed some light on the scene. Dorrance lifted his cigarette lighter and set it on a head-high shelf, still burning.

He took a bandage from the same shelf and started to wind it around Nick's wrist.

"Waste not, want not," said Dorrance. "Even if your blood is tainted, it has succeeded beyond my dearest hopes. I have long dreamed of waking Her."

"It, you mean," croaked Nick.

Dorrance tied off the bandage, then suddenly slapped Nick's face hard with the back of his hand.

"You are not worthy to speak of Her! She is a goddess! A goddess! She should never have been sent away! My father was a fool! Fortunately I am not!"

Nick chose silence once more, and waited for another blow. But it didn't come. Dorrance took a deep breath, then bent under the table. Nick craned his head to see what he was doing but could hear only the rattle of metal on metal.

The man emerged holding two sets of old-style handcuffs, the kind whose cuffs were screwed in rather than key locked. He quickly handcuffed Nick's left wrist to the metal rail of the bed, then did the same with the second set to his right wrist.

"It has been politic to play the disbeliever about your Charter Magic," he said as he screwed the handcuffs tight. "But She has told me different in my dreams, and if She can rise so far from the Wall, perhaps your magic will also serve you . . . and ropes do burn or fray so easily. Rest here, young Nicholas. My mistress may soon need a second drink, whether the taste disagrees with Her or not."

After shaking the handcuffs to make sure they were secure, Dorrance picked up his still-burning cigarette lighter and left, muttering something to himself that Nick couldn't quite hear. It didn't sound entirely sane, but Nick didn't need to hear bizarre mumblings to know that Dorrance was neither the harmless eccentric of his public image or the cunning spymaster of his secret identity. He was a madman in league with a Free Magic creature.

As soon as Dorrance had gone, Nick tested the handcuffs, straining against them. But he couldn't move his hands more than a few inches off the table, certainly not far enough to reach the screws. However, he could reach the pommel of his dagger with the tips of three fingers. After a few failed attempts, he managed to get the blade out, and by rolling his body, he sliced through the rope on his left wrist, cutting himself slightly in the process.

He was trying to move his left ankle up toward his hand when he heard the first distant gunshots and screams. There were more, but they got fainter and fainter, lending hope that the creature was moving farther away.

Not that it made much difference, Nick thought as he rattled his handcuffs in frustration. He couldn't get free by himself. He would have to work out a plan to get Dorrance to at least uncuff him when he returned. Then Nick might be able to surprise him. If he did return. Until then, Nick decided, he should try to rest and gather his strength. As much as the adrenaline coursing through his bloodstream would let him rest, immobilized on a steel operating table in a secret underground facility run by a lunatic, with a totally inimical creature on the loose.

He lay in silence for what he estimated was somewhere between fifteen minutes and an hour, though he was totally unable to judge the passage of time when he was in the dark and so wound up with tension. In that time, every noise seemed loud and significant, and made him twist and tilt his head, as if by moving his ears he could better capture and identify each sound.

There was silence for a while, or near enough

to it. Then he heard more gunshots but without the screams. The shots were repeated a few seconds later, louder and closer, and were followed by the slam and echo of metal doors and then hurrying footsteps. Of more than one person.

"Help!" cried Nick. "Help! I'm tied up in here!"

He figured it was worth calling out. Even fanatical Department Thirteen employees must have realized by now that Dorrance was crazy and he'd unleashed something awful upon them.

"Help!"

The footsteps came closer, and a flashlight beam swung into the room, blinding Nick. Behind its yellow nimbus, he saw two partial silhouettes. One man standing in front of another.

"Get those shackles off and untie him," ordered the second man. Nick recognized the voice. It was Constable Ripton. The man who shuffled ahead, allowing the light to fall on his face and side, was Professor Lackridge. A pale and trembling Lackridge, who fumbled with the screws of the handcuffs. Ripton was holding a revolver on him, but Nick doubted that was why the scientist was so scared.

"Sorry to take so long, sir," said Ripton

calmly. "Bit of a panic going on."

Nick suddenly understood what Ripton had actually been trying to convey with his quick glances back in the guardroom. His uncle's words ran through his head.

It is watched over quite carefully, I assure you.

"You're not really D Thirteen, are you? You're one of my uncle's men?"

"Yes, sir. Indirectly. I report to Mr. Foxe."

Nick sat up as the handcuffs came off, and quickly sliced through the remaining ropes. He was not entirely surprised to see the faint glimmer of Charter Marks on the blade, though they were nowhere near as bright and potent as they'd be near the Wall.

"Can you walk, sir? We need to get moving."

Nick nodded. He felt a bit light-headed but otherwise fine, so he guessed he hadn't lost too much blood to the creature.

"Sorry," Lackridge blurted out as Nick slid off the table and stood up. "I never . . . never thought that this would happen. I never believed Dorrance, thought only to humor him. . . . He said that she spoke to him in dreams, and if it was more awake, then . . . We hoped to be able to discover the secret of waking mental communication. . . . It was—"

"Mind control is what Dorrance thought he could get from it," Ripton said, interrupting him. He tapped his coat pocket. "I've got your diary here. Mind control through people's dreams. And you just went along with whatever Dorrance wanted, you stupid sod."

"What's actually happening?" asked Nick. "Has it killed anyone?"

Lackridge choked out something unintelligible.

"Anyone! It's killed almost everyone down here, and by now it's probably upstairs killing everyone there," said Ripton. "Guns don't work up close to it, bullets fired farther back don't do a thing, and the electric barrier grilles just went *phhht* when it walked up! As soon as I figured it was trying to get out, I doubled around behind it. Now I reckon we follow its path outside and then run like the clappers while it's busy—"

"We can't do that," said Nick. "What about the guests? And the servants—even if they do work for D Thirteen, they can't be abandoned."

"There's nothing we can do," said Ripton. He no longer appeared so calm. "I don't know what that thing is, but I do know that it has already killed a dozen highly trained and fully armed D

Thirteen operatives. Killed them and . . . and drunk their blood. Not . . . not something I ever want to see again. . . ."

"I know what it is," said Nick. "Somewhat. It is a Free Magic creature from the Old Kingdom. A source of Free Magic itself, which is why guns and electricity don't work near it. I would have thought that bullets coming in from farther away would at least hurt it, though. . . ."

"They bounced off. I saw the lead splashes on its hide. . . . Here's a flashlight. You go in front, Professor. Get your key ready."

"We have to try to save the people upstairs," Nick said firmly as they nervously entered the corridor, flashlight beams probing the darkness in both directions. "Has it definitely already got out of here?"

"I don't know! It was through the second guardroom. The library exit might slow it more. It's basically a revolving reinforced concrete-and-steel slab, like a vault door. Supposed to be bombproof—"

"Is there another way up?"

"No," said Ripton.

"Yes," said Lackridge. He stopped and turned, the bronze key gleaming in his hand. Ripton stepped back, and his finger whipped from resting outside the trigger guard to curl directly around the trigger.

"The dumbwaiter!" Lackridge blurted out. "Dorrance has a dumbwaiter from the wine cellar below us here, which goes up through his office to the pantry above."

"What time is it?" asked Nick.

"Half eight," said Ripton. "Or near enough."

"The guests will be at dinner," said Nick. "They won't have heard what's going on down here. If we can take the dumbwaiter to the pantry, we might be able to get everyone out of the house before the creature breaks through to the library."

"And then what?" asked Ripton. "Talk as we go. Head for the office, Prof."

"It's not a Dead thing, so running water won't do much," said Nick as they broke into a jog. "Fire might, though. . . . If we made a barrier of hay and set it alight, that could work. It would attract attention at least. Bring help."

"I don't think the sort of help we need exists around here," said Ripton. "I've never been up north, but I know people in the NPRU, and this is right up their alley. Things like this just don't happen down here."

"No, they don't," said Nick. "They wouldn't have happened this time, either, only Dorrance fed his creature the wrong blood."

"I don't understand," Lackridge said, puffing after them. Now that they were heading for a possible exit, he had gotten more of a grip on himself. "I didn't believe him . . . but . . . Dorrance thought the blood of one of you people with the Charter brand would rouse the creature a little, without danger. Then when we got you to come in for the Forwin Mill investigation, he saw you had a Charter Mark. The opportunity was too good to resist—"

"Shut up!" ordered Ripton. As Lackridge calmed down, the policeman got more tense.

"Dorrance worships the creature, but I don't think even he wanted it this active," snapped Nick. "I can't explain the whole thing to you, but my blood is infused with Free Magic as well as the Charter. I guess the combination is what got the creature going so strongly . . . but it was too rich or something; that's why it's trying to dilute it with normal blood. . . . I wonder if that means that the power it got from my blood will run out. Maybe it'll just drop at some point. . . ."

Lackridge shook his head, as if he still couldn't

believe what he was hearing, despite the evidence.

"It might come back for a refill from you as well," said Ripton. "Here's the office. You first, Professor."

"But what if the creature's in there?"

"That's why you're going first," said Ripton. He gestured with his revolver, and when Lackridge still didn't move, he pushed him hard with his left hand. The bulky ex-boxer rebounded from the door and stood there, his eyes glazed and jowls shivering.

"Oh, I'll go first!" said Nick. He pushed Lackridge aside a little more gently, turned the door handle, and went into Dorrance's office. It was the room he'd been in before, with the big leather club chairs, the desk, and the liquor cabinet.

"It's empty—come on!"

Ripton locked the door after them as they entered the room, and then he slid the top and bottom bolts home.

"Thought I heard something," he whispered. "Maybe it's coming back. Keep your voices down."

"Where's the dumbwaiter?" asked Nick.

Lackridge crossed to a bookshelf and pressed

a corner. The whole shelf swung out an inch, allowing Lackridge to get a grip and open it out completely. The beam of Nick's flashlight revealed a square space behind it about three feet high and just as wide: a small goods elevator or dumb-waiter.

"We'll have to go one at a time," said Ripton. He slipped his revolver into his shoulder holster, laid his flashlight on the desk, and dragged one of the heavy studded leather chairs against the door. "You first, Mr. Sayre. I think it must have heard us, or smelled us, or something; there's definitely movement outside—"

"Let me go!" Lackridge burst out, darting toward the elevator. He was brought up short as Ripton whirled around and kicked him behind the knee, bringing him crashing down, his fall rattling the bottles in the liquor cabinet.

Nick hesitated, then climbed into the dumb-waiter. There were two buttons on the outside frame of the elevator, one marked with an up arrow and one with a down; but as he expected, neither did anything. However, there was a hatch in the ceiling, which when pushed open revealed a vertical shaft and some heavily greased cables. The shaft was walled with old yellow bricks, and some had been removed every few feet to make irregular, but usable, hand and footholds.

Nick ducked his head out and said, "It's electric, not working. We'll have to climb the—"

His voice was drowned out as the metal office door suddenly rang like a bell and the middle of it bowed in, struck with tremendous force from the other side.

"Fire!" Nick shouted as he jumped out of the elevator. "Start a fire against the door!"

He rushed to the liquor cabinet and ripped it open as the creature struck the door again. This second blow sheared the top bolt and bent the top half of the door over, and a dark shape with glowing violet eyes could be seen beyond the doorway. At the same time, Ripton's flashlight shone intensely bright for a second, then went out forever.

The remaining flashlight, left in the elevator, continued to shine erratically. Nick frantically threw whisky and gin bottles at the base of the door, and Ripton struck a match on the chair leg, swearing as it burst into splinters instead of flame. Then his second match flared and he flicked it across to the alcohol-soaked chair, and there was a blue flash and a ball of flame exploded around the door, searing off both Ripton's and Nick's eyebrows.

The creature made a horrid gargling, drowning sound and backed away. Nick and Ripton retreated to the wall and hunched down to try to get below the smoke, which was already filling the room. Lackridge was still slumped on the floor, not moving, the smoke twirling and curling over his back.

"Go!" Ripton coughed, gesturing with his thumb at the dumbwaiter.

"What about . . . ridge?"

"Leave him!"

"You go!"

Ripton shook his head, but when Nick crawled across to Lackridge, Ripton climbed into the dumbwaiter. The professor was a dead weight, too heavy for Nick to move without standing up. As he tried again, an unopened bottle exploded behind him, showering the back of his neck with hot glass. The smoke was getting thicker with every second, and the heat more intense.

"Get up!" Nick coughed. "You'll die here!"

Lackridge didn't move.

Flames licked at Nick's back and he smelled burning hair. He could do nothing more for the professor. He had only reduced his own chances of survival. Cradling his arms around his head, Nick dived into the dumbwaiter.

He had hoped for clean air there, but it was no better. The elevator shaft was acting as a chimney, sucking up the smoke. Nick felt his throat and lungs closing up and his arms and legs growing weaker. He thrust himself through the hatch, climbed onto the roof of the dumbwaiter, and felt about for the hatch cover, slapping it down in the hope that this might stop some of the smoke. Then, coughing and spitting, he found the first missing bricks and began to climb.

He could hear Ripton somewhere up above him, coughing and swearing. But Nick wasn't listening for Ripton. All his senses were attuned to what might be happening lower down. Would the creature come through the fire and swarm up the shaft?

The smoke did begin to thin a little as Nick climbed, but it was still thick enough for him to smash his head into Ripton's boots after he had climbed up about forty feet. The sudden shout it provoked confirmed that Ripton had been thinking about where the creature was as well.

"Sorry!" Nick gasped. "I don't think it's following us."

"There's a door here. I'm standing on the edge

of it, but I can't slide the bloody thing— Got it!"

Light spilled into the shaft as smoke wafted out of it. Hard white gaslight. Ripton stepped through, then turned to help Nick pull himself up and over.

They were in a long whitewashed room lined from floor to ceiling with shelves and shelves of packaged food of all varieties. Tins and boxes and packets and sacks and bottles and puncheons and jars.

There was a door at the other end. It was open, and a white-clad cook's assistant was staring at them openmouthed.

"Fire!" shouted Nick, waving his arms to clear the smoke that was billowing out fast from behind him. He started to walk forward, continuing to half shout, his voice raspy and dulled by smoke. "Fire in the cellars! Everyone needs to get out, to the . . . Which field is closest, with hay?"

"The home meadow," croaked Ripton. He cleared his throat and tried again. "The home meadow."

"Tell the staff to evacuate the house and assemble on the home meadow," Nick ordered in his most commanding manner. "I will tell the guests."

"Yes, sir!" stammered the cook's assistant. There was still a lot of smoke coming out, even though Ripton had managed to close the door to the dumbwaiter. "Cook will be angry!"

"Hurry up!" said Nick. He strode past the assistant and along a short corridor, to find himself in the main kitchen, where half a dozen immaculately white-clad men were engaged in an orderly but complex dance around a number of counters and stove tops, directed by the rapid snap of commands from a small, thin man with the tallest and whitest hat.

"Fire!" roared Nick. "Get out to the home meadow! Fire!"

He repeated this as he strode through the kitchen and out the swinging doors immediately after a waiter who showed the excellence of his training by hardly looking behind him for more than a second.

As Nick had thought, the dinner guests were making so much noise of their own that they would never have heard any kind of commotion deep in the earth under their feet. Even when he burst out of the servants' corridor and jumped onto an empty chair near the head of the table that was probably his, only five or six of the forty guests looked around.

Then Ripton fired two rapid shots into the ceiling.

"Ladies and gentlemen, I do beg your pardon!" shouted Nick. "There is a fire in the house! Please get up at once and follow Mr. Ripton here to the home meadow!"

Silence met this announcement for perhaps half a second; then Nick was assaulted with questions, comments, and laughter. It was such a babble that he could hardly make out any one coherent stream of words; but clearly half the guests thought this was some game of Dorrance's; a quarter of them wanted to go and get their jewels, favorite coats, or lapdogs; and the last quarter intended to keep eating and drinking whether the house burned down around them or not.

"This isn't a joke!" Nick screamed, his voice barely penetrating the hubbub. "If you don't go now, you'll be dead in fifteen minutes! Men have already died!"

Perhaps ten of the guests heard him. Six of them pushed their chairs back and stood. Their movement caused a momentary lull, and Nick tried again.

"I'm Nicholas Sayre," he said, pointing at his

burnt hair and blackened dress shirt, and his bloodied cuffs. "The Chief Minister's nephew. I am not playing games for Dorrance. Look at me, will you! Get out now or you will die here!"

He jumped down as merry pandemonium turned into panic, and almost knocked down the butler, who had been standing by to either assist or restrain him; Nick couldn't be sure which.

"You're D Thirteen, right?" he asked the imposing figure. "There's been an accident downstairs. There is a fire, but there's an . . . animal . . . loose. Like a tiger, but much stronger, fiercer. No door can hold it. We need to get everyone out on the home meadow, and get them building a ring of hay. Make it about fifty yards in diameter, and we'll gather in the middle and set it alight to keep the animal out. You understand?"

"I believe I do, sir," said the butler, with a low bow and a slight glance at Ripton, who nodded. The butler then turned to look at the footmen, who stood impassively against the wall as guests ran past them, some of them screaming, some giggling, but most fearful and silent. He tuned his voice to a penetrating pitch and said, "James, Erik, Lancel, Benjamin! You will lead the guests to the home meadow. Lukas, Ned, Luther, Zekall! You will alert Mrs. Krane, Mr. Rowntree, Mr. Gowing, and Miss Grayne, to have all their staff immediately go to the home meadow. You will accompany them. Patrick, go and ring the dinner gong for the next three minutes without stopping, then run to the home meadow."

"Good!" snapped Nick. "Don't let anyone stay behind, and if you can take any bottles of paraffin or white spirits out to the meadow, do so! Ripton, lead the way to the library."

"No, sir," said Ripton. "My job's to get you out of here. Come on!"

"We can bar the doors! What the—"

Nick felt himself suddenly restrained by a bear hug around his arms and chest. He tried to throw himself forward but couldn't move whoever had picked him up. He kicked back but was held off the ground, his feet uselessly pounding the air.

"Sorry, sir," said Ripton, edging well back so he couldn't be kicked. "Orders. Take him out to the meadow, Llew."

Nick snapped his head back, hoping to strike his captor's nose, but whoever held him was not only extremely big and strong but also a practiced wrestler. Nick craned around and saw he was in the grip of a very tall and broad footman, one he had noticed when he had first arrived, polishing a suit of armor in the entrance hall that, though man-size, came up only to his shoulder.

"Nay, you shan't escape my clutch, Master," said Llew, striding out of the dining room like a determined child with a doll. "Won the belt at Applethwick Fair seven times for the wrestling, I have. You get comfortable and rest. It baint far to the home meadow."

Nick pretended to relax as they joined the column of people going through the main doors and out across the graveled drive and lawn. It was still quite light, and a harvest moon was rising, big and kind and golden. Many of the people slowed down as the sudden hysteria of Nick's warning ebbed. It was a beautiful night, and the home meadow looked rustic and inviting, with the haycocks still standing, the work of spreading the hay into a defensive ring not yet begun, though the butler was already directing servants to the task.

Halfway across the lawn, Nick suddenly arched his back and tried to twist sideways and out of Llew's grip, but to no avail. The big man just laughed.

The lawn and the meadow were separated by a fence in a ditch, or ha-ha, so as not to spoil the view. Most of the guests and staff were crossing this on a narrow mathematical bridge that supposedly featured no nails or screws, but Llew simply climbed down. They were halfway up the other side when there was a sudden, awful screech behind them, a shrill howl that came from no human throat or any animal the Ancelstierrans had ever heard.

"Let me go!" Nick ordered. He couldn't see what was happening, save that the people in front had suddenly started running, many of them off in random directions, not to what he hoped would be safety. If they could get the hay spread quickly enough and get it alight . . .

"Too late to go back now, sir," said Ripton. "Let him go, Llew! Run!"

Nick looked over his shoulder for a second as they ran the last hundred yards to the center of the meadow. Smoke was pouring out of one wing of the house, forming a thick, puffy worm that reached up to the sky, black and horrid, with red light flickering at its base. But that was not what held his attention.

The creature was standing on the steps of the

house, its head bent over a human victim it held carelessly under one arm. Even from a distance, Nick knew it was drinking blood.

There were people running behind Nick, but not many; and while they might have been dawdling seconds before, they were sprinting now. For a moment Nick hoped that everyone had gotten out of the house. Then he saw movement behind the creature. A man casually walked outside to stand next to it. The creature turned to him, and Nick felt the grip of horror as he expected to see it snatch the person up. But it didn't. The creature returned to its current victim, and the man stood by its side.

"Dorrance," said Ripton. He drew his revolver, rested the barrel on his left forearm, and aimed for a moment, before holstering the weapon again. "Too far. I'll wait till the bastard's closer."

"Don't worry about Dorrance for the moment," said Nick. He looked around. The guests were all clustered together in the center of the notional fifty-yard-diameter circle, and only the servants were spreading hay, under the direction of the butler. Nick shook his head and walked over to the guests. They surged toward him in turn, once again all speaking at the same time.

"I demand to know—"

"What is going on?"

"Is that . . . that animal really—"

"Clearly this is not properly—"

"This is an outrage! Who is respons—"

"Shut up!" roared Nick. "Shut up! That animal is from the Old Kingdom! It will kill all of us if we don't keep it out with fire, which is why everybody needs to start spreading hay in a ring! Hurry!"

Without waiting to see their response, Nick ran to the nearest haycock and tore off a huge armful of hay and ran to add it to the circle. When he looked up, some of the guests were helping the servants, but most were still bickering and complaining.

He looked across at the house. The creature was no longer on the steps. There was a body sprawled there, but Dorrance had vanished as well.

"Start pouring the paraffin!" shouted Nick. "Get more hay on the ring! It's coming!"

The butler and some of the footmen began to run around the circle, spraying white petroleum spirit out of four-gallon tins.

"Anyone with matches or a cigarette lighter,

stand by the ring!" yelled Nick. He couldn't see the creature, but his forehead was beginning to throb, and when he pulled his dagger out an inch, the Charter Marks were starting to glow.

Two people suddenly jumped the hay and ran across the meadow, heading for the drive and the front gate. A young man and woman, the woman throwing aside her shoes as she ran. She was the one who had come to his door, Nick saw. Tesrya, as she had called herself.

"Come back!" shouted Nick. "Come back—"

His voice fell away as a tall, strange shape emerged from the sunken ditch of the ha-ha, its shadow slinking ahead. Its arms looked impossibly long in the twilight, and its legs had three joints, not two. It began to lope slowly after the running couple, and for a brief instant Nick thought perhaps they might have a chance.

Then the creature lowered its head. Its legs stretched; the lope became a run and then a blurring sprint that caught it up with the man and woman in a matter of seconds. It knocked them down with its clubbed hands as it overshot them, turning to come back slowly as they flopped about on the ground like fresh-caught fish.

Tesrya was screaming, but the screams

stopped abruptly as the creature bent over her.

Nick looked away and saw a patch of tall yellow flowers near his feet. Corn daisies, fooled into opening by the bright moonlight.

. . . wrapped in three chains. One of silver, one of lead, and one made from braided daisies . . .

"Ripton!"

"Yes, sir!"

Nick jumped as Ripton answered from slightly behind him and to his left.

"Get anyone who can make flower chains braiding these daisies, and those poppies over there too. The maids might know how."

"What?"

"I know what it sounds like, but there's a chance that thing can be restrained with chains made from flowers."

"But . . ."

"The Old Kingdom. Magic. Just make the chains!"

"I knows the braiding of flowers," Llew said, bending down to gently pick a daisy in his huge hand. "As does my kin here, my nieces Ellyn and Alys, who are chambermaids and will have needle and thread in their apron pockets."

"Get to it then, please," said Nick. He looked

across at where the young couple had fallen. The creature had been there only seconds ago, but now it was gone. "Damn! Anyone see where it went?"

"No," snapped Ripton. He spun around on the spot as he tried to scan the whole area outside the defensive circle.

"Light the hay! Light the hay! Quickly!"

Ripton struggled with his matches, striking them on his heel, but others were quicker. Guests with platinum and gold cigarette lighters flicked them open and on and held them to the hay; kitchen staff struck long, heavy-headed matches and threw them; and one old buffer wound and released a clockwork cigar fire starter, an affectation that had finally come into its own.

Accelerated by paraffin, brandy, and table polish, the ring of hay burst into flames. But not everywhere. While the fire leapt high and smoke coiled toward the moon over most of the ring, one segment about ten feet long remained stubbornly dark, dank, and unlit. The meadow was sunken there, and wet, and the paraffin had not been spread evenly, pooling in a hole.

"There it is!"

The creature came out of the shadow of the oaks near the drive. Its strangely jointed legs propelled it across the meadow in a sprint that would have let it run down a leopard. It moved impossibly, horribly fast, coming around the outside of the ring. Nick and Ripton started to run too, even though they knew they had no chance of beating the creature.

It would be at the gap in seconds. Only one person was close enough to do anything—a kitchen maid running with a lit taper clutched in her right hand, her left holding up her apron.

The creature was far faster, but it had farther to go. It accelerated again, becoming a blur of movement.

Everyone within the ring watched the race, all of them desperately hoping that the fire would simply spread of its own accord, all of them wishing that this fatal hole in their shield of fire would not depend upon a young woman, an easily extinguished taper, and an apron that was too long for its wearer.

Six feet from the edge of the hay, the apron slipped just enough for the girl to trip over the hem. She staggered, tried to recover her balance, and fell, the taper dropping from her hand.

Though she must have been shocked and bruised by the fall, the maid did not lie there. Even as the creature bunched its muscles for the last dash to the gap, the young woman picked up the still-burning taper and threw it the last few feet into the center of the dark section.

It caught instantly, fed by the pool of paraffin that had collected in the dip in the ground. Blue fire flashed over the hay, and flames licked up toward the yellow moon.

The creature shrieked in frustration, its hooked heels throwing up great clods of grass and soil as it checked its headlong rush. For a moment it looked as if it might try to jump the fire, but instead it turned and loped back to the ha-ha, disappearing out of sight.

Nick and Ripton stopped and bent over double, resting their hands on their knees, panting as they tried to recover from their desperate sprint.

"It doesn't like fire," Ripton coughed out after a minute. "But we haven't got enough hay to keep this circle going for more than an hour or so. What happens then?"

"I don't know," said Nick. He was acutely aware of his ignorance. None of this would be happening if the creature hadn't drunk his blood. *His* blood, pumping furiously around his body that very second but a mystery to him. He knew nothing about its peculiar properties. He didn't even know what it could do, or why it had been so strong that the creature needed to dilute it with the blood of others.

"Can you do any of that Old Kingdom magic the Scouts talk about?"

"No," said Nick. "I . . . I'm rather useless, I'm afraid. I've been planning to go to the Old Kingdom . . . to learn about, well, a lot of things. But I haven't managed to get there yet."

"So we're pretty well stuffed," said Ripton. "When the fire burns down, that thing will just waltz in here and kill us all."

"We might get help," said Nick.

Ripton snorted. "Not the help we need. I told you. Bullets don't hurt it. I doubt even an artillery shell would do anything, if a gunner could hit something moving that fast."

"Keep your voice down," Nick muttered. Most of the people inside the ring were huddled right in the center, as much to get away from the drifting smoke of the fires as for the psychological ease of being farther away from the creature. But a knot of half a dozen guests and servants was only a dozen yards away, the servants helping the kitchen maid up and the guests getting in the way.

"I meant Old Kingdom help. I sent a message with Malthan. A telegram for him to send to some people who can get a message to the Old Kingdom quickly."

Ripton bent his head and mumbled something.

"What? What did you say?"

"Malthan never made it past the village," Ripton muttered. "I handed him over to two of Hodgeman's particular pals at the crossroads. Orders. I had to do it, to maintain my cover."

Nick was silent, his thoughts on the sad, frightened, greedy little man who was now probably dead in a ditch not too many miles away.

"Hodgeman said you'd never follow up what happened to Malthan," said Ripton. "He said your sort never did. You were just throwing your weight around, he said."

"I would have checked," said Nick. "I would have left no stone unturned. Believe me."

He looked around at the ring of fire. Sections of it were already dying down, generating lots of smoke but little flame. If Malthan had managed to send the telegram six or more hours ago, there might have been a slim chance that the Abhorsen . . . or Lirael . . . or somebody competent to deal with the creature would have been able to get there before they ran out of things to burn.

"Hodgeman's dead now, anyway. He was one of the first that thing got."

"I sent another message," said Nick. "I bribed Danjers's valet to go down to the village and send a telegram."

"Nowhere to send one from there," said Ripton. "Planned that way, of course. D Thirteen keeping control of communications. The closest telephone would be at Colonel Wrale's house, and that's ten miles away."

"I don't suppose he would have managed it anyway—"

Nick broke off and peered at the closer group of people and then at the central muddle, wiping his eyes as a tendril of smoke wafted across.

"Where is Danjers? I don't remember seeing him at the dinner table, and he's pretty hard to miss. What's the butler's name again?"

"Whitecrake," said Ripton, but Nick was already striding over to the butler, who was issuing orders to his footmen, who in turn were busy feeding the fires with more straw.

"Whitecrake!" Nick called before he had closed the distance between them. "Where is Mr. Danjers?"

Whitecrake rotated with great dignity, rather

like a dreadnought's gun turret, and bowed, allowing Nick to close the distance before he replied.

"Mr. Danjers removed himself from the party and left at five o'clock," he said. "I understand that the curtains in the dining room clashed with his waistcoat."

"His man went with him?"

"Naturally," said Whitecrake. "I believe Mr. Danjers intended to motor over to Applethwick."

Nick felt every muscle in his shoulders and neck suddenly relax, as a ripple of relief passed through on its way to his toes.

"We'll be all right! Danjers's valet is bound to have sent that telegram! Let's see, if they got to Applethwick by seven thirty . . . the telegram would be at Wyverley by eight at the latest. . . . They'd get the message on to the Abhorsen's House however they do it. . . . Then if someone flew by Paperwing to Wyverley, they've got those aeroplanes at the flying school there to fly south . . . though I suppose not at night, even with this moon. . . ."

The tension started to come back as Nick came to the realization that even if the Abhorsen or King Touchstone's Guard had already received his message, there was no way anyone could be at Dorrance Hall before the morning, at the very earliest.

Nick looked up from the fingers he'd been counting on and saw that Ripton, Whitecrake, several footmen, a couple of maids, and a number of the guests were all hanging on his every word.

"Help will be coming," Nick announced firmly. "But we have to make the fires last as long as we can. Everything that can burn must be gathered within this ring. Every tiny piece of straw, any spare clothes, papers you may have on you, even banknotes . . . need to be gathered up. Mr. Whitecrake, can you take charge of that? Ripton, a word if you don't mind."

No one objected to Nick's taking command, and he hardly noticed himself that he had. He had often taken the lead among his school friends and at college, his mind usually grasping any situation faster than his fellows did and his aristocratic heritage providing more than enough self-confidence. As he turned away and walked closer to the fire, Ripton followed at his heels like an obedient shadow.

"There won't be any useful help till morning at the earliest," Nick whispered, his voice hardly audible over the crackle of the fire. "I mean Old Kingdom help. Provided Danjers's man did send the telegram."

Ripton eyed the burning straw.

"I suppose there's a chance the fire'll last till dawn, if we rake it narrower and just try to maintain a bit of flame and coals. Do you . . . Is there a possibility that . . . that thing doesn't like the sun, as well as fire?"

"I don't know. But I wouldn't count on it. From the little I heard my friend Sam talk about it at school, Free Magic creatures roam the day as freely as they do the night."

"Maybe it'll run out of puff," said Ripton. "Like you said. Dorrance didn't even expect it to wake up, and here it is running around—"

"What's that noise?" interrupted Nick. He could hear a distant jangling, carried on the light breeze toward him. "Is that a bell?"

"Oh no . . ." groaned Ripton. "It's the volunteer fire brigade from the village. They know they're not to come here, no matter what. . . ."

Nick looked around at the ring of red fire, and beyond that at the vast column of spark-lit smoke that was winding up from Dorrance Hall. No firefighter would be able to resist that clarion call.

"They're probably only the first," he said quietly. "With this moon, the smoke will be visible for miles. We'll probably have town brigades here in an hour or so, as well as all the local volunteers for a dozen miles or more. I'll have to stop them."

"What! If you leave the circle, that monster will be on you in a second!"

Nick shook his head.

"I've been thinking about that. It ran away from me after it drank just a little of my blood. Dorrance was yelling something about getting it other blood to dilute mine. It could easily have killed me then, but it didn't."

"You can't go out," said Ripton. "Think about it! It's drunk enough in the last hour to dilute your blood a hundred times over! It could easily be ready for more. And it's *your* blood that revved it up in the first place. It'll kill you and get more powerful, and then it'll kill us!"

"We can't just let it kill the firemen," Nick said stubbornly. He started to walk to the other side of the circle, closer to the drive. Ripton hurried along beside him. "I might be able to hurt . . . even kill . . . the creature with this."

He pulled out Sam's dagger and held it up. Fire and moonlight reflected from the blade, but there was green and blue and gold there, too, as Charter Marks swam slowly across the metal. Not fully active, but still strange and wonderful under the Ancelstierran moon.

Ripton did not seem overly impressed.

"You'd never get close enough to use that little pigsticker. Llew! Llew!"

"You're not catching me like that again," said Nick, without slowing down. He stowed the dagger away and picked up a rake, ready to make a gap in the burning barrier. A glance over his shoulder showed him the huge-shouldered Llew getting up from where he was braiding flowers. "If I want to go, you're going to let me this time."

"Too late," said Ripton. "There's the fire engine."

He pointed through the smoke. An ancient horse-drawn tanker, of a kind obsolete everywhere save the most rural counties, was coming up the drive, with at least fourteen volunteer firemen crammed on or hanging off it. They were in various states of uniform, but all wore gleaming brass helmets. Several firemen on horseback came behind the engine, followed by a farm truck loaded with more irregular volunteers, who were armed with fire beaters and buckets. Two small cars brought up the rear, transporting another four brass-helmeted volunteers.

"How did they—"

"There's another entrance to the estate from the village by the gamekeeper's cottage. Cuts half a mile off the front drive."

Nick plunged at the fire with the rake, and dragged some of the burning hay aside before he had to fall back from the smoke and heat. After a few seconds to recover, he pushed forward again, widening the gap. But it was going to take a few minutes to get through, and the firemen would be at the meadow before he could get out.

After his third attempt he reeled back into the grasp of Llew, who held Nick as he tried to swipe his legs with the rake, till Ripton grabbed it and twisted it out of his hands.

"Hold hard, Master!" said Llew.

"It's not attacking them!" cried Ripton. "Just keep still and take a look."

Nick stopped struggling. The fire engine had come to a halt as close as the men and horses could stand the heat, some fifty yards from the house. Firemen leapt off onto the lawn and began to bustle about with hoses as the truck and cars screeched to a halt behind them, throwing up gravel. The two mounted firemen continued on toward the meadow, their horses' hooves clattering on the narrow bridge over the ha-ha.

"It'll take the horsemen," said Nick. "It *must* be hiding in the ditch."

But the riders passed unmolested over the bridge and across the meadow, finally wheeling about close enough to the ring of fire for one of them to shout, "What on earth is happening here?"

Nick didn't bother to answer. He was still looking for the creature. Why hadn't it attacked?

Then he saw it through the swirling smoke. Not attacking anyone, but slinking up from the ha-ha and across the meadow toward the drive. Dorrance was riding on its back, like a child on a bizarre mobile toy, his arms clasped around the creature's long neck. He pointed toward the gatehouse, and the creature began to run.

"It's running away!" exclaimed Ripton.

"It's running," echoed Nick. "I wonder where?"

"Who cares!" Ripton exclaimed happily.

"I do," said Nick. He slipped free of Llew's suddenly relaxed grasp, took a deep, relatively smoke-free breath, sprinted forward, and jumped the ring of fire where he'd already made a partial gap.

He landed clear, fell forward, and quickly

rolled in the grass to extinguish any flames that might have hitched a ride. He felt hot but not burned, and he had not breathed in any great concentration of smoke.

Looking back, he saw Ripton and Llew frantically raking the fire apart, but they had not dared to jump after him. He got up and ran toward the lawn, the parked cars, the fire engine, and the burning house.

There was only one reason the creature would flee now. It had nothing to fear from any weapons the Ancelstierrans could bring to bear. It could have stayed and killed everybody and drunk their blood. It must have decided to cut and run because the power it had gained from Nick's blood was waning and it didn't dare drink any more from him. That meant it would be heading north, toward the Old Kingdom, to find fresh victims to replenish its strength. Victims who bore the Charter Mark on their foreheads.

Nick couldn't let it do that.

He reached the rearmost car and vaulted into the driver's seat, deaf to the roar of the fire, the thud of the pumps, and the contained shriek of the high-pressure hoses. Even when Nick pressed the starter button, none of the firemen looked around, the sound of the little two-seater's engine lost amid all the noise and action.

The car was a Branston Four convertible, very similar to the Branston roadster Nick used to rent occasionally when he was at Sunbere. He slapped the gear lever into reverse with the necessary double tap and gently pulled the hand throttle. The little car rolled back onto the lawn. Nick tapped the lever into the first of the two forward gears and nudged forward.

The firemen still hadn't noticed, but as Nick opened up the hand throttle, the car backfired, hopped forward, and stalled. Someone, presumably the owner of the car, shouted. Nick saw a bronze-helmeted head approaching in the side-view mirror. To his left, Ripton and Llew charged up out of the ha-ha.

He depressed the clutch, hit the starter again, and hoped he had the throttle position right. The car backfired once more and leapt six feet forward, and then the engine suddenly hit a sweet, drumming note. The speedometer stopped hiccuping up and down and started to slowly climb toward the top speed of thirty-five miles per hour. A breeze ruffled Nick's hair, undiminished by the tiny windscreen.

The bronze helmet disappeared from the mirror as the car accelerated along the drive. Ripton and Llew got almost close enough to lay a hand on the rear bumper before they, too, were left behind. Ripton shouted something, and a second later, Nick felt something rebound off his shoulder and land on the seat next to him. He glanced down and saw a chain of yellow daisies, punctuated every ten blooms or so with a red poppy.

Nick didn't bother switching on the car's headlights. The moon was so bright that he could even read the dashboard dials and see the drive clearly. What he couldn't see was the creature and Dorrance, but he had to presume they were heading for the front gate. The wall around the estate was probably no great barrier for the creature, but if it didn't need to climb it, he hoped, it wouldn't.

His guess was rewarded as he turned out of the gate and stopped to look in both directions, up and down the lane. It was darker here, the road shadowed by the trees on either side. But on a slight rise, several hundred yards distant, Nick caught sight of the odd silhouette of the creature, with Dorrance still riding on its back. It disappeared over the crest, running very fast and keeping to the road.

Nick sped after it, the little car vibrating as he wrenched the hand throttle out as far as it would go. The speedometer went past the curlicued *35* that indicated the car's top speed and got stuck against the raised letter *n* that completed the word *Branston* on the dial. But even at that speed, by the time he got to the top of the rise, the creature and Dorrance were gone. The lane kept on, with a very gentle curve to the left, so if Nick's quarry was anywhere within a mile, he should have been able to see them in the clear, cool light of the vast moon overhead.

Various possibilities whisked through Nick's mind. The most disturbing was the thought that they had seen him and were hiding off the road, the creature ready to spring on him as he passed. But the most likely possibility quickly replaced that fear. He hadn't seen it at first, because of the trees, but another road joined the lane just before it started to curve away. The creature must have gone that way.

Nick took the corner a little too fast, and the car slid off the paved road and onto the shoulder, sending up a spray of clods and loose asphalt. For a moment he felt the back end start to slide out, and the steering wheel was loose in his hands, as if it were no longer connected to anything. Then the tires bit again, and he overcorrected and fishtailed furiously for thirty yards before getting fully under control.

When he could properly look ahead, Nick couldn't see the creature and Dorrance. But this road only continued for another two hundred yards, ending at a small railway station. It was not much more than a signal box, a rudimentary waiting room, a platform, and the stationmaster's house set some distance away. A single line of track looped in from the southwest, ran along the platform, then looped back out again, to join the main line that ran straight and true a few minutes' walk away.

It had to be Dorrance Halt, the private railway station for Dorrance Hall. There was a train waiting at the platform, gray-white smoke busily puffing out of the locomotive and steam wafting around its wheels. It was a strangely configured train, in that there were six empty flatcars behind the engine, then a private car. Dorrance's private car, with his crest upon the doors.

Nick suddenly realized the significance of the blazon of the silver chain. Dorrance's several-times-great-grandfather must have been the

Captain-Inquirer who found the creature, and the money gained from the sale of a silver chain was part of the current Dorrance's inheritance.

The significance of the empty flatcars was also apparent to Nick. They were there to separate the locomotive from any Free Magic interference caused by the creature. Dorrance had thought out this mode of transport very carefully. Perhaps he had always planned to take the creature away by train. The thing's long-term goal must always have been to return to the Old Kingdom.

Even as Nick pushed the little Branston to its utmost, the locomotive whistled and began to pull out of the station. As the rearmost carriage passed the waiting room, the electric lights outside fizzed and exploded. The train slowly picked up speed, the gouts of smoke from its funnel coming faster as it rolled away.

Nick wrenched the throttle completely out of its housing, drove off the road, raced through the station garden in a cloud of broken stakes and tomato plants, and drove onto the platform in a desperate effort to crash into the train and stop the creature's escape.

But he was too late. All he could do was lock his knee and try to push his foot and the brake pedal through the floor, as the Branston squealed and slid down the platform, prevented from sliding off the end only by a slow-speed impact with a long and very sturdy line of flowerpots.

Nick stood up and watched the train rattle onto the main line. For a moment, he thought he saw the glow of the creature's violet eyes looking back at him through the rear window of the carriage. But, he told himself as he put the flower chain around his neck and then jumped out of the badly dented Branston, it was probably just a reflection from the moon.

A sound from the waiting room made Nick jump and draw his dagger, but he sheathed it again straightaway. A man wearing a railway-uniform coat over blue-striped pajamas was standing in the doorway, staring, as Nick had just done, at the departing train.

"Where's that train going?" Nick demanded. "When's the next train coming here?"

"I . . . I . . . saw a real monster!" said the man. His eyes were wide with what Nick at first thought was shock but slowly realized was actually delight. "I saw a monster!"

"You're lucky it left you alive to remember it," said Nick. "Now answer my questions! You're the stationmaster, aren't you? Get a grip on yourself!"

The man nodded but didn't look at Nick. He kept staring after the train, even as it disappeared from sight.

"Where's that train going?"

"I . . . I don't know. It's Mr. Dorrance's private train. It's been waiting for days, the crew sleeping over at the house . . . then the call to be ready came only an hour ago. It got a slot going north, that's all I know, direct from Central at Corvere. I guess it'd be going to Bain. You know, I never thought I'd see something like that, with those huge eyes, and those spiked hands. Not here, not—"

"When's the next train north?"

"The Bain Flyer," the man replied automatically. "But she's an express. She doesn't stop anywhere, least of all here."

"When is it due to go past?"

"Ten-oh-five."

Nick looked at the clock above the waiting room, but it was electric and so had ceased to function. There was a watch chain hanging from the stationmaster's pocket, so he snagged that and drew out a regulation railway watch. Mechanical clockwork did not suffer so much from Free

Magic, and its second hand was cheerfully moving round. According to the watch, it was three minutes to ten.

"What's the signal for an obstruction on the line?" snapped Nick.

"Three flares: two outside, one on the track," the man said. He suddenly looked at Nick, his attention returned to the here and now. "But you're not—"

"Where are the flares?"

The stationmaster shook his head, but he couldn't hide an instinctive glance toward a large red box on the wall to the left of the ticket window.

"Don't try to stop me," said Nick very forcefully. "Go back to your house and, if your phone's working, call the police. Tell them . . . Oh, there's no time! Tell them whatever you like."

The flares were ancient, foot-long things like batons, which came in two parts that had to be screwed together to mix the chemicals that in turn ignited the magnesium core. Nick grabbed a handful and rushed over the branch line to the main track. Or what he hoped was the main track. There were four railway lines next to each other, and he couldn't be absolutely sure which one

Dorrance's train had taken heading north.

Even if he got it wrong, he told himself, any engineer seeing three red flares together would almost certainly stop. He screwed the first flare together and dropped it on the track, then the other two followed quickly, one to either side.

With the flares gushing bright blue magnesium and red iron flames, Nick decided he couldn't afford explanations, so he crossed the tracks and crouched down behind a tree to wait.

He didn't have to wait long. He had barely looked over his shoulder at the expanding pall of smoke from Dorrance Hall, which now covered a good quarter of the sky, before he heard the distant sound of a big, fast-moving train. Then, only seconds after the noise, he saw the triple headlights of the engine as it raced down the track toward him. A moment later there was the shriek of the whistle, and then the awful screech of metal on metal as the driver applied the brakes, a screech that intensified every few seconds as the emergency brakes in each of the following carriages came on hard as well.

Nick, on hearing the horrid scream of emergency braking and seeing the sheer speed of the approaching lights, suddenly remembered the boast of the North by Northwest Railway, that its trains averaged 110 miles per hour, and for a fearful moment he wondered if he'd made a terrible mistake. It was one thing to risk his life pursuing the creature, but quite another if he was responsible for derailing the Bain Flyer and killing all the passengers on board.

But despite the noise and speed, the train was slowing under total control, on a long straight path. It came to a shrieking, sparking halt just short of the flares.

Even before it completely stopped, the engineer jumped down from the engine and conductors leapt from almost every one of the fifteen carriages. No one got out on the far side, so it was relatively easy for Nick to run from his tree, climb the steps of a second-class carriage, and go inside without being observed—or so he hoped.

The carriage was split into compartments, with a passageway running down the side. Nick quickly glanced into the first compartment. It had six passengers in it, almost the full complement of eight. Most of them were squashed together trying to look out the window, though one was asleep and another reading the paper with studied detachment. For a brief second, Nick thought of going in, but he dismissed the notion immediately. The passengers would have been together for hours, and the appearance of a bloodied, blackened young man with burnt eyebrows could not go unnoticed or unremarked. Somehow, Nick doubted that any explanation he could provide would satisfy the passengers, let alone the conductor.

Instead, Nick looked up at the luggage rack that ran the length of the carriage. It was pretty full, but he saw a less-populated section. Even as he hoisted himself up and discovered that his chosen resting place was on top of a set of golf clubs and an umbrella, the engine whistled twice, followed by the sound of doors slamming and then the appearance of a conductor and two large, annoyed male passengers, who had just come back aboard.

"I don't know what the railway's coming to."

"Wrack and ruin, that's what."

"Now, now, gentlemen, no harm's done. We'll make up our time, you'll see. We're expected in at twenty-five minutes after midnight, and the Bain Flyer is never late. The railway will buy you a drink or two at the station hotel, and all will be right with the world."

If only, thought Nicholas Sayre. He waited for the men to move along, then wriggled into a slightly less uncomfortable position and rearranged the flower chain across his chest so it would not get crumpled. He lay there, thinking about what had happened and what could happen, and built up plan after plan the way he used to build matchstick towers as a boy, only to have them suffer the same fate. At some point, they always fell over.

Finally, it hit him. Dorrance and the creature had gotten away. At least, they'd gotten away from him. His part in the whole sorry disaster was over. Even if Dorrance's special train was going to Bain, they would arrive at least fifteen minutes ahead of Nick. And there was a good chance that Ripton would have made it to a phone, so the authorities would be alerted. The police in Bain had some experience with things crossing the Wall from the Old Kingdom. They'd get help—Charter Mages from the Crossing Point Scouts. There would be lots of people much more qualified than Nick to deal with the creature.

At least I tried, Nick thought. *When I see Lirael . . . and Sam . . . and the Abhorsen—though I hope I don't have to explain it to her—then I can honestly say I really did my best. I mean, even if I had managed to catch up with them, I don't know if I'd have been able to do anything. Maybe my*

Charter-spelled dagger would have worked . . . maybe I could have tried something else. . . .

Nick suddenly felt very tired, and sore, the weariness more urgent than the pain. Even his feet hurt, and for the first time he realized he was still wearing carpet slippers. He was sure his shoes had been wonderfully shined, but by now they would be ash in the ruins of Dorrance Hall.

Nick shook his head at the thought, pushed back on the golf bag, and, without meaning to, fell instantly asleep.

He woke to find something gripping his elbow. Instantly he lashed out with his fist, connecting with something fleshy rather than the scaly, hard surface his dreaming mind had suggested might be the case.

"Ow!"

A young man dressed in ludicrously bright golfing tweeds looked up at Nick, his hand covering his nose. Other passengers were already in the corridor, most of them with their bags in hand. The train had arrived in Bain.

"You've broken my nose!"

"Sorry!" Nick said as he vaulted down. "I'm very sorry! Mistaken identity. Thought you were a monster."

"I say!" called out the man. "Wait a moment. You can't just hit a man and run away!"

"Urgent business!" Nick replied as he ran to the door, weaving past several other passengers, who quickly stood aside. "Nicholas Sayre's the name. Many apologies!"

He jumped out onto the platform, half expecting to see it swarming with police, soldiers, and ambulance attendants. He would be able to report to someone in authority and then check into the hotel for a proper rest.

But there was only the usual bustle of a big country station in the middle of the night, with the last important train finally in. Passengers were disembarking. Porters were gathering cases. A newspaper vendor was hawking a late edition of the *Times*, shouting, "Flood kills five men, three horses. Getcher paper! Flood kills five—"

There'd be a different headline in the next edition, Nick thought, though it almost certainly wouldn't be the real story. "Fire at Country House" would be most likely, with the survivors paid or pressured to shut up. He would probably get to read it over breakfast, which reminded him that he was extremely hungry and needed to have a very late, much-delayed dinner. Of course, in order to eat, he'd need to get some money, and that meant . . .

"Excuse me, sir, could I see your ticket, please?"

Nick's train of thought derailed spectacularly. A railway inspector was standing too close to him, looking sternly at the disheveled, blackened, eyebrowless young man in ruined evening wear with a chain of braided daisies around his neck and carpet slippers on his feet.

"Ah, good evening," replied Nick. He patted his sides and tried to look somewhat tipsy and confused, which was not hard. "I'm afraid I seem to have lost my ticket. And my coat. And for that matter my tie. But if I could make a telephone call, I'm sure everything can be put right."

"Undergraduate, are you, sir?" asked the inspector. "Put on the train by your friends?"

"Something like that," admitted Nick.

"I'll have your name and college to start with," said the inspector stolidly. "Then we can see about a telephone call."

"Nicholas Sayre," replied Nick. "Sunbere. Though technically I'm not up this term."

"Sayre?" asked the inspector. "Would you be . . ."

"My uncle, I'm afraid," said Nick. "That's

whom I need to call. At the Golden Sheaf Hotel, near Applethwick. I'm sure that if there is a fine to pay, I'll be able to sort something out."

"You'll just have to purchase a ticket before you leave the station," said the inspector. "As for the phone call, follow me and you can—"

He stopped talking as Nick suddenly turned away from him and stared up at the pedestrian bridge that crossed the railway tracks. To the right, in the direction of the station hotel and most of the town, everything was normal, the bridge crowded with passengers off the Flyer eager to get to the hotel or home. But to the lonely left, the electric lights on the wrought-iron lampposts were flickering and going out. One after the other, each one died just as two porters passed by, wheeling a very long, tall box.

"It must be the . . . but Dorrance was at least fifteen minutes ahead of the Flyer!"

"You're involved in one of Mr. Dorrance's japes, are you?" The inspector smiled. "His train just came in on the old track. Private trains aren't allowed on the express line. Hey! Sir! Come back!"

Nick ran, vaulting the ticket inspection barrier, the inspector's shouts ignored behind him. All his resignation burned away in an instant. The creature was here, and he was still the only one who knew about it.

Two policemen belatedly moved to intercept him before the stairs, but they were too slow. Nick jumped up the steps three at a time. He almost fell at the top step, but turned the movement into a flèche, launching himself into a sprint across the bridge.

At the top of the stairs at the other end, he slowed and drew his dagger. Down below, at the side of the road, the tall box was lying on its side, open. One of the two porters was sprawled next to it, his throat ripped out.

There was a row of shops on the other side of the street, all shuttered and dark. The single lamp-post was also dark. The moon was lower now, and the shadows deeper. Nick walked down the steps, dagger ready, the Charter Marks swimming on the blade bright enough to shed light. He could hear police whistles behind him and knew that they would be there in moments, but he spared no attention from the street.

Nothing moved there until Nick left the last step. As he trod on the road, the creature suddenly emerged from an alcove between two shops and dropped the second porter at its hoofed feet. Its violet eyes shone with a deep, internal fire now, and its black teeth were rimmed with red flames. It made a sound that was half hiss and half growl and raised its spiked club hands. Nick tensed for its attack and tried to fumble the flower chain off his neck with his left hand.

Then Dorrance peered over the creature's shoulder and whispered something in its ear slit. The thing blinked, single eyelids sliding across to dim rather than close its burning violet eyes. Then it suddenly jumped more than twenty feet—but away from Nick. Dorrance, clinging to it for dear life, shouted as it sped away.

"Stay back, Sayre! It just wants to go home."

Nick started to run, but stopped after only a dozen strides, as the creature disappeared into the dark. It had evidently not exhausted all the power it had gained from Nick's blood, or perhaps simply being closer to the Old Kingdom lent it strength.

Panting, his chest heaving from his exertion, Nick looked back. The two policemen were coming down the stairs, their truncheons in hand. The fact that they were still approaching indicated they had not seen the creature.

Nick sheathed his dagger and held up his

hands. The policemen slowed to a walk and approached warily. Then Nick saw a single headlight approaching rapidly toward him. A motorcycle. He stepped out into the street and waved his hands furiously to flag the rider down.

The motorcyclist stopped next to Nick. He was young and sported a small, highly-trimmed mustache that did him no favors.

"What occurs, old man?"

"No . . . time . . . to explain," gasped Nick. "I need your bike. Name's Sayre. Nicholas."

"The fast bowler!" exclaimed the rider as he casually stepped off the idling bike, holding it upright for Nick to get on. He was unperturbed by the sight of Nick's strange attire or the shouts of the policemen, who had started to run again. "I saw you play here last year. Wonderful match! There you are. Bring the old girl back to Wooten, if you don't mind. St. John Wooten, in Bain."

"Pleasure!" Nick said as he pushed off and kicked the motorcycle into gear. It rattled away barely ahead of the running policemen, one of whom threw his truncheon, striking Nick a glancing blow on the shoulder.

"Good shot!" cried St. John Wooten, but the

policemen were soon left behind as easily as the creature had left Nick.

For a few minutes Nick thought he might catch up with his quarry fairly soon. The motorcycle was new and powerful, a far cry from the school gardener's old Vernal Victrix he'd learned on back at Somersby. But after almost sliding out on several corners and getting the wobbles at speed, Nick had to acknowledge that his lack of experience was the limiting factor, not the machine's capacity. He slowed down to a point just slightly beyond his competence, a speed insufficient to do more than afford an occasional glimpse of the creature and Dorrance ahead.

As Nick had expected, they soon left even the outskirts of Bain behind, turning right onto the Bain High Road, heading north. There was very little traffic on the road, and what there was of it was heading the other way. At least until the creature ran past. Those cars or trucks that didn't run off the road as the driver saw the monster stalled to a stop, their electrical components destroyed by the creature's passage. Nick, coming up only a minute or so later, never even saw the drivers. As might be expected this far north, they had instantly fled the scene, looking for running water or, at the very least, some friendly walls.

The question of what the creature would do at the first Perimeter checkpoint was easily answered. When Nick saw the warning sign he slowed, not wanting to be shot. But when he idled up to the red-striped barrier, there were four dead soldiers lying in a row, their heads caved in. The creature had killed them without slowing down. None of them had even managed to get a shot off, though the officer had his revolver in his hand. They hadn't been wearing mail this far south, or the characteristic neck- and nasal-barred helmets of the Perimeter garrison. After all, trouble came from the north. This most southern checkpoint was the relatively friendly face of the Army, there to turn back unauthorized travelers or tourists.

Nick was about to go straight on, but he knew there were more stringent checkpoints ahead, before the Perimeter proper, and the chance of being shot would greatly increase. So he put the motorcycle in neutral, sat it on its stand, and, looking away as much as he could, took the cleanest tunic, which happened to be the officer's. It had a second lieutenant's single pip on each cuff. The previous wearer had probably been much the same age as Nick, and moments before must have been proud of his small command, before he lost it, with his life.

Nick figured wearing the khaki coat would at least give him time to explain who he was before he was shot at. He shrugged it on, left it unbuttoned with the flower chain underneath, got back on the motorcycle, and set off once more.

He heard several shots before he arrived at the next checkpoint, and a brief staccato burst of machine-gun fire, followed a few seconds later by a rocket arcing up into the night. It burst into three red parachute flares that slowly drifted north by northwest, propelled by a southerly wind that would usually give comfort to the soldiers of the Perimeter. They would not have been expecting any trouble.

The second checkpoint was a much more serious affair than the first, blocking the road with two heavy chain-link-and-timber gates, built between concrete pillboxes that punctuated the first of the Perimeter's many defensive lines, a triple depth of concertina wire five coils high that stretched to the east and west as far as the eye could see.

One of the gates had been knocked off its hinges, and there were more bodies on the ground just beyond it. These soldiers had been wearing mail coats and helmets, which hadn't saved them. More soldiers were running out of the pillboxes, and there were several in firing positions to the side of the road, though they'd stopped shooting because of the risk of hitting their own people farther north.

Nick throttled back and weaved the motorcycle through the slalom course of bodies, debris from the gate, and the live but shaken soldiers who were staring north. He was just about to accelerate away when someone shouted behind him.

"You on the motorcycle! Stop!"

Nick felt an urge to open the throttle and let the motorcycle roar away, but his intelligence overruled his instinct. He stopped and looked back, wincing as the thin sole of his left carpet slipper tore on a piece of broken barbed wire.

The man who had shouted ran up and, greatly surprising Nick, jumped on the pillion seat behind him.

"Get after it!"

Nick only had a moment to gain a snapshot of his unexpected passenger. He was an officer, not visibly armed, wearing formal dress blues with more miniatures of gallantry medals than he should have, since he looked no more than twenty-one. He had the three pips of a captain on his sleeves and, more important, on his shoulders the metal epaulette tags NPRU, for the Northern Perimeter Reconnaissance Unit, or as it was better known, the Crossing Point Scouts.

"I know you, don't I?" shouted the captain over the noise of the engine and rush of the wind. "You tried out for the Scouts last week?"

"Uh, no," Nick shouted back. He had just realized that he knew his passenger too. It was Francis Tindall, who had been at Forwin Mill as a lieutenant six months ago. "I'm afraid I'm . . . well, I'm Nicholas Sayre."

"Nick Sayre! I bloody hope this isn't going to be like last time we met!"

"No! But that creature is a Free Magic thing!"

"Got a hostage, too, from the look of it. Skinny old duffer. Pointless carrying him along. We'll still shoot."

"He's an accomplice. It's already killed a lot of people down south."

"Don't worry, we'll settle its hash," Tindall shouted confidently. "You don't happen to know exactly what kind of Free Magic creature it is? Can't say I've ever seen anything like it, but I only got a glimpse. Didn't expect anything like that to run past the window at a dining-in night at Checkpoint Two."

"No, but it's bulletproof and it gets power by drinking the blood of Charter Mages."

Whatever Tindall said in response was lost in the sound of gunfire up ahead, this time long, repeated bursts of machine-gun fire, and Nick saw red tracer bouncing up into the air.

"Slow down!" ordered Tindall. "Those are the enfilading guns at Lizzy and Pearl. They'll stop firing when the thing hits the gate at Checkpoint One."

Nick obediently slowed. The road was straight ahead of them, but dark, the moon having sunk farther. The red tracer was the only thing visible, crisscrossing the road four or five hundred yards ahead of them.

Then big guns boomed in unison.

"Star shell," said Tindall. "Thanks to a southerly wind."

A second after he spoke, four small suns burst high above, and everything became stark black and white, either harshly lit or in blackest shadow.

In the light, Nick saw another deep defensive line of high concertina wire, and another set of gates. He also saw the creature slow not at all, but simply jump up and over thirty feet of wire, smashing its way past the two or three fast but foolish soldiers who tried to stick a bayonet in it as it hit the ground running.

Dorrance was no longer on its back.

Nick saw him a moment later, lying in the middle of the road. Braking hard, he lost control of the bike at the last moment, and it flipped up and out, throwing both him and Tindall onto the road, but fortunately not at any speed.

Nick lay there for a moment, the breath knocked out of him by the impact. After a minute, he slowly got to his feet. Captain Tindall was already standing, but only on one foot.

"Busted ankle," he said as he hopped over to Dorrance. "Why, it's that idiot jester Dorrance! What on earth would someone like him be doing with that creature?"

"Serving Her," whispered Dorrance, his voice startling both Tindall and Nick. The older man had been shot several times and looked dead, his chest black and sodden with blood. But he opened his eyes and looked directly at Nick, though he clearly saw something or someone else. "I knew Her as a child, in my dreams, never knowing She was real. Then Malthan came, and I saw Her picture, and I remembered Father sending Her away. He was mad, you know. Lackridge found Her for me again. It was as I remembered, Her voice in my head. . . . She only wanted to go home. I had to help Her. I had to . . ."

His voice trailed away and his eyes lost their focus. Dorrance would play the fool no more in Corvere.

"If it wants to go north, I suppose we could do worse than just let it go across the Wall," said Tindall. He waved at someone at the checkpoint and made a signal, crossing his arms twice. "If it can, of course. We can send a pigeon to the Guards at Barhedrin, leave it to them to sort out."

"No, I can't do that," said Nick. "I . . . I'm already responsible for loosing the Destroyer upon them, and I did nothing to help fight it. Now I've done it again. That creature would not be free if it weren't for me. I can't just leave it to Lirael, I mean the Abhorsen . . . or whoever."

"Some things are best left to those who can deal with them," said Tindall. "I've never seen a Free Magic creature move like that. Let it go."

"No," said Nick. He started walking up the road. Tindall swore and started hopping after him.

"What are you going to do? You have the

Mark, I know, but are you a Mage?"

Nick shook his head and started to run. A sergeant and two stretcher bearers were coming through the gate, while many more soldiers ran purposefully behind them. With star shell continuing to be fired overhead, Nick could clearly see beyond the gates to a parade ground, with a viewing tower or inspection platform next to it, and beyond that a collection of low huts and bunkers and the communications trenches that zigzagged north.

"The word for the day is *Collection* and the countersign is *Treble*," shouted Tindall. "Good luck!"

Nick waved his thanks and concentrated on ignoring the pain in his feet. Both his slippers were ripped to pieces, barely more than shreds of cloth holding on at the heels and toes.

The sergeant saluted as he went past, and the stretcher bearers ignored him, but the two soldiers at the gate aimed their rifles at him and demanded the password. Nick gave it, silently thanking Tindall, and they let him through.

"Lieutenant! Report!" shouted a major Nick almost ran into as he entered the communications trench on the northern side of the parade ground.

But he ignored the instruction, dodging past the officer. A few steps farther on, he felt something warm strike his back, and his arms and hands suddenly shone with golden Charter Magic fire. It didn't harm him at all, but actually made him feel better and helped him recover his breath. He ran on, oblivious to the shocked Charter Mage behind him, who had struck him with his strongest spell of binding and immobility.

Soldiers stood aside as he ran past, the Charter Magic glow alerting them to his coming. Some cheered in his wake, for they had seen the creature leap over them, and they feared that it might return before a Scout came to deal with it, as they dealt with so many of the strange things that came from the north.

At the forward trench, Nick found himself suddenly among a whole company of garrison infantry. All one hundred and twenty of them clustered close together in less than sixty yards of straight trench, all standing to on the firing step, looking to the front. The wind was still from the south, so their guns would almost certainly work, but none was firing.

A harried-looking captain turned to see what had caused the sudden ripple of movement among the men near the communications trench, and he saw a strange, very irregularly dressed lieutenant outlined in tiny golden flames. He breathed a sigh of relief, hopped down from the step, and stood in front of Nick.

"About time one of you lot got here. It's plowing through the wire toward the Wall. D Company shot at it for a while, but that didn't work, so we've held back. It's not going to turn around, is it?"

"Probably not," said Nick, not offering the certainty the captain had hoped for. He saw a ladder and quickly climbed up it to stand on the parapet.

The Wall lay less than a hundred yards away, across barren earth crisscrossed with wire. There were tall poles of carved wood here and there, quietly whistling in the breeze among the metal pickets and the concertina wire. Wind flutes of the Abhorsen, there to bar the way from Death. A great many people had died along the Wall and the Perimeter, and the border between Life and Death was very easily crossed in such places.

Nick had seen the Wall before, farewelling his friend Sam on vacation. But apart from a dreamlike memory of it wreathed in fierce golden fire, he had never seen it as more than an antiquity, just an old wall like any other medieval remnant in a good state of preservation. Now he could see the glow of millions of Charter Marks moving across, through, and under the stones.

He could see the creature, too. It was surrounded by a nimbus of intense white sparks as it used its club hands to smash down the concertina wire and wade directly toward a tunnel that went through the Wall.

"I'm going to follow it," said Nick. "Pass the word not to shoot. If any other Scouts come up, tell them to stay back. This particular creature needs the blood of Charter Mages."

"Who should I say—"

Nick ignored him, heading west along the trench to the point where the creature had begun to force its path. There were no soldiers there, only the signs of a very rapid exodus, with equipment and weapons strewn across the trench floor.

Nick climbed out and started toward the Wall. It was night in the Old Kingdom, a darker night without the moon, but the star-shell light spread over the Wall, so he could see that it was snowing there, not a single snowflake coming south.

He lifted the daisy-chain wreath over his head

and held it ready in his left hand, and he drew the dagger with his right. The flowers were crushed, and many had lost petals, but the chain was unbroken, thanks to the linen thread sewn into the stems. Llew and his nieces really had known their business.

Nick was halfway across the No Man's Land when the creature reached the Wall. But it did not enter the tunnel, instead hunkering down on its haunches for half a minute before easing itself up and turning back. It was still surrounded by white sparks, and even thirty yards away Nick could smell the acrid stench of hot metal. He stopped, too, and braced himself for a sudden, swift attack.

The creature slowly paced toward him. Nick lifted the wreath and made ready to throw or swing it over the creature's head. But it didn't attack or increase its pace. It walked up close and bent its long neck down.

Nick didn't take his eyes off it for even a microsecond. As soon as he was sure of his aim, he tossed the wreath over the creature's head. The chain settled on its shoulders, the yellow and red flowers taking on a bluish cast from the crackling sparks that jetted out from the creature's hide.

"Let us talk and make truce, as the day's eye

bids me do," a chill, sharp voice said directly into Nick's mind, or so it felt. His ears heard nothing but the wind flutes and the jangle of cans tied to the wire. "We have no quarrel, you and I."

"We do," said Nick. "You have slain many of my people. You would slay more."

The creature did not move, but Nick felt the mental equivalent of a snort of disbelief.

"These pale, insipid things? The blood of a great one moves in you, more than in any of the inheritors that I have drunk from before. Come, shed your transient flesh and travel with me back to our own land, beyond this prison wall."

Nick didn't answer, for he was suddenly confused. Part of him felt that he could leave his body and go with this creature, which had somehow suddenly become beautiful and alluring in his eyes. He felt he had the power to shuck his skin and become something else, something fierce and powerful and strange. He could fly over the Wall and go wherever he wanted, do whatever he wanted.

Against that yearning to be untrammeled and free was another set of sensations and desires. He did want to change, that was true, but he also wanted to continue to be himself. To be a man, to find out where he fitted in among people, specifically the people of the Old Kingdom, for he knew he no longer could be content in Ancelstierre. He wanted to see his friend Sam again, and he wanted to talk to Lirael. . . .

"Come," said the creature again. "We must be away before any of Astarael's get come upon us. Share with me a little of your blood, so that I may cross this cursed Wall without scathe."

"Astarael's get?" asked Nick. "The Abhorsens?"

"Call them what you will," said the creature. "One comes, but not soon. I feel it, through the bones of the earth beneath my feet. Let me drink, just a little."

"Just a little . . ." mused Nick. "Do you fear to drink more?"

"I fear," said the creature, bowing its head still lower. "Who would not fear the power of the Nine Bright Shiners, highest of the high?"

"What if I do not let you drink, and I do not choose to leave this flesh?"

"Your will is yours alone," said the creature. "I shall go back and reap a harvest among those who bear the Charter, weak and prisoned remnant of my kin of long ago."

"Drink then," said Nick. He cut the bandage

at his wrist and, wincing at the pain, sliced open the wound Dorrance had made. Blood welled up immediately.

The creature leaned forward, and Nick turned his wrist so the blood fell into its open mouth, each drop sizzling as it met the thing's internal fires. A dozen drops fell; then Nick took his dagger again and cut more deeply. Blood flowed more freely, splashing over the creature's mouth.

"Enough!" said the voice in his mind. But Nick did not withdraw his hand, and the creature did not move. "Enough!"

Nick held his hand closer to the creature's mouth, sparks enveloping his fingers, to be met by golden flames, blue and gold twirling and wrestling, as if Charter Magic visibly sought dominance over Free Magic.

"Enough!" screamed the silent voice in Nick's head, driving out all other thoughts and senses, so that he became blind and dumb and couldn't feel anything, not even the rapid stammer of his own heartbeat. "Enough! Enough! Enough!"

It was too much for Nick's weakened body to bear. He faltered, his hand wavering. As the blood missed the creature's mouth, it staggered, too, and fell to one side. Nick fell also, away from it, and the voice inside his head gave way to blessed silence.

His vision returned a few seconds later, and his hearing. He lay on his back, looking up at the sky. The moon was just about to set in the west, but it was like no moonset he had ever seen, for the right corner of it was diagonally cut off by the Wall.

Nick stared at the bisected moon and thought that he should get up and see if the creature was moving, if it was going to go and attack the soldiers in order to dilute his blood once again. He should bandage his wrist, too, he knew, for he could feel the blood still dripping down his fingers.

But he couldn't get up. Whether it was blood loss or simply exhaustion from everything he'd been through, or the effects of the icy voice on his brain, he was as limp and helpless as a rag doll.

I'll gather my strength, he thought, closing his eyes. *I'll get up in a minute. Just a minute . . .*

Something warm landed on his chest. Nick forced his eyes to open just enough to look out. The moon was much lower, now looking like a badly cut slice of pumpkin pie.

His chest got even warmer, and with the warmth, Nick felt just a tiny fraction stronger. He opened his eyes properly and managed to raise his head an inch off the ground.

A coiled spiral made up of hundreds of Charter Marks was slowly boring its way into his chest, like some kind of celestial, star-wrought drill, all shining silver and gold. As each Mark went in, Nick felt strength return to more far-flung parts of his body. His arms twitched, and he raised them too, and saw a nice, clean, Army-issue bandage around his wrist. Then he regained sensation in his legs and lifted them up, to see his carpet slippers had been replaced with more bandages.

"Can you hear me?" asked a soft voice, just out of sight. A woman's voice, familiar to Nick, though he couldn't place it for a second.

He turned his head. He was still lying near the Wall, where he'd fallen. The creature was still lying there, too, a few steps away. Between them, a young woman knelt over Nick. A young woman wearing an armored coat of laminated plates, and over it a surcoat with the golden stars of the Clayr quartered with the silver keys of the Abhorsen.

"Yes," whispered Nick. He smiled and said, "Lirael."

Lirael didn't smile back. She brushed her black hair back from her face with a golden-gloved hand, and said, "The spells are working strangely on you, but they are working. I'd best deal with the Hrule."

"The creature?"

Lirael nodded.

"Didn't I kill it? I thought my blood might poison it. . . ."

"It has sated it," said Lirael. "And made it much more powerful, when it can digest it."

"You'd better kill it first, then."

"It can't be killed," said Lirael. But she picked up a very odd-looking spear, a simple shaft of wood that was topped with a fresh-picked thistle head, and stepped over to the creature. "Nothing of stone or metal can pierce its flesh. But a thistle will return it to the earth, for a time."

She lifted the spear high above her head and drove it down with all her strength into the creature's chest. Surprisingly, the thistle didn't break on the hide that had turned back bullets; it cut through as easily as a hand through water. The spear quivered there for a moment; then it burst, shaft and point together, like a mushroom spore. The dust fell on the creature, and where it fell, the flesh melted away, soaking into the ground. Within seconds there was nothing left, not even the glow of the violet eyes.

"How did you know to bring a thistle?" Nick asked, and then cursed himself for sounding so stupid. And for looking so pathetic. He raised his head again and tried to roll over, but Lirael quickly knelt and gently pushed him back down.

"I didn't. I arrived an hour ago, in answer to a rather confused message from the Magistrix at Wyverley. I expected merely to cross here, not to find one of the rarest of Free Magic creatures. And . . . and you. I bound your wounds and put some healing charms upon you, and then I went to find a thistle."

"I'm glad it was you."

"It's lucky I read a lot of bestiaries when I was younger," said Lirael, who wouldn't look him in the eye. "I'm not sure even Sabriel would know about the peculiar nature of the Hrule. Well, I'd best be on my way. There are stretcher bearers waiting to come over to take you in. I think you'll be all right now. There's no lasting damage. Nothing from the Hrule, I mean. No new lasting effects, that is. . . . I really do have to get going. Apparently there's some Dead thing or other farther south—the message wasn't clear. . . ."

"That was the creature," said Nick. "I sent a

message to the Magistrix. I followed the creature all the way here from Dorrance Hall."

"Then I can go back to the Guards who escorted me here," Lirael said, but she made no move to go, just nervously parted her hair again with her golden-gloved hand. "They won't have started back for Barhedrin yet. That's where I left my Paperwing. I can fly by myself now. I mean, I'm still—"

"I don't want to go back to Ancelstierre," Nick burst out. He tried to sit up and this time succeeded, Lirael reaching out to help him and then letting go as if he were red-hot. "I want to come to the Old Kingdom."

"But you didn't come before," said Lirael. "When we left and Sabriel said you should because of what . . . because of what had happened to you. I wondered . . . that is, Sam thought later, perhaps you didn't want to . . . that is, you needed to stay in Ancelstierre for some person, I mean reason—"

"No," said Nick. "There is nothing for me in Ancelstierre. I was afraid, that's all."

"Afraid?" asked Lirael. "Afraid of what?"

"I don't know," said Nick. He smiled again. "Can you give me a hand to get up? Oh, your hand! Sam really did make a new one for you!"

Lirael flexed her golden, Charter-spelled hand, opening and closing the fingers to show Nick that it was just as good as one of flesh and bone, before she gingerly offered both her hands to him.

"I've had it for only a week," she said shyly, looking down as Nick stood not very steadily beside her. "And I don't think it will work very far south of here. Sam really is a most useful nephew. Do you think you can walk?"

"If you help me," said Nick.

Introduction to Under the Lake

For someone who doesn't like the Arthurian mythos, I am in the odd position of having written two "Arthurian" stories (the other one is "Heart's Desire," also in this collection). At least, I always think I'm not very fond of the whole Arthur thing, believing there are already too many stories and books that have mined the canon. But I love T. H. White's *The Once and Future King*. I love Mary Stewart's *The Hollow Hills* and *The Crystal Cave* (while not being partial to the two later sequels). I like the Arthurian elements in Susan Cooper's The Dark Is Rising sequence. I would especially love to see again a television cartoon series from my childhood called *King Arthur and the Square Knights of the Round Table*. I know there are many other fine Arthurian or Arthurian-influenced books.

So I must not have a problem with Arthurian legend as such. My dissatisfaction probably lies in the way that the legends are used over and over again in the same way: the same stories told with little or no variation of character, plot, theme, or imagery.

The Lady of the Lake is one example of a clichéd character. How many times has she appeared as a beautiful woman, rising out of the water to hand over Excalibur and help out the forces of good? Not to mention being dressed in silken samite.

Finding something new in an Arthurian character was the first thing I thought about when I was asked to write a story for an Arthurian-themed collection (after writhing about in horror, that is, and initially declining the invitation). Several months later, as the deadline approached, I started thinking about the Lady of the Lake. What would it be like living way down deep? Why would she choose to live there? What if she wasn't actually a lady? Or, better still, not even human? And why would she help Arthur? What if she wasn't good at all? What if she was a real monster, like a very smart psychopath?

The story came from there. The anthology I wrote it for never proceeded, adding insult to injury. I'd written an Arthurian story against my better judgment, and all for nothing. But stories share a characteristic with humans, in that they often get second, third, or even more chances. For "Under the Lake," that came with publication in *The Magazine of Fantasy & Science Fiction*, and I was on the record as having committed Arthuriana.

UNDER THE LAKE

MERLIN HAS COME again, down to where the light has gone and there is only darkness. Darkness and pressure, here where the water is as cold and hard as steel. He is bright himself, so bright that he hurts my eyes and I must lid them and turn away. Merlin uses that brightness, knowing that I cannot bear it, nor bear him seeing the creature I have become.

That is his strength, and it is the reason I will ultimately give him what he wants. For Merlin has power, and only he can give me what I need. He knows that, but as in any negotiation, he does not know at which point he will win. For I have two things that he seeks, and he has the price of only one.

I think he will choose Excalibur, for even he finds it difficult to think down here, under the lake. We can both see the strands of time that unravel from this choice, but I do not think Merlin sees as far as I in this darkness. He will choose the sword for his Arthur, when he could have the Grail.

I admit the sword seems more readily useful. With the scabbard, of course. But Merlin's sight does not see behind, only forward, and what he has learned of the sword is only a small part of the story.

If he chose to be less blinding, I might tell him more. But the light is cruel, and I do not care to prolong our conversation. I will merely cast my own mind back, while he talks. It is as effective a means as any to avoid the spell he weaves so cleverly behind his words. Only Merlin would seek to gull me so, even though he should know better. Let him talk, and I will send his spell back. Back into time, when I walked under the sun, in the land that was called Lyonnesse.

Back into time, when the barbarians first landed on Lyonnesse's sweet shores, and the people came to me, begging for a weapon that would save them. They had no fear of me in those days, for I had long held a woman's shape, and I had never broken the agreement I made with their ancestors long ago. Not that they ever sought me out in times of peace and plenty, for they also remembered that I did nothing without exacting a price.

As I did when they asked me to make a sword, a sword that could make a hero out of a husbandman, a warrior of an aleswiller, a savior from a swineherd. A sword that would give its wielder the strength of the snow-fed river Fleer, the speed of the swifts that flew around my hill, and the endurance of the great stone that sat above my hidden halls.

They were afraid of the barbarians, so they paid the price. A hundred maidens who came to my cold stone door, thinking they would live to serve me in some palace of arching caverns underearth. But it was their lives I wanted, not their service. It was their years I supped upon to feed my own, and their blood I used to quench the sword. I still thought of humans as I thought of other animals then, and felt nothing for their tears and cries. I did not realize that as I bound the power of river, swifts, and stone into the metal, I also filled the sword with sorrow and the despair of death.

They called the sword Excalibur, and it seemed everything they had asked. It took many months before they discovered it was both more and less. It was used by several men against the barbarians and delivered great victories. But in every battle the wielder was struck with a battle madness, a melancholy that would drive him alone into the midst of the enemy. All would be strong and swift and untiring, but eventually they would always be struck down by weight of numbers, or number of wounds.

The people came to me again, and demanded that I mend the madness the sword brought, or make the wielder impossible to wound, so the sword could be used to its full effect. They argued that I had not fulfilled the bargain and would pay no more.

But I sat silent in my hill, the barbarians still came in their thousands, and there were few who dared to wield Excalibur, knowing that they would surely die.

So they brought the two hundred youths I had demanded. Some even came gladly, thinking they would meet their sweethearts who had gone before. This time I was more careful, taking their futures from them without warning, so there was no time for pain, despair, or sadness. From their hair I wove the scabbard that would give the wearer a hundred lives between dawn of one day and dawn the next.

I knew nothing of human love then, or I would have demanded still younger boys, who had no knowledge of the girls who came to my hill the year before. The scabbard did make the bearer proof against a multiplicity of wounds, but it also called to the sword and held it like a lover, refusing to let go. Only a man of great will could draw the sword, or a sorcerer, and there were few of those in Lyonnesse, for I disliked their kind. Many a would-be hero died with Excalibur still sheathed upon his belt. Even a hundred lives is not enough against a hundred hundred wounds.

Each time, the sword and scabbard came back to me, drawn to the place of their making. Each time I returned them to the good folk of Lyonnesse, as they continued their largely losing war against the barbarians. Not that I cared who won one way or another, save for tidiness and a certain sense of tradition.

Many people came to me in those times of war, foolishly ignoring the pact that spoke of the days and seasons when I would listen and spare their lives. Consuming them, I learned more of humanity, and more of the magic that lurked within their brief lives. It became a study for me, and I began to walk at night, learning in the only way I knew. Soon, it was mostly barbarians I learned from, for the local folk resumed the practice of binding rowan twigs in their hair, and they remembered not to walk in moonlight. Once again children were given small silver coins to wear as earrings. Some nights I gathered many blood-dappled coins but garnered neither lives nor knowledge.

In time the barbarians learned too, and so it was that a deputation came to me one cold Midwinter Day, between noon and the setting of the sun. It was composed of the native folk I knew so well, and barbarians, joined together in common purpose. They wanted me to enforce a peace upon the whole land of Lyonnesse, so that no man could make war upon another.

The price they were prepared to pay was staggering, so many lives that I would barely need to feed again for a thousand years. Given my new curiosity about humankind, the goal was also fascinating, because for the first time in my long existence, I knew not how it could be achieved.

They paid the price, and for seven days a line of men, women, and children wound its way into my hill. I had learned a little, for this third time, so I gave them food and wine and smoke that made them sleep. Then as they slept, I harvested their dreams, even as I walked among them and drank their breath.

The dreams I took in a net of light, down through the earth to where the rocks themselves were fire, and there I made the Grail. A thing of such beauty and of such hope began to form that I forgot myself in the wonder of creation, and poured some of my dreams into it too, and a great part of my power.

Perhaps some of my memory disappeared in the making of the Grail, because I had forgotten what my power meant to the land of Lyonnesse. All that long climb back from the depths of the earth I gazed at what I had made, and I thought nothing of the rumbling and shaking at my feet. Down there the earth was never still. I did not realize that its mutterings were following me back into the light.

I emerged from my hill to find the deputation gone, panicked by the ground that shook and roared beneath them. I held the Grail aloft, and shouted that it would bring peace to all who drank from it. But even as I spoke, I saw the horizon lift up like a folded cloth, and the blue of the sky was lost in the terrible darkness of the sea. The sea, rising up higher than my hill or the mountains behind, a vast and implacable wave that seemed impossible—till I realized that it was not the sea that rose, but Lyonnesse that fell. And I remembered.

Long ago, long ago, I had shored up the very foundations of the land. Now, in my making of the Grail, I had torn away the props. Lyonnesse would drown, but I would not drown with it. I became a great eagle and rose to the sky, the Grail clutched in my talons. Or rather, I tried to. My wings beat in a frenzy, but the Grail would not move. I tried to let it go, but could not, and still the wave came on, till it blocked out the very sun and it was too late to be flying anywhere.

It was then I knew that the Grail brought not only peace but judgment. I had filled it with the dreams of a thousand folk, dreams of peace and justice. But I had let other dreams creep in, and one of those was a dream that the white demon that preyed upon them in the moonlit nights would be punished for the deaths she wrought, and the fear she had brought upon the people.

The wave came upon me as I changed back to human shape, crushing me beneath a mountain wall of water, picking me up, Grail and all, for a journey without air and light that crossed the width of Lyonnesse before it let me go. I was broken at the end, my human form beyond repair. I took another shape, the best I could make, though it was not pleasing to my or any other eyes. It is a measure of the Grail's mercy that this seemed sufficient punishment, for only then could I let it fall.

I did let it go, but never from my sight. For now, even waking, I dreamed of all the folk of Lyonnesse who died under the wave, and only the Grail would give me untroubled rest. Years passed, and I slithered from sea to river to lake, till at last I came here, following the drifts and tumblings of the Grail. I was not surprised to find that Excalibur awaited me, still sheathed and shining, despite its long sojourn in the deep. It seemed fitting that everything I made should lie together, both the things and the fate. Even the Grail seemed content to sit, as if waiting for the future I could not see.

I cannot remember when Merlin first found me here, but it is not so strange, given our birthing together so long ago. He has studied humanity with greater care than I, and used his power with much more caution.

There! I have left his spell behind with my drowned past, and now we shall bargain in earnest. He will give me back my human shape, he says, in return for the sword. He knows it is an offer I cannot refuse. What is the sword to me, compared to the warmth of the sun on my soft skin, the colors that my eyes will see anew, the cool wind that will caress my face?

I will give him the sword. It will bring Arthur triumph but also sorrow, as it has always done, for his victories will never be his own. The scabbard too, will save him and doom him, for a man who cannot be wounded is not a man whom a woman can choose to love.

Merlin is clever. He will not touch the sword himself, but will tell me when I must give it up to Arthur. Only then will I receive my side of the bargain. It is curious to feel expectation again, and something that I must define as hope.

Even the brightness seems less wearing on my eyes, or perhaps it is Merlin who has chosen to be kind. Yes, now he talks of the Grail, and asks me to give it up. Merlin does not understand its nature, I think, or he would not be trying to get it for himself.

The Grail will wait, I tell him. Go and fetch

your king, your Arthur. I will give him the sword, the scabbard too, and may he use them well.

Merlin knows when to wait. He has always been good at waiting. He leaps upward in a flurry of light and I slide back into my cave, to coil around the hollow that contains my treasures. The Grail was there yesterday, but not now. If I thought Merlin had stolen it, I would be angry. Perhaps I would pursue him, up into the warmer, lighter waters, to see if his power is as great as what remains of mine.

But I will not, for I know the Grail has left me without Merlin's tricks or thievery, as it has left a thousand times before. I have always followed it in the past, seeking the relief it gave. Now I think time has served that same purpose, if not so well. Time and cold and depth. It slows thought, and dulls memory. Only Merlin's coming has briefly woken me at all, I realize, and there lies the irony of our exchange.

I will give the sword to Arthur, but without the Grail I do not think I will long remain in human shape. The Grail taught me guilt, but it also drank it up. Without it, I shall have to think too much and remember too much. I will have to live with a light that blinds me, until at last I have used up all the lives of Lyonnesse that lie within my gut.

No. The Grail has gone. When Excalibur is likewise gone, I shall return to the darkness and the cold, to this place where a dull serpent can sleep without dreaming. Till once again I must obey the call of strength and sorrow, of love and longing, of justice and of peace. All these things of human magic, that I never knew till I made the sword and scabbard, and never understood until I made the Grail.

INTRODUCTION TO CHARLIE RABBIT

"Charlie Rabbit" was written while the (second) Iraq war was brewing but before it had begun, specifically for the War Child charity anthology *Kids' Night In*. War Child (www.warchild.org) is a network of independent organizations working across the world to help children affected by war. The royalties donated by the authors from the *Kids' Night In* anthology have been used to help children in all kinds of war-torn areas to get schooling, medical attention, and much more.

In "Charlie Rabbit" I wanted to tell a story, of course, but also to communicate a snapshot of some small children caught up in a war. A non-specific war, because the children suffer no matter what the war is about, or where it is, or who is fighting it. Often children in a war have little or no idea of what is really going on. They simply suffer the consequences.

I've thought a lot about war and conflict and read a lot about it, from military history to personal accounts. I served in the Australian Army

Reserve for four years (a part-time force like the American National Guard), so I have a little understanding of what it means to be a peacetime soldier. Back then, there were a lot of Vietnam veterans still serving, and I listened to them, and I thought about what might happen if I had to go to war, too, and I have thought about it since.

But until I sat down to work out what I was going to write for the War Child anthology, I had never considered the particular horror of being a child in a country at war: totally powerless, totally vulnerable, and totally innocent.

"Charlie Rabbit" is my attempt to help other people think about the actual children who are affected by war, even if they survive. Children just like your own, or the kids next door, or the children at the school across the road.

Children who would like to have two parents, peaceful lives, and a Charlie Rabbit.

Charlie Rabbit

Abbas woke to the scream of sirens. Half asleep, he tumbled out of the upper bunk and shook his brother, who was asleep below.

"Joshua! Get up!"

Joshua opened one eye, but he didn't move any other muscle. He was six, and unruly. Abbas, who was eleven, felt practically grown up by comparison.

"I don't want to go down the hole," complained Joshua. He still hadn't opened his other eye.

Abbas pulled the bedclothes back and dragged Joshua onto the floor. Charlie Rabbit, who had been under the blankets, fell out too. His long floppy ears sprawled across Abbas's bare feet, till Joshua grabbed his constant companion and hugged him to his chest.

"It's a cellar, not a hole, and we have to go now!"

Joshua lay on the floor and shut both eyes. Abbas hauled him up into a sitting position, but Joshua was as floppy as Charlie Rabbit's ears. As soon as Abbas let go, Joshua slumped down again.

"Mum!" shouted Abbas, a touch of panic in his voice. He could feel a rapid, regular vibration through the walls and floor, and could hear something like distant thunder beneath the shrieking sirens. But it wasn't thunder. The cruise missiles were hitting the south side. The next wave would strike much closer to home. He had to get Joshua to the shelter.

"Mum!"

There was no answer. Abbas, still half asleep, felt a sudden pain of memory. Their mother had been wounded in a daylight air raid that afternoon, and had been taken away. To a hospital, Abbas desperately hoped, if there was one left. His grandparents were supposed to come over, but they hadn't arrived by nightfall. Abbas had put Joshua to bed and then, much later, had fallen into an exhausted sleep himself.

He tried not to think about what might have happened to Grandpa and Gramma, in the same way he tried not to think about his father, who had been drafted eighteen months before. The single postcard they had gotten from him was still pinned to the wall of their room, its edges curled, the ink fading.

No one could help him, Abbas realized. He had to look after Joshua by himself.

"You stay, then!" Abbas shouted. He snatched Charlie Rabbit from Joshua and ran to the door. "Charlie Rabbit will come with me."

"Wait!" squealed Joshua. He jumped up and reached for his rabbit. But Abbas held it above his head and ran for the stairs. Joshua followed, pleading and clutching at his brother's pajamas to make him stop. Somehow they made it down the stairs together, without Abbas losing his pajamas or his temper.

The cellar was entered through a trapdoor in the kitchen that led to a long, narrow ladder. As Abbas flung the trapdoor open, there was a terrible booming crash outside. The whole house shook, and a storm of dust and pieces of plaster rained down from the ceiling. The light near the stove sparked and went out, leaving them in darkness. Joshua lost his balance and fell over, almost rolling into the trapdoor. Purely by luck, Abbas got in the way, and they lay tangled together on the floor.

"Down the ladder!" shouted Abbas as Joshua started to howl. He wrestled the little boy around and lowered him down by feel.

"Charleeee! Charleeee!" screamed Joshua. He hung on to the ladder with one hand while he clawed at Abbas with the other, trying to grab Charlie Rabbit.

"Charlie's coming too! Climb down! Down!"

Another missile hit nearby. Abbas felt the impact through his whole body. It took a moment for him to realize that it had knocked him senseless for a few seconds. He was still on the kitchen floor, but he couldn't feel the trapdoor—or Joshua. He couldn't hear anything either, because it felt as if a school bell were going off deep inside his ears.

Blinded and deafened, he was so disoriented it took several seconds of panicked reaching around before he realized he was backed up against the fridge. That meant the trapdoor should be over to the right. He crawled in that direction and felt his probing fingers drop into the open trapdoor. But where was Joshua?

There was an electric lantern at the foot of the ladder. Abbas realized he had to get it before he could look for Joshua. He lowered himself through the trapdoor as another missile hit nearby. This time Abbas saw the flash, which meant the blackout curtains over the windows were gone. Or perhaps the whole wall had fallen over. Hastily he stepped down, dragging the trapdoor shut behind him, though it did little to muffle the sound of explosions.

Abbas's hearing started to come back before he reached the foot of the ladder. A distant, piercing voice penetrated his aching ears. Joshua's voice.

"It's dark! Where's Charlie? Charlie!"

"Stay still!" instructed Abbas, far too loudly, over the ringing in his ears. "I'll find Charlie after I get the light."

He felt around behind the ladder. The emergency box was there, and the large electric lantern they used to take camping. Years ago, when there were still holidays and you could leave the city without a special pass.

Abbas switched the lantern on. Nothing happened, and a sob began to rise in the boy's throat. They had saved those batteries especially, kept them for exactly this sort of emergency. They couldn't have gone dead. . . .

A faint glow appeared before the sob could

leave Abbas's mouth, and slowly grew till it became a bright, white light. Abbas turned the sob into a cough and looked around. Joshua was already picking up Charlie Rabbit. The little boy was dirty but otherwise seemed unhurt, though he must have fallen halfway down the ladder.

"Nothing hurts?" asked Abbas.

Joshua shook his head and hid his face in Charlie Rabbit's ears.

Abbas looked around. The "hole" had been an ice cellar, long ago, and was really only a cave dug into the thick clay below the house. Where the ice blocks had once been stacked, there was now a makeshift shelter, an A-frame made from two heavy tabletops with the legs cut off, bolted together at the top and sandbagged at the bottom and each end.

Another missile exploded close by, the ground shivering from the impact. More dust fell from the ceiling.

"Into the shelter," gasped Abbas, as he pushed his brother toward the wooden A-frame. For once, Joshua did as he was told, even taking the lantern from Abbas, who turned back and picked up the heavy emergency box. It contained a couple of old blankets, some food, and a bottle of water.

Abbas had taken only two steps toward the shelter when a cruise missile hit the house next door. The explosion shattered the whole street, smashing every house like a sledgehammer coming down on matchstick models.

The earth under Abbas's feet rolled, and all the air around him was sucked up with a terrible scream. He was lifted up, then thrown forward, almost to the shelter. He landed hard, on his side, but had no time to think about the pain. The scream of air dissipated, but in its place came a terrible groaning noise, an almost human expression of pain, though it was far louder than any human sound.

It was the house. Abbas looked up and saw the floor above bulge down, every beam protesting under a terrible strain. The whole building was about to collapse.

Without hesitation. Abbas threw the emergency box toward the shelter and flung himself after it, an instant before the space where he'd been was hit by a huge ceiling beam.

As the beam fell, the floor above gave way and the ruins of the house came pouring down, a great dumping of broken wooden beams, floor planks, plaster, roof tiles, and chimney bricks, mixed in with furniture, books, even the bathtub.

The wooden walls of the shelter boomed and shook as the cascade of ruin continued. Abbas pushed Joshua all the way to the back as debris began to flow in through the shelter entrance, preceded by a thick wave of dust; cloying, sticky dust that made it almost impossible to breathe and dimmed the light of the lantern.

Joshua screamed as debris continued to crash down. Abbas was about to tell him to shut up, when he realized he was screaming too. Abbas forced himself to stop, shutting the scream inside as he crawled to the far end of the shelter, dragging his little brother and Charlie Rabbit with him.

Joshua's screaming became a choking sob as the sound of the falling debris diminished. Abbas kept holding him, as much for his own comfort as his brother's. Both of them jumped and shivered every time the shelter was hit by something particularly large. Would it hold? Could it hold?

It did hold. Eventually the crashing descent of debris stopped. A little more spread in through the entrance, but there were no more terrifying booms and thuds upon the shelter.

Joshua's sobs slowed. He coughed and mumbled a few words. It took Abbas a few seconds to work out that he'd asked, "Are we dead?"

"No, we're . . ." began Abbas. He had to stop and cough before starting again. There was so much dust that he could barely breathe, let alone talk.

"Not dead!" he gasped. "Don't move. I'll . . . get water."

He crawled across to the emergency box. It was buried under bits of broken wood and plaster rubble, but Abbas managed to dig through and retrieve it. Beyond the box, the entrance to the shelter was completely blocked with debris. There was no way out.

Abbas tried to open the water bottle, but his hands were shaking too much. He put the bottle between his knees and tried again, and managed to unscrew the cap. He took a cautious swallow and spat out a mouthful of muddy dust. Then he held the bottle for Joshua, making sure his brother could not drink too much or spill it.

"More!" demanded Joshua.

Abbas shook his head and screwed the lid tight.

"No more for now," he said quietly. "Later."

Joshua's lower lip trembled but he didn't protest. He just held Charlie Rabbit tighter, his small face crumpled in shock and puzzlement.

Abbas wiped the dust off the lantern. The light brightened, but that didn't help. It lit up a tiny pocket of clear space, just big enough for the two of them to crouch in.

They were completely buried under the ruins of the house.

From the continuing tremble he could feel through the floor, Abbas knew that there were still missiles falling, though they were striking farther away. That meant there would be little or no chance of rescue. There were already thousands of destroyed houses. No one would search under this one. No one knew they would be here.

Joshua mumbled something, the words lost in Charlie Rabbit's ears.

"It's okay," said Abbas. He wished he sounded more convincing. He cleared his throat and tried again. "We're safe here, now."

"Where's Mum?" asked Joshua, more audibly. "I want Mum."

Abbas closed his eyes for a second. *I have to be brave. I have to be brave.*

"She's okay too. She'll . . . she'll come and get us in the morning."

"When is it morning?"

"Not for a long time. Try to go back to sleep."

Joshua stared at his brother.

"Can't sleep."

"I'll tell you a story."

"A Charlie Rabbit story?"

"Uh, I suppose. Let me try and remember the story for a second."

Joshua nodded his agreement. He loved stones.

Abbas didn't try to think of a story. He tried to think about what they could do. He had to remember everything his father had told him about the shelter, about what to do. But it was over a year ago, and he hadn't paid attention—

"Who else is in the story?"

"What?"

"Who else is in the story, besides Charlie?"

Abbas shook his head. He couldn't think, but Joshua needed a story. He had to be distracted from their situation.

"There were two boys," he said. "Their names were—"

"Abbas and Joshua!"

"Okay, Abbas and Joshua. They lived long ago in a city of white flowers, in a beautiful and peaceful kingdom. Everyone was happy, and there was plenty to eat and good things to drink, like hot chocolate. Abbas and Joshua went to a school that had lots of books and teachers for every subject. But one day a terrible giant appeared and demanded that everyone in the city hand over half their gold or—"

"He would eat them?"

"No . . . he would destroy their city. The giant was so big and so horrible that the people had no choice. Abbas and Joshua had no gold, but their parents had to give up half their life's savings to the giant. The giant took the gold and went away, and everyone was happy again."

"Didn't they ask Charlie Rabbit for help?"

"No, not yet. They thought if they gave the gold, the giant would go away. But the next year the giant came back again, and this time he had brought his friends. Three huge giants who stamped and shouted and demanded all the gold that was left or they would smash the people into little pieces."

"Why didn't they fight? I bet Abbas and Joshua would fight."

"They couldn't fight. The giants were too big, and they could throw huge rocks from far away. So the people of the city handed over their gold and hoped that they would never see the giants again."

"But the giants came back?"

"Yes, the giants came back. This time they didn't ask for gold. They said they were going to smash the city into little bits and there was nothing anyone could do about it—"

"Except Charlie Rabbit!"

"Yes, but no one knew where Charlie Rabbit was. He'd gone away and he hadn't come back."

"But he did!"

"Well, first of all Abbas and Joshua decided to go looking for him. But before they could leave, the giants started to throw rocks at the city. Huge rocks, bigger than houses, that fell down from the sky, smashing everything to bits.

"Abbas and Joshua were in their house when the first rock struck. They knew they couldn't go out, so they climbed down a ladder into a cave. There was a secret tunnel from the cave that came out beyond the city walls. But while they were still in the cave, a really big rock hit directly above them!"

Joshua took a sharp intake of breath. His eyes were huge, staring at Abbas, waiting for what happened next.

"The cave collapsed all around the two boys. They were trapped."

"What happened then?"

"Then . . ." Abbas began, but he couldn't go on. His mouth trembled and he felt tears start in his eyes. "Then . . ."

"Then Charlie Rabbit came back," said Joshua, eagerly taking over the story. "Charlie Rabbit smelled the boys in the tunnel, and he dugged them up. Then Charlie Rabbit jumped over to the giants and he kicked them with his big foots. *Wham! Wham! Wham! Wham! Wham!* The giants ran away and everyone was happy and Charlie Rabbit ate a carrot."

Abbas nodded. "Yes . . . that was what happened."

"I'm going to sleep now," announced Joshua. He dragged one of the old blankets out of the box and curled up on it. "Wake me up when Charlie Rabbit comes to dig us out."

"I will," said Abbas. He felt truly helpless. If only there were a secret tunnel, or a real Charlie Rabbit . . .

Secret tunnel. Another way out.

Abbas remembered what his father had said. There *was* another way out. The shelter backed onto the old ice chute, which had been used long ago to slide the ice blocks from the street down to the cellar.

Abbas took a deep breath, then coughed it away. There was too much dust for deep breaths. Or maybe the air was running out. He took a shallower breath and edged around Joshua to the back of the shelter. The wall there looked just like the hard clay of the other walls.

Abbas tapped it and was rewarded with a hollow sound. He let out a sobbing half laugh and started to scrape. There was a wooden hatch behind the clay, one so rotten that it crumbled at his touch. Abbas attacked it eagerly, pulling at the wood in a frenzy, ignoring the splinters.

There was a narrow chute beyond the hatch. Abbas crawled a little way up it, then looked back at Joshua, marveling at his little brother's ability to sleep. Should he wake him? Or should he make sure the chute was clear all the way to the street?

Abbas hesitated, then edged back down. As he backed into the shelter again, he heard Joshua sit up. And there was another noise, something rustling in the debris. A sound he couldn't quite place.

"Abbas! It's wet!"

It took Abbas a second to turn around in the confined space. By the time he could see, he could already feel the water around his ankles. It was freezing cold, and rising very quickly.

Broken water pipe. Maybe a big one. A water main. We have to get out!

"It's okay, Josh," Abbas said quickly. He picked up the lantern and showed Joshua the entrance. "I've found the tunnel. The secret tunnel. You go up first. Quickly."

Joshua scrambled up into the ice chute. Still sleepy, he didn't pick up Charlie Rabbit. Abbas started after him but at the last moment grabbed the rabbit. Joshua would want it for sure, later.

Water burbled around Abbas's knees as he climbed up into the chute. It was rising very quickly, far too quickly. Abbas pushed at Joshua's legs to make him go faster.

"Hurry up!"

They crawled up at least thirty feet, with the water always lapping at Abbas's feet, sometimes even catching up to his knees. Joshua's speed varied, and Abbas had to keep pushing at him.

Then Joshua stopped altogether and let out a howl of protest as Abbas shoved at his legs.

"What's wrong? Keep going!"

"Can't," said Joshua.

Abbas shone the light up. He could see the top hatch. But it was broken and hanging down, and where the open air should be, there was a huge slab of concrete, its reinforcing wires hanging down like severed tree roots.

It was the roof of the bus shelter from across the street. It must have been blown off and come straight down on the ice chute exit. Now there really was no way out.

Abbas twisted around. The water was slowly swirling around his thighs. Cold, dark water, constantly rising.

"Lie on your side," instructed Abbas. Joshua rolled over, and Abbas crawled up next to him. They could both just fit that way, though it was a squeeze. Charlie Rabbit was once again between them, and Joshua gratefully grabbed his ears.

Abbas worked the lantern around and shone it on the concrete slab that blocked their way. There was a small gap in one corner, not much larger than a softball. Abbas reached out and tried to crumble the concrete edges, but that only made his fingers bleed.

"Can . . . can you fit through there?" Abbas asked his brother hopefully. The water was up to his knees again, despite the extra yards he'd gained by moving next to Joshua.

Joshua shook his head. The gap was far too small.

Abbas put his hand against the wall. He couldn't feel any explosions. The missile strike must be over. The civil defense teams would be out. But how could he attract their attention quickly enough? They'd be drowned in ten or twenty minutes.

"Help!" he shouted, the word leaping out of his mouth almost without him thinking about it. Joshua flinched at the noise. "Help!"

The sound echoed back from the concrete and the rising water, but Abbas knew it had not penetrated aboveground. No one could hear him.

"I'm cold," whimpered Joshua. "It's wet."

"I'm trying to get help," said Abbas. "I'm trying—"

"Charlie Rabbit—"

"Shut up about Charlie Rabbit!" screamed Abbas. He grabbed the rabbit and pulled its ears apart, trying to rip it in his desperate anger. "Charlie Rabbit is a toy!"

Joshua started to sob again—deep, wracking sobs that shook his whole body.

Abbas stopped pulling Charlie Rabbit's ears and stared at its big-eyed, long-nosed, furry face. Charlie Rabbit was a toy. A very fancy toy.

"Ssshhh, it's okay," Abbas said more gently. "I'm sorry. Charlie Rabbit is going to help us."

Joshua's sobs became a sniffle.

"He is?"

"He is," confirmed Abbas. He tore off a long piece of wood from the broken hatch and propped it against the gap in the concrete block. Then he opened the panel on the back of Charlie Rabbit. "Only we have to sit in the dark for a while, because Charlie needs the batteries from the lantern. Can you be brave for Charlie Rabbit?"

"Yes . . ."

Abbas set Charlie down between them, turned off the lantern, and took out the carefully hoarded batteries one at a time.

One slip now, one battery dropped down the chute . . . I must concentrate . . . this has to work. . . .

He got the batteries in, slid the switch to "maximum," and closed the panel. Would Charlie still work? Even if he did, would it help? The water was up to his waist now, and it was so cold, he couldn't feel his legs anymore.

"Joshua," he whispered. "Feel for Charlie. Twist his nose."

He heard Joshua move. Then there was a sudden light and a burst of sound. Charlie Rabbit twitched, and his eyes shone with a deep, bright green glow; his paws went up and down, and his internal speaker began to hum.

Abbas pushed Charlie Rabbit into the gap above, then used the broken timber to shove the toy through, into the open air. As it emerged, the rabbit started to sing its trademark song:

"Hoppity, hoppity, hoppity me,
I'm as happy as I can be
Carrot, lettuce, radishes, too,
I'm Charlie Rabbit, how do you do?
Hoppity, hoppity, hoppity through,
Let's all be happy, too—"

The song suddenly stopped.

Abbas waited, holding his breath, hoping that he would hear the stupid song start again, or someone call out to them, or something. But there was nothing. The chill water was up under his arms, rising even more swiftly now.

"Joshua," said Abbas quietly, "crawl up as far

as you can and put your face against that hole. Pull your legs up, out of the water."

"Charlie Rabbit will get help," said Joshua confidently as he curled into a small ball.

"Yes," said Abbas in the darkness. He closed his eyes and let his head rest on the ground, close to the water that was caressing his neck. He was so cold now, he couldn't really care what happened. "Charlie Rabbit will get help."

"Hoppity, hoppity, hoppity through, Let's all be happy, too," sang Joshua. "Hoppity, hoppity . . . Abbas!"

"What?"

"Look, Abbas! Light!"

Abbas opened his eyes. The concrete block was rising up, rising into the air. Harsh, white electric light spilled down the chute, so bright he had to shield his eyes. Hands came reaching down to take Joshua, and then Abbas was lifted out himself, water spilling out onto the street behind him. Loud voices were all around him, shouting, asking questions, too much noise for Abbas to make any sense of it, save for one small voice that cut through everything. Joshua's voice, shrill in the night.

"Charlie! I want my Charlie Rabbit!"

Introduction to From the Lighthouse

Both my memory and my records are rather blank on this story. I thought I wrote it specifically for the 1998 anthology *Fantastic Worlds* (edited by Paul Collins), but when I checked the copyright date for "From the Lighthouse," I found it was 1996, and all the other stories were 1998. Which suggests the story appeared somewhere else first, and I do have a faint niggling memory that it did see print somewhere obscure before being collected in *Fantastic Worlds*.

This completely destroys my explanation of the origins of the story. When I thought it first appeared in *Fantastic Worlds,* I was going to say that I must have started with landscape because of the anthology title, with the idea of an island in the ice, protected by a Summer Field. I'm pretty certain that the setting came first, and some of the details of the place and its people, but it can't have been sparked by the anthology title.

This is one of my notionally science fiction

stories, in that it features technology and some vague explanation of that technology, but it still has the feel of fantasy. Perhaps it is science fantasy, a handy label for one of the many borderlands of the overlapping genres. I've never written any "hard" science fiction, in which the science can bear rigorous examination or is a real extrapolation of current knowledge. I'd like to think that this is not just laziness and a lack of intellectual stamina, but rather a love of story, which always is paramount to me. Having to make the science work as well as everything else just seems too hard. I like to read it, though, which suggests that I am actually just lazy.

I suspect that I originally intended to revisit this setting in another story, and I do have a faint recollection of jotting down some notes about the island and its people. But those notes are lost, seemingly like everything else related to "From the Lighthouse," apart from a few letters having to do with *Fantastic Worlds*. But as I haven't revisited the oasis island of Lisden for about a decade, I guess it can wait until I find a story welling up out of my subconscious that wants or needs to be set there, at which time I can reinvent everything I made up before.

FROM THE LIGHTHOUSE

1. ARRIVAL

EVERYONE GATHERED AT the wharf when the gold-hulled ice cruiser docked. Not because they'd been told to, though some people thought there had been some sort of instruction, or invitation. It was simply curiosity.

The Kranu hunters had met the yacht some five relgues offshore and, finding the Kranu refusing to rise through the hot holes and the day dull, had formed up around it as an escort. The villagers, seeing the hunters skating in two lines on either side of a great vessel with sun-colored sails, had naturally come to see the hunters' prize.

Marcus Kilman saw it quite differently. From the poop of the *Mercurial Gadfly* he waved left-handed, in the manner of a ruler to newfound vassals. His right hand crept finger by finger between the buttons of his crisp white suit. In his gold-heeled boots he was five foot one, and thanks to a nightly exercise with lead sinkers his earlobes were almost pendulous enough to be handsome.

When the *Mercurial Gadfly* finished tying up at the wharf that poked out of the island's Summer Field into the ice, the crew paraded on the foredeck, the ex-Senatorial Navy bosun plying his whistle in what Kilman believed to be a salute, but was actually the opening bars of the theme from the comic opera *The Great Kranu from the Deep*. As always, the crew smirked solemnly, laughter submerged in hacking coughs. Kilman frequently had his Bonesman check them for lung rot or throat curse. He was afraid of any kind of infection, physical or intellectual. The Bonesman never found either sort aboard Kilman's ship.

Kilman descended from the poop, reappearing at the gangway. The waiting crowd of islanders, silent out of politeness rather than awe, pleased him immensely. Respect! At last he had found somewhere untainted by egalitarian ideals. He would be king, and they would be his peasantry.

"People of Lisden!" he declaimed, his voice breaking pitch like a badly blown trumpet. "I am

Marcus Kilman, and I have purchased this island. I am your new owner."

The islanders greeted this disclosure with equanimity. Kilman had allocated ten seconds for rapturous applause but resumed speaking after only six seconds of embarrassing silence.

"People of Lisden! I will bring you a new era of peace and prosperity, lower taxes, and good government."

This provoked a reaction of sorts. A murmur ran through the audience like a water spider skidding from lily to lily or, in this case, from each mainland speaker in the crowd. Lisden already had peace; as much prosperity as they could handle without having greed; taxes were nonexistent, as the Kranu cooperative provided all services from its profits (if any); and the only government was the board of the cooperative, which included every adult islander. Theoretically, there was a mainland government department that looked after their affairs, and the Humble and Obedient Senate of the People beyond that, but both had lost the Lisden file years ago, and consequently denied the island's existence.

Kilman saw this reaction as suppressed joy at the good news, and was about to launch into further grandiose announcements when a woman stepped out of the crowd and onto the gangplank. She was much younger than Kilman—but the sort of woman who could be anywhere between sixteen and thirty and very striking in looks and stature. She was at least six foot two, and looked taller in her plain black dress, with a long silver scarf draped over one shoulder like an arrow, emphasizing her height.

"Sir," she said, in Mainland so untainted by accent that it was clearly not her native tongue. "May I ask from whom you purchased this island?"

"Why, little lady," Kilman answered, looking down on her from the high end of the gangplank, hoping she wouldn't come up any farther, "I purchased this island from the Lisden Fish Export Company, for the sum of one point seven five million gold bezants."

"Ah," said the woman, who knew that the Lisden Fish Export Company had been superseded by the Lisden Fish Enterprise Cooperative one hundred seventy-six years ago, and so couldn't sell anybody anything. She turned and spoke briefly to the crowd in their native tongue, explaining that the poor short man with the badly fitting toupee was a crazy millionaire who'd been the victim of a confidence trickster. They should humor him, provided it was not too difficult. Spare him embarrassment, she asked. Be kind, and in due course we will tell him the truth about his purchase.

The crowd nodded, waved, or spoke their agreement and dispersed, laughing and talking among themselves. Kilman watched his audience disappear, disgruntlement showing in the folds of flesh about his mouth.

"Why are they going?" he snapped. "I didn't say that they could go."

"They're going to prepare a proper welcome for our new owner," the woman invented, seeing that he was quite hurt, and a little angry.

She felt sorry for him, having to wrap an ego the size of the legendary Great Kranu Hunter of Remm in flesh not much bigger than the Kranu lures the hunters put down the hot holes. She took a few steps back down the gangplank and slumped a little.

"Who are you anyway?" the proud owner of Lisden asked as she retreated. He suddenly felt an interest in her now, even an incipient fondness. She wasn't as arrogant-looking as he'd first thought.

"My name is . . . in Mainland, you would say Malletta, or Maryen . . . even perhaps Margon."

"Okay, Margalletta," said Kilman, who only

ever remembered numbers properly. "Why don't you get hold of a wheeler and show me over my new property?"

"It would be my pleasure," replied Margalletta (as she was now resigned to being named). She slumped a little more, and gripped the rail of the gangplank as if overcome by weakness.

2. SIGHTSEEING

WHEELERS—AND THEIR theoretically impossible system of motivation that relied on a refusal to rotate at the same speed as the planet—had not arrived in Lisden. There was a steam car instead, a two-hundred-year-old vehicle of doubtful provenance. It had been locally repaired several times, so the panel work, while distinctive, was no longer representative of any particular manufacturer. Similarly, any badges, ornamental exhausts, or hood ornaments it might once have had were long gone. A stuffed parrot hung from the khatcatcher at the front of the boiler, but this was clearly not a factory-issue embellishment.

Margalletta sat, or rather slumped, behind the wheel. Kilman sat in the back. Instead of leather upholstery he had a fringed carpet. Margalletta told him this was a local tradition—the island's ruler always had such a carpet: lining a chariot; as a saddle blanket for horse or camel; or under the howdah of an elephant. Kilman was pleased by this image, unable to discern that it was a complete fabrication. The only elephants or camels ever seen on Lisden appeared in several very old books.

For all its odd appearance, the steam car was mechanically sound. Once it had built up sufficient pressure for the safety valve to scream alarmingly, Margalletta engaged all six drive wheels and shot off up the road, taking the corners that switchbacked up the island's central mountain with considerable elan, choosing whichever side of the road took her fancy.

Kilman, enquiring about road safety in a voice of blustering, ill-concealed fear, was informed that this was the only vehicle, and everyone knew she was taking him up the mountain. So there was no danger from horse-drawn vehicles or the occasional camel. Oh yes, the ceremonial camels had bred in the wild. . . .

Kilman kept his nose perpendicular to the window. Looking for camels, but also seeing the deep blue-gray-green of the sea suddenly meeting the blue sheen of ice; the picturesque fishing village nestled at the apex of a triangular bay; the orange and lemon orchards rising up the terraced slopes. All of it safely maintained by the Summer Field that made this oasis possible amid the vast sea of ice that had sprung up millennia ago as the result of a misguided application of a Winter Field. The ancient savants who had invented both were very successful at starting the fields, and phenomenally unsuccessful at turning them off.

Not that anyone would want to turn off Lisden's field. Or banish it, since no one really knew what made the Fields occur. Some said mirrors in the sky, and others fire or ice elementals mixed together.

Kilman certainly didn't want to change his oasis. Despite being obscure, it was only eighteen days' sail from the Republic, and there was a growing desire among the wealthy citizens for travel and well-regulated adventure.

Lisden would perfectly meet the demand of this new industry. In his imagination he saw hostelries spring up all along the coast, and houle gardens. There would be khat netting parties and Kranu hunts with steam harpoons. The lemon groves would give way to a dalliance maze, where masked frolics could be conducted, with refreshments and prophylactics sold at exorbitant prices.

Margalletta, sharp eared and sharp eyed, heard him whispering to himself, and saw the thick mouth move, saliva wetting the lower lip, as if he were about to moisten his finger to count money. She no longer felt sorry for him. Instead, a slight twinge of alarm caused her to open the power venturi farther and accelerate rather violently out of a turn. Kilman didn't really own the island, but he thought he did, and to such a man, that might be enough to eventually make it so.

"There is a lookout at the top of the mountain," Margalletta announced as she slowed to negotiate another corner. "You will be able to survey the whole of the island from there . . . the entirety of your realm."

"My realm . . ." Kilman repeated, his chin thrusting out and up, right hand once again thrusting between the third and fifth gleaming bronze jacket button. "My conquest!"

Margalletta suppressed a shrug of distaste.

"Conquest" indeed! The man was more unpleasant than she had thought, and clearly not an object of pity. He was also dangerous. Kilman's wealth gave him a weapon—and he lacked both the morality and the sense to use it wisely.

Still, by calling the island his conquest, he had clarified Margalletta's role.

To have a conquest, one must conquer an enemy. If he had truly conquered the island, she would be his enemy. Now, though he only thought he'd conquered the island, it might still become a reality. Margalletta would be his enemy then, so she might as well think and act like an enemy now. Logic was not her strong point, but she rarely needed it, having intuition and common sense instead.

"This road will have to be widened," Kilman pronounced a few minutes later, as they bounced around yet another bend. "At least four lanes. Of maybe we could get one of those cable-car things . . . you know."

Margalletta did know. Unlike most of the islanders, her parents had dragged her around many parts of the globe, believing travel to be far superior to a school education.

One of her most unpleasant memories was of

being stranded for hours in an antique clockwork cable car, swaying a hundred span above an icy crevasse, the wind screeching through a gap under the ill-fitting door. It had taken everyone on board six hours to rewind the mechanism, taking it in turns. She still had nightmares about cold, heights, and a slowly turning key.

Her silence did not dissuade Kilman from further musings. A few corners on, with perhaps a third of the mountain still to come, he suddenly sat up like a spring-wound Archimedes jumping out of a model bathtub.

"A railway! It could circle all the way around, with stops every forty-five degrees of circumference. Viewing platforms. Bars. A summit restaurant. The Kilman Express."

"A railway?" asked Margalletta. "There was one once. A clockwork rail, to take the tailings from the glazmium mine."

"Glazmium! No one told me about glazmium!" Kilman squawked. Fear and greed were evenly balanced in his voice, but the scales were teetering. Margalletta decided to give them a push.

"Oh, there's no glazmium now," she said brightly. "Only the waste from the mine. We used it as infill for the breakwater. And the village.

Not to mention this road."

Kilman was silent for a while; then Margalletta saw him take out a slightly soiled dove from his right sleeve and shake it awake.

It was one of the new paper-and-blood doves, short-lived but swift. He whispered to it with his habitual secrecy and cast it out the window. The wind shook it into life and it grew plump, winging down to the waiting ship.

Margalletta drove with newfound glee. She had defeated him so easily, with a lie about as digestible as a logy Lisden haddock.

On the next corner, the dove was back. Obligingly it flew into Kilman's lap and expired, becoming paper again, with a message shining wet and red upon the sheet.

"The breakwater and the village?" murmured Kilman, reading the message. "Well, I guess it must have been mighty low-grade glazmium. My Bonesman on the *Gad* says his skull hardly chatters. Was it buried a long time ago, Miss Margalletta?"

The unexpected counterattack is the most effective. Margalletta flinched, nodded halfheartedly, and sat up straighter, taller by several inches. Kilman disgusted her now and, being cleverer than she thought, frightened her more too. For his part, Kilman felt her shadow fall across him and increase as she stretched. His previous good feeling, dissipated by the glazmium scare, ebbed further. He was tired of the road, tired of the car, and tired of its driver.

"How long till we get to the damn top?" he asked, querulous, as if he'd missed his breakfast by several meals. "And what's there anyway?"

"I believe I mentioned the view," Margalletta replied stiffly. "It is most spectacular from the lighthouse."

"Lighthouse! Why didn't you say so? I love lighthouses!"

He did, too, though Kilman had never actually bothered to set foot in one. He liked pictures of lighthouses, and the idea of lighthouses. The only thing wrong with lighthouses was that they cost money instead of making it. That was why they were the natural monopoly of governments. In Kilman's worldview everything that cost money and produced no revenue was the business of the Republic.

He was unaware that the Lisden lighthouse was a great revenue producer. It had begun life as the folly of a Lirugian colonial governor, grown to maturity under a Hamallish one, and been bastardized by a Treton, who used it as a gull-shooting platform. But as far as anyone living could remember, its main purpose was as a giant trellis for passion-fruit vines, and its biannual crop was flavorsome, heavy, and lucrative.

To Kilman, at first sight, it just looked as if it were painted a particularly rich green. He didn't really see it anyway, for his imagination had added gas flares, spelling out KILMAN'S OBSERVATORIUM in letters of fire. It would be huge, a landmark for all the visitors to the island, seen from every angle, the backdrop of every organized and expensive activity. . . .

He didn't even notice the vines as they parked next to the entrance, and Margalletta jumped out to unlock the lighthouse door.

3. Departure

"THE LIGHTHOUSE IS sixty-four merads, or 189 spans high," Margalletta said, as she trod purposefully up the winding stairs. "There are two hundred seventy-seven steps, of varying height, due to the different building techniques employed and different builders over the seventy-seven hundred years it was under construction."

"Where's the altivator?" asked Kilman, chuckling to show it was a joke. He knew about lighthouses. He had open-cut diagrams of them. Books with plans. A snow dome featuring a famous lighthouse on some rock in the Boratic Ocean. He forgot its name.

Margalletta led the way at a cracking pace, rejoicing at the wheezing noises behind her, praying he would have a heart attack. Not that she believed in a single God, though most of the islanders did. Just in prayer. It was good for you, even if it didn't work.

Kilman wheezed, but it was only cosmetic. No heart attack was in the offing, and none eventuated. They both reached the top breathless and red-faced, but with arteries intact and pounding. Margalletta opened the door, pulled-back hair encountering the wind and defeating it aided by a large black comb and rigid preparation that morning. Kilman's toupee, less disciplined, rose from his scalp and flapped like a hatch on a hinge, till he clapped one hand upon it and pushed past

Margalletta in an urgent, embarrassed rush.

She waited for a few minutes, then closed the door and went down. Fortunately, the steam car was on the opposite side from the balcony door, so there would be no need for further panel work. The passion fruit hadn't fared so well, as Margalletta discovered when she walked around—the vines were all torn away near the top. There was a particularly nasty bare patch, just where the balcony railing would have been, if only the Treton governor hadn't dismantled it for being Hamallish and getting in his field of fire.

Curiously enough, one of Mr. Kilman's blood-and-paper doves had fallen out of his other sleeve and seemed unharmed by the fall. Margalletta picked it up and whispered into its ear, breath bringing it slowly to life.

"Hello. Is that Mr. Kilman's ship? I'm afraid there's been an accident. I gave Mr. Kilman some bad news about his purchase, and he . . . he . . ."

Margalletta released the dove into the wind and let them imagine her sobbing. She watched it fly down to the golden ship and she laughed, laughed madly, the sound twining up around the lighthouse like the vines and off into the bright blue sky of summer.

INTRODUCTION TO THE HILL

"The Hill" was written for an interesting international publishing scheme, in which a bunch of publishing houses in Europe and Allen & Unwin in Australia decided to simultaneously publish the same collection of short stories in English and four European languages, with the theme of the new millennium.

I was one of two Australian writers invited to participate, and I wrote "The Hill" in an attempt to try to tell an overtly Australian story—something I'm not known for, since nearly all my work is set in imagined worlds. This proved to be somewhat problematical, particularly when in the first drafts of "The Hill," I made the major characters part Aboriginal and tried to interweave a backstory involving Aboriginal myth and beliefs about land. I knew this would be difficult to pull off, but I didn't expect my Australian publisher's reaction, which was basically that, as a white Australian, I simply couldn't use either Aboriginal characters or

Aboriginal myth. My initially simplistic attitude was that, as a fantasy writer, I should be able to draw on anything from everywhere for inspiration; that I could mine any history, myth, or religion.

After some discussions with both the publisher and an Aboriginal author, I realized that the issue was more complex, and that many Aboriginal people would feel that I was not inspired by their myth but was appropriating something valuable, one of the few things of value that hadn't been taken over in the process of colonization. It would be particularly hurtful because, as an Australian, I should know that some Aboriginal people would consider this yet another theft.

So the fantasy element of "The Hill," inspired by some Aboriginal myths, was removed, and I rewrote it in a more straightforward way. However, given the constraints of the multilingual publishing schedule, and some misunderstanding along the way, the original version of the story is the one that got translated and is in the Norwegian, French, Spanish, and German editions. Only the English-language version is different.

I'm still not quite sure where I stand on the matter of allowable use of myth, legend, and history, save that if I do decide at some point to seek inspiration from the rich traditions and lore of the Australian Aboriginal people, I will ask permission first.

The Hill

Rowan sniffed as the awful hospital smell met him at the front door of the Home. A mixture of antiseptic and illness, hope and despair, churned by air-conditioning that was always slightly too cool or slightly too hot.

He ignored the reception desk, which was easy, since no one was there, and went straight up the stairs, leaping two at a time, unconscious of the old eyes that watched him, remembering when steps were not beyond them.

His great-grandfather's room was the first on the left after the nurses' station, but no one was there. Rowan stuck his head around to make absolutely sure, then continued on to the television room at the end of the hall. He slowed as he approached, reluctant as ever to see the group of old people who suffered so much from Alzheimer's or senile dementia that they couldn't speak or move themselves, so they just sat watching the TV.

Or at least had their faces pointed toward the set. Rowan wasn't sure they saw anything.

They were there, but his great-grandfather wasn't. Sister Amy was helping one of the old ladies sit back up. She saw Rowan and gave him a smile.

"Come to see your great-grandpop, then?" she asked. "He's out in the garden."

"Thanks," said Rowan. "Is he . . . ?"

"He's having one of his good days," said Amy. "Bright as a button, bless him. I only hope I do as well at his age. If I even get that far, of course. Now, up we go, Mrs. Rossi!"

Mrs. Rossi dribbled all over Amy's shoulder as she was lifted up. Rowan mumbled a good-bye and fled, wanting to get out into the fresh air as quickly as possible. He was glad Great-grandad was having a good day. It would make everything much easier. On his bad days, the old man wouldn't talk, or possibly couldn't talk—and he didn't seem to hear anything either.

But as Amy said, he was still a wonder, even on his bad days. When he wanted to talk, he talked intelligently and clearly. When he wanted to walk, he walked, with the aid of two canes. But he was most remarkable for his age. Albert Salway was the oldest person in the Home, the oldest person in the city, the oldest in the state, maybe even the oldest in the country. He had been born in the last decade of the nineteenth century, and now he was only a day away from the beginning of the twenty-first. He was 108 years old and was actually Rowan's great-great-grandfather. But he always said that was too many greats, and anyway, he preferred Rowan to call him Bert.

He was sitting on the bench next to the roses, watching them sway slightly in the breeze, petals ruffling. As always when he went outside, he was properly dressed in moleskin trousers, a flannel shirt, tweed coat, and hat. His two blackwood canes were propped up against the bench, their brass handles bright in the sun.

"Hello, Bert," said Rowan. He sat down and they shook hands, the old man's light and brittle in the boy's, the pressure of his fingers very light, their skin barely touching. Bert smiled, showing his gold tooth on one side and the gap on the other. Apart from the gap and the gold incisor, he still had all his own teeth. Bert had outlived four dentists who couldn't understand the healthiness of his mouth, and many more doctors who couldn't believe his age and condition.

"You've got troubles, my boy," said Bert. "I can see it in your face. Is it school?"

"No," replied Rowan. He coughed and cleared his throat, uncertain of how to go on.

"Hmmm," said Bert. "Something you don't know how to tell me. Is it a girl?"

"No," said Rowan, embarrassed. "It's Dad."

"Ah," said Bert, letting out a whistling sigh. "What's my great-grandson done now?"

"He's . . . he's selling the Hill," Rowan blurted out. He knew he had to tell Bert, but he was afraid the news would hurt the old man badly. Maybe even kill him.

Bert stared at him, his sharp brown eyes seeming to look through Rowan and off into the distance. *To the Hill*, Rowan thought. The Hill was all that remained of their family property. A great saddleback of earth and stone, crowned by a forest of ancient gum trees, lording over the flat farmland around it.

The Hill was the center and the most important part of the 5,000 acres that had belonged to the Salways since 1878.

"He can't sell that land," said Bert finally.

"But he has!" exclaimed Rowan. "I heard him telling Mum about it last night. He's getting three million dollars and we're all moving to Sydney. But I don't want to go. And I don't want the Hill to go, either."

"He can't sell that land," repeated the old man. He started to struggle up, his crooked, shrunken hands taking up the canes. "Give me a hand, Rowan."

"What are you going to do?" asked Rowan anxiously.

"We're going to pack my stuff," said Bert, leaning forward onto his canes, Rowan steadying him as he took his first step. "Then we're going to move back to the Hill. I'll need you to get a few things, Rowan. It's been a few months since I've been up there."

"You've been up there that recently?" asked Rowan, almost letting go of him in surprise. "How? I mean, Dad wouldn't even take me this year. I had to cycle last time, and it took three hours. He shouted at me when I got back and told me to keep away from it."

"Taxi," said Bert. He didn't have a lot of breath to talk when he was walking.

They had a bit of trouble getting out of the Home, but Bert had known the Matron—or Guest Health Services Director, as she was now called—

for a long time. They spoke together briefly, then she even phoned for the taxi herself.

"Make sure he doesn't get wet or cold," she said to Rowan as she helped Bert into the car. "Good luck, Bert."

They stopped on the way to get some food, bottled water, blankets, and kerosene for the old stove in the shack. Bert had quite a lot of money with him. Old fifty-dollar notes, the paper ones that were replaced by the smaller polymer variety years before. The checkout girl didn't want to take them at first, particularly from Rowan, but when he showed her Bert waiting in the taxi and explained that he didn't like the "new money," she relented.

It took half an hour by taxi to get to the Hill. Rowan had expected the gate to be locked and had worried about the climb up the track for Bert, but it was not only unlocked, it was open. The track looked a bit rough, but the taxi driver said it wasn't his cab so he wasn't worried.

"Besides," he added, "if a big Mercedes like that can make it up, we can."

He pointed through the windscreen, and Rowan and Bert saw that there was a very large dark blue Mercedes parked next to the shack. Two men were standing next to it. Rowan recognized his father and felt the lump of anxiety that had been in his stomach all day flower into panic. He didn't recognize the other man, the one in the suit and glittering sunglasses.

"Dad's here already!" exclaimed Rowan.

"Not for long," said Bert. "Just park up next to the shack, will you, mate?"

Rowan felt himself instinctively crouching down as they approached and both men looked over to see who it was. Both looked puzzled; then his dad's face bloomed red as anger sent the blood swirling around his nose and cheeks. He stormed over and yanked the door open, pulling Rowan out by his shirt collar.

"What the bloody hell are you doing, son?" he shouted.

"He's helping me," said Bert, who was being helped out the other door by the taxi driver. "Let him go, Roger. Then you and your friend have got two minutes to get off my property."

"Your property?" said the man in the suit, smiling. He looked at Roger. "I don't think so."

Bert laughed, his gold tooth gleaming.

"Another smart arse from the city who hasn't done his homework," he said. "Perhaps I should introduce myself. I'm Albert Salway."

"Salway?" said the man. "Salway!"

He looked at Roger Salway, the smile and his relaxed slouch gone. He was angry too, now.

"What's his relationship to you, Roger? Does he have any claim over this land?"

"He's my great-grandfather," muttered Roger, not meeting the other man's eyes and not answering his question either.

"It's my land," repeated Bert. "Has been for nearly seventy years. And like I said, you have one minute to get off my property."

"Well, we seem to have got off on the wrong foot," said the businessman, trying to smile again. "Let me introduce myself. I'm John Ragules, representing FirstLaunch Space Services. We plan to build a satellite launching facility in this area—a spaceport. We need this hill, for . . . well, we call it the ski launch component."

Rowan listened in astonishment. This was the first he'd heard of the Hill being used to help launch satellites. His fascination with space was almost as great as his love for the Hill, and for a moment he found himself thinking of how fantastic it would be to have a spaceport close to home. Then he remembered that they would be moving to Sydney anyway, and that the spaceport could be built only if he lost the Hill.

"The Hill's not for sale," said Bert. "Plenty of other places you can build your spaceport, Mr. Ragules. Places already ruined."

He leaned on one cane and gestured with the other, a wide sweep that encompassed all the huge gray gum trees that stood around like an army of giants, whispering in the wind.

"There's trees here that are hundreds of years old," said Bert. "Animals that have fled here from the farms and the city. Birds you don't find anywhere else anymore. There are stories here, in the stone and the red dirt, in the bark and the leaves, in the ants and the spiders, the wallabies and the kookaburras. You build a spaceport and they will all be gone, forever. You've got thirty seconds now. Roger, you can hand over the key to the gate as well."

"Like hell I will," said Roger. He stormed over to the old man and seemed about to shake him, till he saw the taxi driver watching with an unblinking stare, the tattoo of a snake on his forearm twitching up and down. Instead he bent over and whispered, "We can sell this place for three million dollars, Bert! Three bloody million! We'll never get offered that kind of money again."

"The land isn't for sale," Bert said. "We don't need a spaceport here, anyway!"

"What are you talking about, you old fool!" spat Roger. "Three million! And I *will* sell it, even if I have to have you declared senile and incompetent!"

"It still won't be yours to sell," said Bert. He lifted a cane and gently tapped Roger's shin. "Now get off my land."

"I'll be back!" shouted Roger, the heat in his face now spread like a rash to his neck and ears. "I'll be back with a court order to make me your guardian and stick you back in that Home for as long as it takes for you to finally bloody croak. I should have done it years ago!"

He seemed almost about to push Bert again, then he suddenly whipped around and made a beeline for Rowan, who scrambled behind the nearest tree.

"As for you, you'll get a hiding when we get home!" he roared, lunging around the trunk. But Rowan was already fleeing farther into the bush, pushing blindly through the scrub, crashing through spiderwebs, small tree branches, and spiky shrubs. When he felt he was far enough away, he turned back to look, the pain of dozens of tiny scratches building into the greater pain he felt deep inside.

"I'm not going back!" he screamed. "I'm never going back."

The only answer was the sudden well-modulated sound of the Mercedes engine, followed by the noise of its wheels on the gravel near the gate. Then there was silence, the silence of the bush. Wearily, Rowan found a clearer path back to the shack.

The taxi driver was helping Bert to an old chair he'd pulled out of the shack, and was unloading all the gear. When Rowan started to help him, he offered his hand to shake.

"Name's Jake," he said. "Your dad's a rotten bastard, isn't he? You'll have to watch out for him."

"I'm Rowan," said Rowan. "Yeah. It's lucky you were here, or he might have gone for Bert as well."

"How long you planning to stay out here?" asked Jake as they took the last blanket out and he slammed the trunk shut.

"I don't know," said Rowan, shrugging to hide his anxiety. "I guess it depends on Bert."

He looked over to where the old man seemed to have fallen asleep in his chair, facing the trees, his canes propped out widely, almost like oars.

"He looks a bit old to be camping out," said Jake dubiously. "Do you reckon your dad'll be able to have him declared senile or whatever?"

"He's one hundred and eight," said Rowan proudly. "And he's always been much tougher than anyone thinks. He's got a lot of friends in town, too, people who've known him all their lives. I reckon Dad'll find it hard work to get Bert out of the way."

"Legally, maybe," said Jake, looking over to the old man. "He might try something else, though. Listen, how about I come back up later to see if you're okay?"

"I don't know. . . ." said Rowan, eyeing the snake tattoo. Jake seemed like a nice bloke, and he certainly had prevented his dad from running amok. But he'd seen all Bert's money—

"I'd just like a chance to talk to Bert," added Jake. "I mean, it's not every day you get to talk to someone who was around last century. Hell, tomorrow he'll have lived in three different centuries! Maybe I could bring my wife as well?"

"Okay," agreed Rowan after a further slight

hesitation. He guessed it would be safer than being here alone with Bert. "See you later then."

"We'll come up after I get off work. About eight."

"Sure," agreed Rowan. He thought of his father and added, "Come earlier, if you like."

When Jake left, Rowan checked on Bert, who seemed to be okay. He was just sitting, starting at the bush, blinking occasionally and humming to himself. Rowan left him alone and went in to sweep the shack clean and get the spiders and ants out of the old hammocks.

He was sweeping away vigorously when he heard a car again. Keeping the broom, he went out, his heart already beating faster. As Rowan had feared, it was his father, in the old red utility truck. The vehicle screeched to a stop at the gate, and Roger jumped out to open it.

"What'll we do?" whispered Rowan, edging over to stand next to Bert.

"Whatever has to be done," said the old man, sighing. "You know, when I was a boy, Rowan, the bush went all the way to town. There were no cars, no airplanes, no radio, no television, no computers. At your age I hadn't even seen a telephone. When the twentieth century began, I didn't think things would change much. I was wrong, of course. We'll be in the twenty-first century tomorrow, and now everybody expects change. Change, change, change, without thinking what it'll cost in things that can't be replaced. I saw your face when that man said he'd build a spaceport here. You wanted it, didn't you?"

"Not if it takes the Hill," said Rowan anxiously, still looking down the track. "They can build it somewhere else. But what'll we do about Dad? He'll kill me!"

"No, he won't," said Bert. "Help me up."

As soon as he was upright, the old man started shuffling off into the bush. Rowan walked along next to him, trying to anticipate a fall. Behind them, Roger Salway jumped back into the truck, and it accelerated up the path.

"Where are we going?" asked Rowan. "He'll catch us for sure!"

"I want him to catch up with us," said Bert. "At the right place."

He hesitated then, looking around at the rocks and the huge gums, as if he'd forgotten where he wanted to go. Then the glint came back into his eyes and he shuffled off to the right, Rowan following him, most of his attention focused behind them. His father was already out of the truck and running, crashing through the bush without even looking for a path.

As far as Rowan could see, Bert was just making it easier for Roger to beat him up in secret. They were out of sight of the shack now, on the forward slope of the hill. Worse, there was nowhere to run to from here. The slope fell off rapidly into a series of rocky cliffs, and Rowan didn't want to even try to climb down with his father up above throwing rocks or something. Bert wouldn't be able to climb at all, anyway.

"This is it," said Bert as Rowan was desperately trying to think of something to do. He could just lie on the ground, he supposed, and hope his father didn't kick him too much.

"What?" asked Rowan. He'd missed whatever Bert said.

"This is it," said Bert, pointing to a crevasse in the rock ahead, so narrow it was hard to see in the fading light. "We'll just zip across this log. I bet your dad doesn't remember the Narrow."

Rowan looked at the crevasse they'd always called the Narrow. It looked dark and nasty, a thin mouth stretching all the way across the hill. It wasn't that deep. He'd climbed up and down it many times. When Rowan was a small child, his father had helped him up and down, standing in the cool, fern-lined shadows below. "Course he'll remember!"

"No he won't," said Bert. "If he remembered, he wouldn't be trying to sell up."

Hesitantly, the old man put his foot out on the ancient fallen log that bridged the Narrow.

"Bert . . ." Rowan started to say, but the words slipped away from him as Roger came puffing through the bush, his face red and twisted with rage. Fearfully, Rowan scuttled across the log.

Roger barreled on, sticks snapping under his feet, branches whipped back by his passage. He was bellowing, waving his fists, fists that Rowan knew would happily connect with him. He might even be so crazy mad with anger that he would hit Bert.

"Don't!" Rowan shouted. "Don't!"

He wasn't sure if his shout was a warning about the Narrow or a feeble attempt to turn away all that concentrated fury and those terrible fists.

It didn't matter, because Roger was too far gone in his rage to listen. One second he was right in front of them, his face as red as the setting sun, his mouth pouring out words that were so twisted up they sounded like an animal's howl.

Then he was gone, and there was sudden silence.

Bert shuffled to the edge of the crevasse and looked down. After a second Rowan looked too, shutting one eye because that might somehow make whatever he saw easier to cope with.

"He's alive, anyway," said Bert, as a whimper came up out of the Narrow. "You all right down there, Roger?"

Rowan held his breath while he waited for an answer. Finally it came. A small voice, the rage all drained away.

"I think . . . I think I've busted my wrist."

"Forgot about the Narrow, didn't you?" said Bert conversationally. "You used to climb up and down it enough as kid. Was it you or your dad who broke his arm down there?"

"Dad," said Roger. He seemed a bit dazed, thought Rowan. He hadn't heard his father speaking so quietly for ages.

"And now you've done your wrist," said Bert. "Losing any blood? Anything else broken?"

"No," said Roger shortly. "Just my wrist."

"Must run in the family," Bert said to Rowan, peeling back his sleeve to show a faded scar along his forearm. "Not a break. Cut it open mucking around down there."

"I can't climb out by myself," said Roger. They couldn't even see him now, the way the night had poured into the Narrow. The stars were getting brighter overhead, a great swathe of them that you couldn't see in the city, where they were swamped by artificial light.

"I guess you can't," said Bert. "So you might as well sit down and listen while I tell you a few things."

"I'm listening," said Roger. Rowan could hear him moving about, settling down on one of the ledges.

"First, no one's selling the Hill," said Bert. "Not while I'm alive, and not after it, either. I had a team of fancy lawyers work out how to make sure of that more than ten years ago. The family will be trustees, no more. If you'd bothered to ask, I would have told you.

"Second, I reckon your temper is getting out of hand. I've got a bit of money put by. Not three million, but a tidy sum. I'm going to leave it all to Rowan. If he feels like it, he might give you some.

So if it's money you're after, you'd better learn to talk to your son instead of throwing your weight around. You'll live longer too. Bad for the heart, getting angry."

There was a really long silence after Bert stopped talking.

Rowan looked at the stars, unable to believe what he was hearing. The Hill not to be sold. His father having to talk to him instead of hitting him.

After a few more minutes when Roger still didn't say anything, Bert went back across the log bridge, his old arms outstretched for balance. Rowan walked behind him, quite close, so he could steady him if necessary.

"Where are you going?" asked Roger. There was a hint of panic in his voice.

"Thought we'd leave you to think about things for a while," said Bert. "We've got a visitor coming up. It's New Year's Eve, remember?"

"What about me?"

"We'll be back next century," said Bert. "Course, you still have to agree to behave yourself."

He chuckled a bit then, and started up the hill.

"Wait!" called Roger. "I agree! I agree!"

Bert kept walking. Rowan looked at him, then back at the Narrow. His father was calling him now, desperation in his voice. In the distance, he could hear a car approaching. It had to be Jake in the taxi, back a bit early.

"Come on," said Bert. "We'll go meet Jake. We can come back for Roger later."

"But," said Rowan, "what about Dad?"

"We won't leave him too long," said Bert. "Just long enough for him to work out what he can do."

"Like what?" asked Rowan nervously.

"Like nothing," said Bert. "That's what I want him to work out."

"So everything's going to be all right?" asked Rowan.

Bert shrugged. Then he shakily held out his arms, as wide as they would go, taking in Rowan, the Hill, the night, and the stars.

"You can never guess what a new year will bring, even when you've seen more than a hundred of them," he said. "Sometimes you see what's coming and can't do a thing about it. Sometimes you can."

He paused and took a deep breath of the

eucalyptus-scented air, closed his arms around his great-great-grandson, and added, "Out here, right now, I reckon maybe everything will be as close to all right as it can possibly get."

INTRODUCTION TO LIGHTNING BRINGER

I always enjoy watching electrical storms, though I prefer to do so from inside a house, behind a nice glass window. The undesirability of becoming more closely acquainted with lightning was brought home to me once, when lightning struck a drainpipe a few yards away from me. I'm not exactly sure what happened, because I found myself sitting on the very wet mat outside the back door, with spots dancing before my eyes and my ears ringing. My friend inside told me that the whole house had shaken and the thunderclap had made everything rattle; she thought I must have been killed when she ran through the kitchen and saw me slumped against the door.

Despite this near miss, I remained fascinated by lightning, as anyone who has read even one or two of my books can probably tell. A few weeks before I wrote this story, I was held spellbound by a television documentary on lightning. In this documentary, they had amazing film that showed the "streamers" that flow up from anything vertical.

These streamers actually make the connection with the lightning leaders coming down from the thunderclouds. I saw ghostly streamers rising from trees and buildings, from weathercocks, and, most importantly, from people.

The taller and stronger the streamer, the more likely that it will connect with the storm. When it does, there is an electrical discharge down from storm to ground, through the conductor. If the conductor is a metal lightning rod, that's okay. But people are not so well equipped to deal with bolts of energy that at their core are as hot as the surface of the sun.

I vaguely knew how lightning worked, but it wasn't until I saw these strange, luminous streamers rising out of vertical structures that it really made sense. At the same time, I was struck with the way the streamers varied, even between people of the same height. Some people just had stronger streamers.

I also knew that there were people who tended to get struck by lightning quite a lot, but who still survived. I had a dim memory of a man who was struck by lightning seven times over quite a few years. He was apparently going to the post office to mail the proof of his many lightning strikes to the *Guinness Book of World Records* when he was hit by an eighth lightning bolt. He survived that as well, though his clothes were burned off and some of his papers singed.

Put together, all this gave me an idea about people who could see the streamers and who could manipulate electrical energy in various ways. Small, secret ways, like changing the electrical energies in people's minds, or big, flashy ways, like calling down lightning. That was the central idea. Then I had to find a story to use that idea.

At the time my most pressing need was for something to submit to the anthology *Love & Sex*, edited by Michael Cart, so I was also trying to work out a story that would concern sex. Mixing up my ideas about controlling minds and lightning with sex and love seemed like it might produce an interesting story. "Lightning Bringer" is the result.

Lightning Bringer

It was six years ago when I first met the Lightning Bringer, on a cloudy day just a few weeks past my tenth birthday.

That's when I invented the name, though I never spoke it, and no one else ever used it. Most of the townsfolk called him "Mister" Jackson. They didn't know why they called him mister, even though he looked pretty much like any other hard-faced drifter. Not normally the sort they'd talk to at all, except maybe to order off their property—once they were sure the police had arrived.

I knew he was different the first second I saw him. It's like a photograph stuck in my personal album, that memory. I walked out the school gate, and there he was, leaning against his motorcycle. His jet black motorcycle that looked like a Harley-Davidson but wasn't. It didn't have any brand name or anything on it. He was leaning against it, because he was tall, two feet taller than me, easily six foot three or four. Muscles tight under the black T-shirt, the twin blue lightning tattoos down his forearms. Long hair somewhere between blond and red, tied back under a red-and-white-spotted bandanna.

But what I really noticed was his aura. Most people have dim, fuzzy sorts of colors that flicker around them in a pathetic kind of way. His aura was all blue sparks, jumping around like they were just waiting to electrocute anyone who went near.

The guy looked like trouble. Then he smiled, and if you couldn't see the aura, that smile would somehow make you think that he was all right, the biker with the heart of gold, the drifter who went around helping out old folk or whatever.

But I saw part of the energy go out of his aura and into the smile, flickering out like a hundred snakes' tongues to touch and spark against the dull colors of the people around him.

He charmed them, that's what. I saw it happening, saw the tongues coming out and lighting up the older kids' gray days. And then I saw all the electric currents come together to caress one student in particular: Carol, the best-looking girl in the whole school.

Of course I was only ten back then, so I didn't

really appreciate everything Carol had going for her. I mean, I knew that she had movie-star looks, with the jet black hair and the big brown eyes, and breasts that went out exactly the right amount and a waist that went in exactly as it should and legs that could have been borrowed from a Barbie doll. But it was sort of secondhand appreciation at that stage. I knew everyone thought she looked good, but I didn't really know why myself. Now I can get really excited thinking about the way she looked when she was playing basketball, with that tight top and the pleated skirt . . . at least till I remember what happened to her. . . .

She was looking especially good that day. With hindsight, I reckon she'd found out that she was really attractive to men, picking up a certain confidence. That air of the cat that's worked out it's the kind of cat that's always going to get the cream.

When the Lightning Bringer's smile reached out for her, her eyes went all cloudy and she kind of sleepwalked over to him, as if nothing else even existed. They talked for a while; then she walked on. But she looked back—twice—and that electricity kept flowing out of the drifter, crackling around her like fingers just aching to undo the big white buttons on the front of her school dress.

Then she was around the corner, and I realized everyone else had gone. There was just me and the man, leaning against his bike. Watching me, not smiling, the blue-white tendrils pulling back into the glowing shell around him. Then he laughed, his head pulled back, the laughter sending a stream of blue-white energy up into the sky.

That laugh scared the hell out of me, and I suddenly felt just like a rabbit that realizes it's been staring into the headlights of an oncoming truck.

Like a lot of rabbits, I realized this too late. I'd hardly got one foot up, ready to run, when he was suddenly looming over me, fingers digging into my shoulders like old tree roots boring into the ground. Like maybe he'd never let go till his fingers plunged through the flesh, squishing me like a rotten apple.

I started to scream, but he shook me so hard, I just stopped.

"Listen, kid," he said, and his voice was scraped and raw, like maybe he'd drunk a bottle of whiskey the night before, on top of a cold. "I'm not going to hurt you. You can *see*, can't you?"

I knew he wasn't talking about normal eyesight. I nodded, and he eased off his grip.

"I'll tell you something for free," he said, real serious. He bent down on one knee and looked me right in the eye, except I ducked my head, so I had only about a second of that fierce, yellow-eyed gaze burning into my brain.

"One day you can be like me," he whispered, voice crawling with little lightnings, power licking away at my head. "You saw how that girl looked at me? I'm going to have her tonight. I can get any woman I like—or any man, if I was that way inclined. No one can touch me either. I do what I want. You know why? Because I was born with the Power. Power over things seen and unseen, Power over folk and field, Power over wind and water. You've got it too, boy, but you don't know what it can do yet. It can go away again if you don't look after it right. You've got to keep it charged up. You've got to use it, boy. That's the truth. You have to feed the Power!"

Then he kissed me right on the forehead, fire flaming through my skull, and I could smell my hair burning like a hot iron, and I was screaming and screaming and then the world spun around and around and I wanted to throw up but instead I lay down and everything went black.

When I came to, the Darly twins were turning

my pockets inside out, looking for money. I was still pretty dizzy, but I punched one while I was still on the ground, and he fell back into the other one, so I got up and kicked them both down the street.

That made me feel better, and I thought maybe the worst of the day had happened and it could only get better from there.

But I was wrong.

I was real restless that night. Everybody was. The air was hot and sticky, with thunderheads hanging off on the horizon, black and grumbling but not doing anything about moving in to break the heat. There was nothing on television either, and we all sat there flicking between channels and complaining, till Mom lost her temper and tried to send everyone to bed. Including Dad, but he lost his temper too and they had a shouting fight, which was rare enough to send us shocked to bed.

I remember thinking that I wouldn't be able to get to sleep, but I did. For a while, anyway. I had this awful dream about the Lightning Bringer, how he was creeping through the house and up the stairs, blue sparks jumping around the bent-back toes of his boots. Then just as those lightning-tattooed arms were reaching down, fingers spreading around my neck, there was this incredibly loud burst of thunder, and I woke up screaming.

The thunder was real, drowning my scream and bringing a cold wind that rattled the shutters in counterpoint to the bright flashes of lightning behind them. But the rest was just a dream. There was no one there except my brother, Thomas, and he was asleep.

Still, it shook me up pretty bad. I can't think why else I would've gone to the window and looked outside. I mean, if you have a nightmare, normally that's the last thing you do, just in case you see something.

Well, I saw something. I saw the Lightning Bringer on his motorcycle, parked out in our street, looking right up at the window. He had Carol with him; her arms tightly wrapped around his well-built, leather-clad chest. She had a bright red jacket on and jeans, and a red woolen hat instead of a helmet. She looked like the sort of helper Santa Claus might choose if Santa read *Penthouse* a lot.

The Lightning Bringer smiled at me and waved. Then he mouthed some words, words I understood without hearing, words that seemed to enter my brain directly, punctuated by the distant lightning.

"I can have anything I want, boy. And you can be just like me."

Then he revved up the bike and they were gone, heading up the road to the mountain, the lightning following on behind.

I never saw Carol again, and neither did anyone else. They found her a few days later, burned and blackened, her fabled beauty gone, life snuffed out.

"Struck by lightning," said the coroner. "Accidental death."

No one except me had seen her with the Lightning Bringer. No one except me thought it was anything but a tragic accident. She'd been foolish to go out walking in the thunderstorm, stupid to be out that late at night anyway. Some people even said she was lucky it was the lightning that got her.

I was the only one who knew she didn't have a choice, and it wasn't any ordinary lightning that killed her. But I didn't tell anyone. Who could I tell?

I'd like to say that I never thought of the Lightning Bringer after that day—and what he'd said—but I'd be lying. I thought about him every day for the next six years. After I got interested in girls, I think I thought about him every five minutes. I tried not to, but I just couldn't shake the memory of how Carol had looked at him. I wanted a girl like Carol to look at me like that, and do a whole lot more besides.

I used to think about the Lightning Bringer before school dances when I just couldn't get a date. Which, to be honest, was all the school dances up until about two months ago. Then I met Anya. Okay, she didn't look at me like Carol had looked at the Lightning Bringer, and she didn't look like Carol. But she was pretty, with sort of an interesting face and clever eyes, and she used to know what I was thinking without me saying anything. Like when I'd want to undo the back of her bra strap and just slide my hand around, and she'd shift just enough so I couldn't reach—before I even started to do anything.

Which was frustrating, but I still really liked her. She had an interesting aura, too, a bit like apricot jam. I mean apricot jam–colored, and quite thick, not like most of the fuzzy, thin auras I saw. I often wondered if she could see auras too and what mine looked like, but I was too embarrassed to ask her. Which was a bit of a problem, because I was too embarrassed to talk about sex with her either, and I knew that this was probably half the reason why she kept shifting around when I tried to put my hands places that seemed quite normal to go. And why she never let me kiss her for more than a minute at a time.

I mean, I think she would have if I'd talked to her about it. Maybe. Once I ignored her trying to pull away and I just kept kissing, sticking my tongue in even harder and putting my hands down the back of her jeans. Then she started jiggling about, and I thought it meant she was getting excited, till I realized it was sort of panic and she was just trying to get loose of me. I let go and said sorry straight away because I could see in her aura she was really frightened, and I'd gotten sort of scared as well. Anyway, she was mad at me for a week and wouldn't let me even hold her hand for two weeks after that.

It was only a few days after we had gotten back to the holding-hands stage that the Lightning Bringer showed up again. Outside the school, on his black motorcycle, just like he'd done six years before. I felt my heart stop when I saw him, as if something from a nightmare had just walked out into the sun. An awful fear suddenly becoming real.

Which it was, because this time he was smiling at Anya. My Anya! And all those electric tendrils were reaching out for her, blue-spark octopus tentacles, wrapping around and caressing her like I wanted to do but didn't know how.

I tried to hold her back, but she ignored me, and I felt these shivers going through her, like when a dog's fur ripples when you scratch in exactly the right place. Then she pulled her hand out of mine and pushed me away, and I saw her looking at the Lightning Bringer just like Carol had six years before, with her mouth slightly open and her tongue just whisking around to leave her lips wet and her chest pushed forward so the buttons went tight. . . .

I screamed and charged at the man, but he just laughed, and the blue energy came gushing out with his laughter, smacking into me like a fist, and I went down, winded. He laughed again, beating me with Power, so all I could do was crawl away and vomit by the bushes next to the gate. Vomit till there was nothing to come up except black bile that choked and burned till it felt like it was taking the skin off the inside of my mouth and nose.

When I finally got up, the Lightning Bringer and Anya were gone. For a second I thought maybe she'd gone home, but I knew she hadn't. She didn't stand a chance. If the Lightning Bringer wanted her, he'd take her. And he'd do whatever he wanted with her, till he got tired and then she'd be just like Carol. An accidental-death-by-lightning statistic.

I think it was then that I realized that I didn't just like Anya, I was in love with her. I'd been petrified of the Lightning Bringer for six years, terrified of what he could do, and of the darker fear that I might somehow be like him.

Now all I cared about was Anya and how to get her back, back safe before the thunderclouds in the distance rolled over the town and up the mountain. Because I knew that was where the Lightning Bringer had gone. I felt it, deep inside. He'd gone to get closer to the clouds, and he'd gone to call a storm. It was answering him, the charge building up in the sky, answering the great swell of current in the earth. Soon they would come together.

I think it was about this time that I completely flipped out. Totally crazy. Anyway, the Darly twins later said they saw me running along the mountain road without my shirt, bleeding from scratches all over and frothing at the mouth. I think they made up the frothing, though the scratches were certainly true.

Basically, I turned into a sort of beast, just following the one sense that could lead me to Anya. I could tell where she'd gone from the traces of her apricot aura and the blue flashes left by the Lightning Bringer. They were intermingled, too, and in some deep recess of my mind I knew that they were kissing and those tree-strong hands were roaming over her, her own clasped tightly around him as they'd never been properly clasped around me.

I think it was that thought that started the animal part of me howling . . . but I stopped soon enough, because I needed the breath, just as the first thunderheads rolled above me with the snap of cold air and a few fat drops of rain, the lightning coming swift and terrible behind.

I ran even faster, pain stitching up my side, eating into my lungs, and then I was staggering out onto the lookout parking area, and there was the black motorcycle silhouetted against the lightning-soaked sky. I looked around desperately, practically sniffing the aura traces on the ground. Then I saw them, the Lightning Bringer pressing his black-clad body against Anya, her back on the granite stone that marked some local hero's past.

She was naked, school dress blown to the storm winds, lips fastened hungrily to the man, arms clasped behind his head. I watched, frozen, as those arms sank lower, hands unzipping his leather trousers, then fingers lacing behind muscular buttocks.

He raised her legs around him, then thrust forward, his hands reaching toward the sky. With my strange sight I saw streamers fly up from his outstretched fingers, streamers desperately trying to connect with the electric feelers that came questing down from the sky. When they did connect, a million volts would come coursing down through the man's upraised arms—and through Anya.

I ran forward then, leaping onto the Lightning Bringer's back, lifting my hands above his, making the streamers he'd cast my own. He stumbled, and Anya fell away from him, rolling partly down the hill.

Then the lightning struck. In one split, incandescent second it filled me with pure light, charging me with Power, too much Power to contain, Power that demanded a release. It was an ache of pleasure withheld, the moment before orgasm magnified a thousand times. It had to be released before the pleasure burned all my senses away.

Suddenly I knew what the Lightning Bringer knew, knew how I could have not only the Power, but the ecstasy of letting part of it run through me to burn its way, uncaring, as I took my pleasure.

"You see!" he crowed, crouching before me, shielding his eyes from the blazing inferno that my aura had become. "You see! Take her, spend the Power! Feed her to the Power!"

I looked down at Anya, seeing her naked for the first time, her pale skin stark against the black tar of the parking area. She was frightened now, partly free from the Lightning Bringer's compulsion.

I started toward her and she screamed, face crumpling. And somewhere in the midst of all the burning, flowing Power I remembered her fear—and something else, too.

"I love her," I said to the Lightning Bringer. Then I kissed him right in the middle of his forehead.

I don't know what happened next because I was knocked unconscious. Anya says that both of us turned into one enormous blue-hot ball of chain lightning that bounced backward and forward all across the parking area, burning off her bangs and melting both the motorcycle and the bronze plaque on the stone. It didn't leave anything at all of the Lightning Bringer.

When I came to, I was a bit disoriented because I had my head in Anya's lap and I was looking up at her—but since her bangs were gone, I didn't know who she was for a couple of seconds. She had her dress back on again too, or what was left of her dress. It had some really interesting tears, but I was in no state to appreciate them.

"You'd better go," I croaked up at her, my voice sounding horribly like the Lightning Bringer's. "He might be back."

"I don't think so," she said, rocking me backward and forward as if I needed to be soothed or something. I liked it, anyway.

"I'm just like him," I whispered, remembering when I wouldn't stop kissing her, remembering the feel of the Power, wanting to use it to make myself irresistible, to slake its lust and my own on her, make her just a receptacle for pleasure. . . .

"No, you're not," she said, smiling. "You always gave me the choice."

I thought about that for a second, while the dancing black spots in front of my eyes started to fade out and the ringing in my ears quieted down to something like school bells.

"Anya . . . can you see auras?" I said.

"Sometimes, with people I know well," she whispered, bending down to kiss me on the eyes, her breast brushing my ear.

"What color's mine?" I asked. It seemed very important to know, all of a sudden. "It's not blue and kind of . . . kind of . . . electric, is it?

"No!" she answered firmly, bending over to kiss me properly on the lips. "It's orange, shot with gold. It looks a lot like marmalade."

INTRODUCTION TO DOWN TO THE SCUM QUARTER

This is the oldest piece of my work you will find in this book. Written in either 1986 or 1987, it was published in two Australian gaming magazines, *Myths and Legends* and then *Breakout!* It is not a story as such, but an interactive narrative experience: in other words, a "Choose Your Own Adventure" in which the protagonist's story proceeds according to the choices the reader makes, which direct him or her to read particular paragraphs.

But unlike the "Choose Your Own Adventure" or "Fighting Fantasy" books, it is not a serious interactive narrative that is on offer. "Down to the Scum Quarter" is a loving parody of the paragraph-choice game format. It's also something of an homage to one of my favorite books, *The Three Musketeers* by Alexandre Dumas, and to the best movie version of that book, done as two films: *The Three Musketeers* and *The Four Musketeers*, directed by Richard Lester, from scripts by George McDonald Fraser (whose own novels are also excellent).

Because much of my work is serious and can be quite grim, people are sometimes surprised that I also write humorous stories and that I like to make people laugh when I talk to audiences. I also try to have moments of humor and lightness even in my grimmest novels, because life has moments of laughter and comedy even amid darkness and despair. Similarly, when writing humorous stuff, I approach it seriously and try to mix in enough solid, "real" stuff to underlie the comic material.

"Down to the Scum Quarter" I wrote purely for myself, and then I looked around to see if I could find somewhere to publish it. It may be sad to admit it, but even seventeen years later a lot of it still makes me laugh. Possibly because the whole concept of the paragraph adventure game lends itself to parody.

And speaking of such, I should alert interested readers to the fact that there are three or four paragraphs in "Down to the Scum Quarter" that you will never be directed to by other paragraphs. Paragraphs 96 and 97 are two examples. When I wrote those two, I thought there was a story waiting to be written from them, and even now I suspect there still is.

But enough of this rambling. Lady Oiseaux has been kidnaped and the night is yet young. Strap on your rapier, slap on your plumed hat, and sally forth!

Down to the Scum Quarter
A Farcical Fantasy Solo Adventure

How to Play

1. **Decide whether** you're going to cheat or not. Most people cheat in solo adventures, even if they don't admit it. If you're not going to cheat, get a six-sided die.
2. Go down to the local costume rental shop and get a Three Musketeers outfit. This is called "getting into character."
3. If you're old enough, stop by the liquor store on the way back and pick up a few bottles of cheap red wine.
4. Rent a video of *The Three Musketeers*. Start watching it, and practice knocking the tops off the wine bottles with your plastic rapier. This is called "getting the atmosphere."
5. Give up after you break the rapier, and open a bottle with a corkscrew. Drink all of it.
6. Read "The Prelude."

7. Select five items from the list of equipment (unless cheating, in which case you presume you always have exactly what you need).
8. Go to "The Adventure Begins!"
9. Carefully evaluate the situation, choose a course of action, and go to the paragraph indicated, rolling a die when necessary.

The Simple Method:
Get a 6-sided die, and ignore steps 2–5.

The Prelude

YOUR BEAUTIFUL mistress, the Lady Oiseaux, has been kidnaped. There is only one slim clue that may lead you to her—a brief message, scrawled in pale gold eye paint across the side of her hijacked palanquin:

Oh! This is awful! I am being kidnaped!
They are taking me to sell to a desert
chieftain at an auction, which I think
is going to take place at midnight

somewhere near the river, and I'll miss the party tonight. And I was going to wear my new dress with the ruby chips sewn on cloth of gold, and the peacock feather fan from . . .

Those few words, and the "For Sale" brochure you hold in your kid-gloved hand, lead you to suspect that Lady Oiseaux is being held at the infamous Quay of Scented Rats—a floating bordello now stuck in the mudflats of the River Sleine.

Pausing only to slip your trusty rapier into its scabbard, you draw your cloak around you and erupt out into the shadows of the night—toward the Sleine—and the vicious, nasty, disgusting . . . (roll of drums) . . . Scum Quarter of the Old City!

You walk a few yards with considerable bravado and then whip back to your townhouse. Only a complete fool would go down to the vicious, nasty, disgusting Scum Quarter without pistols and a dagger or two. Maybe you should call in on the lads at the Fencing Academy . . . but there's no time. Select five items from the following list before once again slinking out into the shadows of the night. . . .

Dagger
Pistol (with powder & balls for five shots)
Bag of 20 gold bezants
Portrait of Lady Oiseaux (3'6" square)
Scented handkerchief
Halberd
20' rope
Repeater watch
Bottle El Superbeau Cognac
2 pairs silk stockings
A glove puppet of Cyrano de Bergerac
Small plaster saint
Bottle Opossum perfume
Five-pronged fish spear

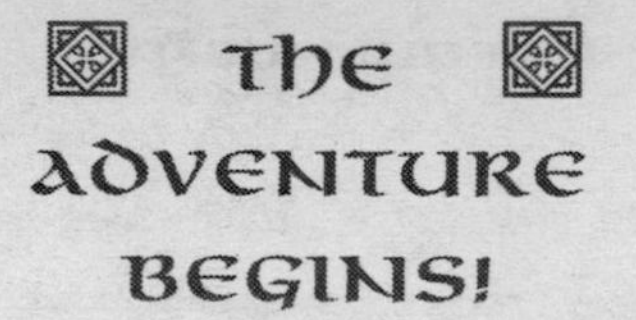

The Adventure Begins!

1 Moving from shadow to shadow down the wide Boulevard of the Muses, you feel very much like the intrepid adventurer hurrying to rescue his beloved lady. You are so caught up in this delightful little daydream that you don't notice the six Watchmen following your erratic shadow-to-shadow progression down the street till you go one shadow too many and find yourself caught in the glare of their lanterns.

If you are carrying a halberd or five-pronged fish spear, Go to 50

If you aren't carrying either of these, Go to 30

2 Who do you think you are—the unnatural offspring of the Three Musketeers and Michael York? Roll one die.

1–3 At least you feinted toward somebody's

left eye. Pity it was your own. Then you stuck your rapier in your left foot. . . . The bravo takes pity on you and lets you limp away. Minus one on all future combat rolls due to both stupidity and injury. Go to 52

4 *Both of you fence away quite competently, crying "Caramba!" and "Take that! And that! And this little one! And that that." Eventually you become so tired, you lean on your swords and just whisper: "Aha—foul blaggard!" etc. The bravo gets bored of this first, and leaves. You rest briefly, then continue on your way.* Go to 52

5–6 *Your fencing master would be proud—there's always a first time. You feint, parry, and riposte as if you knew Errol Flynn intimately when you were a young boy—and tried to keep him at a distance. The bravo is struck several times and retires bleeding to the nearest laundress. You continue on your way.* Go to 52

---

3 Descending to the next floor, you find yourself in a barbershop, the walls lined with mirrors. There are four doors, sixteen

reflections, and a trapdoor.

Do you go through the door marked with a tiger? Go to 85

Or the door marked with a lady? Go to 39

Or through the door marked with both a lady and a tiger? Go to 34

Or the one with two ladies and a tiger? Go to 92

Or through the trapdoor, which is marked with a lamb chop? Go to 58

---

4 It's not very nice up the Emperor August's nostril. Four or five hundred bats seem to have used it as a toilet for about a century. You wait inside for several minutes, then emerge as a grotesque mound of bat guano. The balloon is still there, but whoever is in it doesn't recognize you. Add one to all future combat rolls due to your repellent exterior. You head south. Go to 54

---

5 You smile sickeningly and cross over to the tiger, mumbling "nice pussums . . . good kit-e-kat. . . ." You reach down to scratch its stomach, and it grabs you with both paws and bites your head off. As your soul becomes a delicate butterfly and floats off to the transit lounge, you feel that this would never have happened if you had read *The Jungle Books* as a child. The End.

6 THE WESTERN WALL

Originally built to hold out the barbarians, the Western Wall fell into disrepair when the barbarians became civilized and bought the city in an underhanded real-estate deal. Now only a crumbling ruin inhabited by thieves, cutthroats, and defrocked clergymen, the wall is rarely visited by anyone else.

You remember this as a defrocked clergyman bears down on you, swinging his incense pot with deadly intent.

Do you get out your five-pronged fish spear, leer evilly, and say: "How many prongs do you want, and where do you want them?" Go to 77

Run back to the Arc de Tribump? Go to 99

---

7 You stand in the line before the main entrance to the Quay of Scented Rats—a vast, overdecorated houseboat that is now firmly embedded in the mudflats of the Sleine. At the front of the line two burly men (who look suspiciously like beavers) demand the five-bezant entry fee.

Do you pay them? Go to 55

Say, "Back off, bucktooth. I'm with Scum Quarter Vice"? Go to 36

Offer them the bottle of El Superbeau cognac? Go to 17

---

8 Hanging by one hand, you tie the rope to the sail and climb down to the next one. From this one you climb through a window to the inside of the mill. Go to 35

9

You wrench the door open and leap through it. But will you evade the tiger? Roll one die.

1–3 Damn! The doorknob would be stiff. . . . You half turn to meet your doom like a brave warrior, but the tiger smashes you to the floor, and you let out a pitiful little shriek instead. Fortunately, this is the exact cry of an orphan tiger cub! The tiger stands back, bemused, while you crawl across the room and out through the exit. Go to 79

4–6 The door slams shut just as the tiger slams against the other side. You lean against it, sweating in fear. Go to 79

10

You wrench open the bottle of Opossum perfume and scatter a few drops toward the awful hag. A beautiful aroma fills the room, and she steps back, spitting and cursing. "Back, foul fiend!" you cry, throwing a few more drops, which burn through her outstretched arm like acid—so you throw the whole bottle and bolt for the exit. You don't look back. Go to 79

11

Just as you are about to flèche across the room and drive your rapier through the poor unsuspecting woman's heart, a great gong rings . . . and time stops. As the echoes of the gong die away, a disembodied voice fills the room with the weary pronouncement, "The Age of Chivalry Is Now Officially Dead." Time suddenly resumes, but your heart isn't in the wild attack, so you merely lunge at the tiger. It backs off snarling; you circle around to the other door and duck through it. As you leave, the woman throws the voodoo doll at your head. Subtract one from all future combat rolls due to wax burns on your face. Go to 79

12

FISHGUT ALLEY

And you thought the Street of

Fishmongers smelt bad. Obviously this is where all the fish guts end up after the beggars have tried to eat them—for the second time. At the other end of the alley, a hulking giant of a man is standing, a spiked club in his hand.

Do you approach him for directions to the Sleine? Go to 57

Or return to the Street of Fishmongers? Go to 41

13

As your hand touches the hilt of your rapier, you start, and the eyes in your head bulge dramatically. The hag is wearing the Black Apron of a Master of Cleaver-Fu—a deadly martial art you cannot possibly cope with! Go to 62

14

There really is nothing like just messing about in boats. Pitting one's strength against the vicious tidal bores that sweep up the river, or the onrush of sewage from the city that sweeps down. But lo! There on the port bow you see a heavily decorated houseboat, firmly embedded in the mudflats. The heavy use of purple fur around the windows (and fake gold trim on the gutters) convinces you this must be the infamous Quay of Scented Rats.

Do you heroically leap from your boat as you pass the Quay of Scented Rats, do a triple somersault in the air, and land upon its sleazy deck with an air of casual arrogance? Go to 64

Or cautiously pole up to one end, tie up your boat, and sneak aboard like a rat? Go to 26

15

You emerge into a long corridor lined with various prints of the activities of the Quay of Scented Rats. To your right there is a door marked "Auction Goods." To your left there is a door marked "Not the Auction Goods."

Do you go left? Go to 80

Or right? Go to 23

16 The River Sleine

You sneak past the hustlers of the Southgate and out through a postern. Before you lie the winding, deep blue waters of the River Sleine, alive with wildfowl amid the teeming rushes. . . . Then your eyes clear and you realize you are looking at a picture tacked to the postern door. You open it, and there before you lies the turgid, coal black watercourse that makes slimy pollution look good—the true River Sleine. Steps lead down toward the river, and you think you can see a boat tied up at the bottom.

Do you go down? Go to 27

Or turn back, you coward, only to be killed by a lightning-struck albatross falling out of the sky? (This is called a premonition.) Go to 45

17

"Before we descend to crass commercial transactions," you say suavely, "you may care to have a drop of . . . El Superbeau cognac." You hold the bottle in front of them as they drool and reach out with grasping fingers—then fling it into the Sleine! The two guards hurl themselves into the slime, desperate to reach it before it gurgles away into the murky depths. Seconds later, you are flattened as a horde of eager customers storms across the bridge. You get up wearily and hobble after them. Go to 61

18

The merchant reels back, a garfish sticking out of his left ear. Bleating with fear, he crashes into another merchant's stall. Within seconds, the Place of Plaice becomes a whirling mass of rioting merchants, customers, and airborne tubs of fish. You have to get out! You run toward the Arc de Trihump. Go to 99

19

Roll one die.

1–3 The man in black is entranced.

Your fingers manipulate Cyrano's arms brilliantly, and his rapier flickers back and forth, gleaming in the light from the two-hundred-watt chandelier above. Z draws closer and closer . . . then you strike. The puppet's sword shears off half of Z's mustache! Shrieking, he bursts past you, smashes through the door, and runs away. Go to 100

4–6 You are a little nervous, and Cyrano moves jerkily, producing a very second-rate display of swordsmanship. Z watches for a while, then exclaims: "Non! Non! Ziss iz not ze way ze Thibault iz exerzized! Give eet to me!" You hand over the puppet. Soon Z is totally occupied, putting Cyrano through the seventy-seven Lunges of Señor Ricardo. You slink past. Go to 100

20

"Twenty!" you exclaim, exhibiting profound knowledge of history that hasn't happened yet, the current year being a sort of alternate 1624. Still, "What's an anachronism between friends?" you mutter to yourself. Z takes this as a riddle and begins to knead his forehead in deep thought. Six hours later, still unable to answer your question, he overexerts his brain and faints away. You step over his unconscious form and go through the door. Go to 100

21 AVENUE OF CHAMPIGNONS

A broad and leafy avenue, much frequented by bands of rioters from the Green and Blue factions of the donkey-cart races. Many bravos stalk the avenue, seeking opponents from rival factions.

Are you wearing a blue one-piece body stocking? Go to 33

Are you wearing something else? Go to 33 anyway

22

You stand there, gaping. The shadow of the balloon looms closer and closer, and the stench of manure is overpowering. A man in a pinstriped suit looks out at you and says, "Nah—he hasn't got what it takes," and the balloon flies on. Sometimes it pays to be a ninny. Go to 54

23

You open the door marked "Auction Goods" only to be confronted by the giggling eunuch you may have been unlucky enough to see earlier. The thin, sickly man accompanying him carries a gladstone bag in one hand and a gleaming scalpel in the other. The eunuch titters, "That's him, Doc!" and leaps forward to pinion you in his blubbery arms.

Do you trip the eunuch, use him as a springboard, hurtle through the air, head butt the doctor, somersault, and land on your feet whistling "Dixie"? Go to 68

Or pirouette gracefully and bolt back through the door? Go to 47

24

Your rapier is barely out of its scabbard before the black-clad man has reduced your clothing to tatters. Little "z"s have been cut in every available piece of cloth and leather. Your trousers fall down.

Do you attempt to continue this rather farcical duel? Go to 73

Or say, "Sorry—wrong door," and back out, holding up your trousers with both hands, rapier clutched between your teeth? Go to 94

25

"You sure it's only a five-pronged fish spear?" asks the Sergeant. "Because a six-pronged fish spear is a different kettle of . . ."

"Halberds?" you suggest.

"Right. That's a different kettle of halberds. Now, be on your way."

You leave the Sergeant and his men discussing what a kettle of halberds would actually look like, and proceed to the Street of Fishmongers. Go to 41

26 You pole to the southern end of the gaudy monstrosity and carefully tie up your boat. Several guards look over the railing at you, but you remember your Mandrake lessons well. A few hypnotic passes convince them you are a harmless moron who thinks he's a rat. Squeaking feverishly, you swarm up the bowline and onto the deck—then it is but the work of moments to chew a gaping hole in a nearby door. Go to 44

27 You leap into the boat just like Captain Silver used to—but he only had one leg, so it was excusable. Eventually you get upright again, ship the oars, hoist the topgallants, splice the mainbrace, cast off, and purl three. That all taken care of, you push off with a piece of old stick and head downstream. Far off, you can see pink lights on the water and smell cheap scent. There lies the infamous Quay of Scented Rats. You pole on. Go to 14

28

Roll one die.

1–2 As you poke out your tongue, you slip on some slimy fish and bite the end off this valuable appendage. The pain is intense! You drop your rapier and stagger about howling. The hulking giant runs away in terror. Go to 95

3–4 To cut a long story short, the hulking giant gets in a few good blows and gives you a black eye before you see him off with some little cuts to the face. Subtract one from all future combat rolls due to partial blindness. Go to 95

5–6 The tongue goes out . . . the rapier goes in. The hulking man is surprised. So are you—you nervously let go of your rapier. The giant staggers off with it still in his chest. You chase after him, and pull it out when he falls over and expires. A quick search gains you a silver Bixby—a pair of long-handled biscuit tongs. Go to 95

29 The tigers settle back down as you sit, and the two women explain that they're playing a local variation of poker, where a red two is called the tiger and can be used as any other card. There are a number of other special rules, but you're sure you can get the hang of it. Roll one die.

1–3 You lose all your money and possessions, except for your clothes and rapier. You're sure there's cheating going on, but every time you try to look more closely at the others, or under the table, the tigers come and breathe heavily in your ear, licking their chops and slavering. After an hour you retire gracefully through the other door, declining their offer of "just another hand." Go to 79

4–5 You know they're cheating after about fifteen minutes. Those tigers are reading your cards and signaling to the women by twitching their whiskers. With this knowledge, you keep your losses to a minimum—and lose half your money. After about ten hands, you get up to "stretch your dealing hand," and dash through the other door, the tigers hot on your heels. Go to 79

6 Ah, those long days spent visiting your grandfather in Cell 3B of The Pastille (an infamous lozenge-shaped prison) at last reap their reward. You use all your dear grandpapa's tricks and win twenty-eight bezants over sixteen hands. You bow gracefully, thank the ladies for the game, and saunter to the exit, gloating over your newfound wealth. Go to 79

30

"Wot, I say, wot 'ave we 'ere, then?" says the Watch Sergeant, in the peculiar patois spoken by Watchmen everywhere. "Oi (I) fink (think) we might 'ave (have) a Nimoy (person in search of something) 'ere (at this location) . . . perhaps (perhaps) searching (looking) for his lost (mislaid) demoiselle (lady who drinks a lot of sweet white wine)." While the other Watchmen are trying to translate the Sergeant's words with their Watch Patois/English phrasebooks, you slink past and continue on your way. Go to 41

31 The Carved Heads of Past Emperors

The Carved Heads of Past Emperors were once ranked as the four-hundred-sixteenth wonder of the world. Now only twenty of the sixty heads carved into the Eastern Wall have any discernible features. You scan them briefly, but the Montgolfier is still approaching from behind.

Do you hide up the stone nostril of Emperor August the 10th? Go to 4

Climb the profile of HIH Alfredo (known as "Alfredo the Chinless")? Go to 89

32

The hag raises her cleaver as you reach inside your doublet, then drops it on the floor as you proffer the silk stockings. "Just what I wanted for my thuggee lessons!" she exclaims, swiftly making the stockings into a noose and looking around for a test neck. But you are long gone, running like a young colt (i.e., on shaky legs), through the other door. Go to 79

33

As you casually saunter down the avenue in your unobtrusive blue body stocking (or whatever), a bravo leaps out, brandishing his rapier. You have only a moment to realize that he is dressed entirely in green before combat is upon you.

Do you tremble with fear, knock your knees together, and start blubbering? Then, when he starts laughing, whip out a pistol and blow the smirk off the blaggard's face? (You must have a pistol.) Go to 76

Or feint toward his left eye, parry in sixte, and riposte over your shoulder, plunging your rapier through the knave's heart? Go to 2

34

A harsh-faced woman looks up from her voodoo doll as you enter and screams, "A burglar! Sic him, Tiggums!" A tiger leaps down on you from a platform above the door.

Do you run back through the door? Go to 9

Flèche across the room and run the woman through? Go to 11

Shoot the tiger with your pistol? Go to 43

---

35 You are now on one of the floors of the windmill. It is an eerie place, all white with flour dust, and the sound of the creaking sails and machinery echoing in every nook and cranny. Strange cogs and mechanical arms move back and forth, and a central drive-shaft turns with uncanny speed.

There is a piece of paper lying on the floor. Do you pick it up? Go to 60

Or ignore it, trip, and fall down the central driveshaft into the grinding stones below? Go to 70

---

36 They look at you, taking in your cheap cloak, three-bezant haircut, muddy boots, and distinct lack of a Ferrari red palanquin. "Make that ten bezants, for trying to be smart," says one, crushing a rock and snorting the fragments to show how tough he is.

Do you pay ten bezants? Go to 55

Go back to the end of the line? Go to 7

Or follow the river westish, hoping to find another way to the Quay of Scented Rats? Go to 52

37

Your arms get more and more tired, the wind comes up, and it starts raining. You almost fall several times. Then, in desperation, you start to climb down. Unfortunately, you slip, slide down the windmill's roof, and out . . . down at least forty feet. Fortunately, the hunchback breaks your fall . . . and you break both your legs. You crawl away before the hunchback regains consciousness. For you, this adventure is over, and you are about to embark upon another. (See "The Ferocious Bill of Orthopedic Surgeon Fu Manchu" Adventure 27 in this series.)

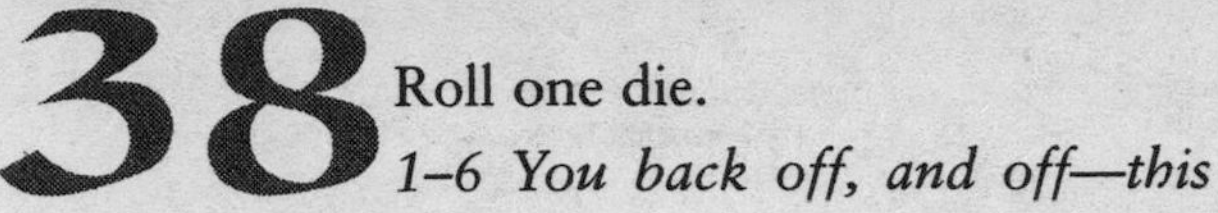

Roll one die.

1–6 You back off, and off—this guy twirls his club so fast, you think he may moonlight as a windmill. He drives you back to the Place of Plaice before losing interest. Go to 83

There is a heavily clawed mannequin in the opposite corner, and a low, menacing growl from a platform above the door. Go to 85

40

The tiger stops in its tracks and looks from side to side, as if to see if anybody is watching. Then it rolls on its back and starts making purring sounds.

Do you go over and scratch its stomach? Go to 5

Or run like a million zephyrs (windily) to the other door? Go to 79

41

The Street of Fishmongers

This street really stinks. Rotten fish guts, rotten gutfish, and people who smell like they died at sea several years ago—and look like they died several centuries ago. You hurry through, with a fold of your cloak stuffed up each nostril—all the fashion in the Street of Fishmongers.

Toward the end of the street, a porcelain model of a toadfish points toward Fishgut Alley, and a statue of a naked mermaid (with rotating flukes) beckons toward the Place of Plaice.

If you walk toward Fishgut Alley, Go to 12

If you stroll toward the Place of Plaice, Go to 83

42

As you say "No thanks," the agent's forked tail and horns break out of his pinstriped suit. He draws a pitchfork from his shoulder holster . . . just a little too late. There is a flash of blue lightning, and the

"Choose Your Own Adventure" agent is now no more than a patch of oily scum. A white-suited man strolls up, the gold wings on his breast pocket gleaming in the sun. He blows the smoke from a magnum pen and slips it back into his pocket. "Get on with it," he says. "Finish up—I need the money."

You nod and head south. Go to 54

43

As the tiger leaps, you draw your pistol in one smooth motion, wind the wheel lock faster than a speeding bullock cart, prime it quicker than a flash of lightning, aim, and . . . Roll one die.

1–3 *Congratulations. All these frantic motions have hypnotized the tiger. It is staring at you, its eyes great circles of disbelief. This puts you off, so you don't fire but edge past to the other door.* *Go to 79*

4–6 *It springs on you before you can fire, so you have to do all the winding, priming, and so forth at the same time as being savagely mauled by a four-hundred-pound Bengal tiger! It's lucky you're a hero—you fire, the tiger dies, and you get to live out the rest of your tragic life with the terrible scars the tiger has inflicted. You staunch the blood where your little finger is bleeding, and eye the scratch marks with depression. Absolutely bound to scar, you think sadly, as you head for the other door.* Go to 79

44 THE SALON

You open the door of the Salon, enter, and quickly close it behind you. It is very dim inside, and your eyes take several seconds to adjust. There is a sort of snuffling sound in one corner, and you start to draw your rapier before you realize it is . . . seductive breathing. Your eyes adjusted, you see the fabled courtesan Yvette lying on a couch, her fishnet stockings gleaming against the red plush. She languidly stretches out one slim arm and beckons to you.

Do you abandon your mission, shout, "Every man for himself," and fling yourself upon her? Go to 67

Allow her to seduce you, pay her, then resume

your search for your true love? Go to 53

Call on Sir Galahad, the Pure Knight, to help you fight temptation? Go to 71

45

You turn back toward the Southgate. Lightning flashes across the sky. Thunder resounds throughout the postern tunnel in which you are sheltering from falling albatrosses. An ancient mariner appears and shoots you with his crossbow. The last words you hear are the senile old fool saying: "That's funny. I could have sworn it was an albatross. Must have been the lightning. . . ." The End.

46

The Bittern approaches and circles lazily, just out of reach of your rapier. You think you've got it beat and start to edge across the square. At that precise second the Bittern strikes, jabbing you savagely in the left buttock. Shrieking, you run across the square, hand clamped to your backside to guard against the infamous second strike. Go to 93

47

You slam the door behind you and brace yourself against it as the tremendous bulk of the eunuch slams against it.

Do you wait for him to charge again, then let the door fly open? Go to 75

Or fire your pistol (if you have one) through the door? Go to 87

48

You start sweeping the halberd viciously back and forth like some sort of deranged lawn mower—but this only makes the giant man angry. His shirt splits up the back, his eyes and muscles bulge, and he puts on a pair of glasses. You stare aghast as he grabs the swinging halberd and breaks it into several pieces, then advances upon you with a particularly sharp splinter, grinning inanely . . . but this is all a product of your fevered imagination. You shouldn't swing that halberd so vigorously! Actually, he ran away as soon as you got the halberd out. Go to 95

49

Hampered by the body, the hag fails to intercept you. She howls abuse as you speed past, through the door, up the stairs, and out. Go to 79

50

"Ullo, ullo, ullo," says the Sergeant of the Watch. "Wot 'ave we 'ere then, sunshine? Is that an 'alberd sticking up out of your cloak?"

Do you—

Say "No, it's a five-pronged fish spear"? Go to 25

Say "Yes, I am going to visit my mother-in-law"? Go to 72

Say "Take that, garboil!" and attack? Go to 65

51

You lose your grip as you fumble one-handed for the saint, and you begin to fall. Fortunately, your shining white heroic teeth manage to clench on the sail. You pray for a miracle (silently), but the effort is too much. You drop the plaster saint and grab the sail. The saint falls on the hunchback's head; he looks up and activates the windmill again. You descend gracefully, land with elan, and cross yourself. The hunchback head butts you in a very sensitive region (he couldn't reach higher) and drops a pile of plaster shards on your doubled-up form. You hobble away, groaning. Go to 54

52

The Southgate

A grim complex of towers, barbicans, murder holes, and dungeons, the Southgate Fortress was transformed into an amusement arcade several years ago. Now, from the Wheel of

Fortune to the Headless Ventriloquist, you'll find fun at the Southgate. Only twenty bezants for the whole family—forty if you don't want the kids back at the end of the day . . . but this is all meaningless hype to you. Your mind is set on rescuing the fair lady . . . what was her name? . . . Oiseaux. You ignore the Southgate, and go

South (sort of). Go to 16

Sort of east. Go to 88

53

Nice try, but it's money up front at the Quay of Scented Rats. As you cannot possibly have the hundred bezants Yvette demands, she rings a little bell. Moments later, an enormous eunuch servant appears and escorts you back to the Main Hall of the bordello. Go to 61

54 QUAY OF SCENTED RATS (LANDWARD SIDE)

At last you have reached the Sleine! You can't see

it through the ramshackle warehouses and wharves, but that odor of muddy decay and raw sewage could only be the river. On the other side of the warehouses, you can just see a ramshackle bridge and the hundred lanterns that spell out "S en ed R ts" (there should be a hundred forty lanterns). Loosening your rapier in its scabbard, you stride on. Go to 7

55

The guards take your bezants with suspicion, subject them to their beaverlike teeth, then reluctantly stamp the back of your hand with today's date and the scented rat symbol of the bordello. They let you pass onto the rickety bridge, and warn you not to approach the old troll who lives underneath. You cross the bridge speedily and enter . . . the Quay of Scented Rats. Go to 61

56

Roll one die.

1–3 *You're running full tilt when you realize you can no longer hear the Bittern. You slow, look around, and see that it has gone into whisper mode, gliding along and changing direction by means of small puffs of air from its beak. Too late, you start to run again . . . and it strikes you savagely in the balls. You can't believe how lucky that was . . . you hardly ever carry tennis balls around in your pockets. Lucky you were planning to have a game this morning. Relieved, you put on speed.* Go to 93

4–6 *You cross the square miles ahead of the Bittern—which, in fact, turns out to be a harmless Tittern. Very similar, but the Tittern's beak is non-rigid, and the feathers on the back of its neck are more golden, and have a barred pattern. Its feeding habits are also markedly different, particularly on Wednesdays, when the Tittern is a familiar sight at the kitchen doors of many fashionable restaurants, pecking at paté de fois gras and trying to get the dregs out of champagne bottles. It is here that the Tittern's remarkable flexible beak comes into its own. A Tittern found trapped in a bottle of Pom Derryong '47 had a beak seven inches long (extended), and three inches long when rolled up on top of its head . . . but you have no time for ornithological observations. On to 93*

57

You approach the hulking giant. Close up, you see that he has a greenish tinge—but then the smell of this place is enough to make anyone sick.

"Excuse me, peasant," you say nicely. "Point me to the River Sleine and be damned quick about it."

He growls, burps, and raises his club to attack.

Do you run back to the Place of Plaice? Go to 83

Calmly fix him with your steely gaze, poke your tongue out, and finish him off with a single lunge? Go to 28

Back off and look for an opening? Go to 38

Get out your halberd (if you have one) and go for his kneecaps? Go to 48

58 You drop down a long chute, accelerating through several twists and curves, then explode out into a dimly lit room. A cackling old hag is lifting a body from another chute, a huge, evil-smelling pot is bubbling on a central stove, there are pastry pie shells laid out on the table, and a big autographed picture of a nasty-looking barber is in the corner.

Do you run for the door? Go to 49

Try and climb back up the chute? Go to 78

Attack the hag with your rapier? Go to 13

59 MA'S FIELD

Heading north by northwest, you arrive in Ma's Field—a small patch of greenery, where many aged women farm market gardens. At the other end of the field, a resplendent red-and-gold Montgolfier is drifting along, with a man throwing primitive fertilizer over the side—it is obviously one of those new-fangled crop-dusting balloons. It drifts closer, and the occupant seems to take an interest in you.

Do you run away toward the Carved Heads of Past Emperors? Go to 31

Stand there like a ninny? Go to 22

60

You hold the piece of paper to the light from the window—or you would, if the window were there. You stare around the solid, windowless walls, and then back to the paper. In the dim, unearthly light, you see it is an invitation—an invitation to "spend the rest of your days in Monsieur Moorcock's Mill of Mazes." You sigh heavily and open the nearest trapdoor. Why, oh why, you ask yourself, is there a maze in every adventure? Go to 3

61

The Great Hall

You enter the Great Hall of the Quay of Scented Rats and are stricken with awe! The basilica of St. Peter's, the Hanging Gardens of Babylon, the Fabled City of Gold—they cannot compare . . . as they are far more awe-inspiring. But the Great Hall is a splendid exhibition of bad taste. Purple fur lines the walls and floor, growing like some sort of fungus between the huge plaster sculptures of Aphrodite and Eros. Glass Cupids swing on chains of worn silver-plated steel and tangle in the papier-mâché ferns. Red plush couches line the walls, where gentlemen and lady customers leaf through the catalogues of men and women of ill repute and an old madam constantly sprays the lot with gallons of cheap scent from a mammoth atomizer.

Do you stride through the Hall and out the door at the other end? Go to 44

Or stride through the Hall and out the door at the other end, feeling as if your life is somehow being manipulated by unearthly powers? Go to 44

62

You draw your rapier, expecting certain death at the monstrously skilled hands of a Cleaver-Fu Master. But the hag is strangely motionless, and you realize that by some quirk of fate, you will be spared. You edge past the hag and out the door. Go to 79 (Please note: Only one quirk of fate allowed per adventure.)

63

You pass the tiger in an adrenline-assisted blur. Obviously it was just trying to lull you into a false sense of security, because it leaps at you, snarling, as you pass. You wrench the other door open and fall out into the street, babbling, "Nice Mr. Tiger. Nice Tiger, don't bite. I give to the World Wildlife Fund. Sixty bezants every full moon. At least I will. Starting next year. Honest, Mr. Tiger . . ." You stop babbling as you realize the door has swung shut behind you. Go to 79

64

As your boat makes its closest approach to the houseboat, you leap from its prow! Roll one die.

1–2 Splosh! You manage to perform one and a half somersaults before entering the Sleine at an obtuse angle. Various courtesans, gigolos, and guests come to the rail of the houseboat and laugh as you are dragged away by the current, thrashing and cursing. Mortally embarrassed, you decide to sink to the bottom of the Sleine and end it all. However, when you do sink to the bottom, it is so disgusting that you change your mind and swim ashore. *Go to 7*

3–5 As you leap, you wisely decide to dispense with the somersaults, and your leap carries you to the prow of the houseboat, where you cling for dear life. You prepare for another leap onto the deck, but that last one really took it out of you, so you slither under the rails and crawl across the deck instead. *Go to 44*

6 You hurtle eighteen feet into the air, do three full somersaults, flourish your hat, and land on the deck in front of several guests of the establishment. Astounded, they can merely gasp as you calmly light a cigarillo and stride toward the Salon door. *Go to 44*

As you struggle to get the halberd out from under your cloak, the

Sergeant steps back, and all four Watchmen lower their blunderbusses and fire.

Your last thought before you shuffle off this mortal coil is whether you left the mulled wine on the fire. Maybe it's boiled dry. . . . The End.

66

You treacherous little worm! Okay—leave Lady Oiseaux to the tender mercies of a desert chieftain. Don't sample the delights of the Quay of Scented Rats or . . . or . . . words fail me. I hope you get a part as Minotaur bait in "Theseus Does Knossos: Choose Your Own Adventure 288." And you can leave the El Superbeau cognac behind.

67

You fling yourself toward the lovely Yvette, only to be met by an upraised knee. You bounce back, whimpering, and she calmly rings a little bell. An enormous eunuch servant enters, giggles, and picks you up. "A new recruit for uth, Mithtreth," he lisps. She smiles, and you are carried away, still whimpering. Go to 90

68

Failure! You go for the trip, but the eunuch isn't as slow as he looks! In the blink of an eye, he has you in a half nelson! You struggle uselessly in the eunuch's deceptively strong grasp. The doctor snaps open his gladstone bag, pulls out a pair of shears, and grins evilly. Suddenly, adrenaline you never knew you had shoots through every muscle in your body, transforming you into someone who makes Arnie Schwarzenegger look like a wimp. Roaring with berserk fury, you pick the three-hundred-pound eunuch up over your head and throw him at the doctor, before smashing through the wall into an adjoining room. Go to 93

I demand twenty bezants for my ruined clothes, you ghastly lump of lard!" you cry indignantly at the merchant. He rubs his hands together obsequiously, offers four trillion billion humble pardons, and begins to bargain with you.

Five minutes later, you leave without the bezants, but with your clothes replaced by a bright blue one-piece, sealskin body stocking with bronze buttons, which the merchant assures you will be the perfect disguise for the riverside slums. You walk toward the Arc de Trihump, glad that you got the better of the merchant. Go to 99

70

Could you really be that stupid? You trip, recover, and just manage to grab hold of the trapdoor's iron ring—saving yourself from certain death. Shaking with relief, you crawl back and pick up the piece of paper. Go to 60

You cry out: "Sir Galahad, come to my aid!" Suddenly, a white light fills the room, there is an explosion of white petals, a miniature snowstorm hurtles past, and there is the knelling of a great bell. A man appears and bows. He is six feet six inches tall, incredibly handsome, and has a smile that blinds at thirty paces. It can only be . . . Sir Galahad! He takes one look at Yvette (who sits up and puts on her Ray-Bans), and says, "Right! I'll take care of this one!"

Yvette says, "Yes please!" and you exit, with the slight suspicion that Galahad might not be as pure as everyone thought. Then you see him getting his prayer book out and pointing to a particular illustrated psalm, so you know he will reform the fallen woman. You open the other door and dash through it, in search of Lady Oiseaux! Go to 15

72

The Sergeant raises his eyebrows for a moment, then waves you on. You walk past, down to the Street of Fishmongers, which marks the beginning of the Scum Quarter. Behind you, the Watch are discussing halberds and, possibly, mothers-in-law.

"Of course, you've got to get in with an overhand. . . ."

"Nah, what you do is get one with a six-foot handle. . . ." Go to 41

73

There's no point beating about the bush on this one. I'll tell it to you straight, without circumlocution, shilly-shallying, or avoiding the subject. It's bad news, but what isn't these days? What with the price of El Superbeau up to four hundred bezants the tun, the king frolicking in orange orchards, the country going to the dogs . . . it's all bad news. Oh yes . . . Z——O kills you. Right through the heart. *Thock!* And it's all over . . . and you were so close to success. . . . The End.

74

You hear the groans and moans of the eunuch and the doctor on the other side of the splintered wall. Dimly, you hear your brain telling you this is going to really hurt later. There is another door.

Do you wrench open the other door? Go to 80

Or take advantage of your berserk strength to smash through the adjacent wall? Go to 93

75

You hear the eunuch backing off, then galumphing forward to batter the door. You fling it open and step aside, as a huge blubbery mass hurtles past and smashes against the other door. The doctor, seeing his protector lying unconscious on the floor, begs for mercy.

"Where are the auction goods?" you ask sternly. Shaking, he points at the door marked "Not the Auction Goods." You nod and continue to stare at him. The slight smile you learned from Clint Eastwood creeps across your face, and you take the shears from his nerveless fingers and click them twice. He looks aghast and faints. You use the shears to trim the end of your Van Dyke beard, then go to the other door, stepping on the unconscious eunuch. Go to 80

76

Roll one die for a highly realistic resolution of this situation.

1–3 He doesn't start laughing. Your eyes clouded with forced tears, and mind numbed by the effort of concentrated blubbering, you hardly notice his rapier has cut you from your guggle to your zatch (don't ask). You blubber for real . . . then it is all over. Your last thoughts are of the stupid guidebook that said this dopey maneuver never failed. The End.

4–6 He guffaws. He nearly chokes with laughter. His eyes pop out of his head. Before you can even draw your pistol, he's lying on the ground, kicking his legs and giggling inanely. You stop blubbering and continue on your way. Go to 52

77

If you don't have a fish spear, your head is bashed in by the ex-priest. Tempus has fugited. The End. That's it.

If you do have a fish spear, roll one die.

1–3 Your spear is longer than the ex-priest's thurible. He is pronged several times before retreating.

4–5 You entangle the thurible's chain in your prongs and whip it away. Bereft of his weapon, the defrocked clergyman retires to contemplate the infinite.

6 You trip; the thuribler hits you with his thurible. It doesn't hurt that much, but the incense makes you feel sick. He steals your fish spear.

Unless you are deceased, you return to the Arc de Trihump. Go to 99

78

You try to climb back up the chute, but it is too steep. From behind you comes the sound of a body being tipped into the pot. You turn, and the hag is advancing upon you brandishing a cleaver. Your stomach churns as you realize that she is wearing the Black Apron of a Master of Cleaver-Fu.

Do you have two pairs of silk stockings? *Go to 32*

Or a bottle of Opossum perfume? Go to 10

Or will you draw your rapier and try and fight your way past? Go to 62

79

Once again, you stand outside the mill. A hunchback looks at you curiously, then wanders off, muttering, "She gave me water. I ordered wine. . . ."

You may go north by northwest. Go to 59

Or south by southwest. Go to 54

80

You wrench open the door, and there before you is a great gate of bronze, studded with rubies and emeralds. In front of the gate stands a mighty Djinn, clutching a scimitar of mirrored steel in a fist of Herculean proportions . . . oops, that's "Down to the Sleazy Sandpits of Samarkand," Adventure 31 in this series. Actually . . .

You wrench open the door, revealing an

antechamber. There is another door, marked "Secret—The Real Auction Goods." You step into the room, and the door swings shut behind you with an audible click that certainly means it is now automatically locked. A man steps out of the shadows, brandishing a rapier. You have only a moment to take in his black hat, black mask, black shirt, black trousers, black boots, black cape, "Z" signet ring, and stupid little mustache before he cries, "En garde!"

Do you swear at him in Spanish and lug out your own rapier? Go to 24

Whip out your glove puppet of Cyrano de Bergerac, entrance him with an impromptu display of puppet swordsmanship, then stick the puppet's sword up his nose? Go to 19

Say, "Violence is the last resort of the incompetent, you childish fellow!" and attempt to walk past? Go to 86

81

This was originally a brilliant paragraph detailing a combat with an enraged Purple-Assed Baboon. However, when

Adventure 46, "Down to the Chlorophyllic Jungle," ran short, it had to go over to it. Also, if you are reading this, you must be cheating.

82

Eighty-two was also a brilliant paragraph, describing the awesome Slime Serpent that was going to emerge from the Sleine at a strategic moment. Once again, that paragraph had to go over to "Down to the Chlorophyllic Jungle." Honestly, I don't know how Steve Jackson and Ian Livingstone do it. They must be good with numbers or something. . . .

83

PLACE OF PLAICE

This is the upmarket part of the Street of Fishmongers—a pleasant, open area, strewn with rancid squid carcasses and buckets of prawns left out in the sun. Smiling merchants offer you slightly fresher wares.

You walk through haughtily, oblivious to this crass business—when, without warning, a fat merchant emerges from behind a crate and knocks you down with his enormous silk-wound belly!

Do you leap up and stick the fellow with a convenient garfish? Go to 18

Leap up and demand twenty bezants for the damage to your clothes? Go to 69

Lie there and hope he doesn't tread on you? Go to 98

84

You grab hold of one of the windmill's sails and are soon lifted high above the city. It is a somewhat tiring mode of sightseeing, but most educational. You have never seen the city's dumps, ruins, broken sewers, and slums laid out in all their splendor before. As the sail reaches the top of its arc, a hunchback emerges from the mill below, says, "She gave me water," and stops the sails. You are left dangling seventy feet above the ground, and your arms are getting tired.

Do you have twenty feet of rope? Go to 8

Or a plaster saint? Go to 51

If you have neither, Go to 37

---

85 As you open the door, a fully grown Bengal tiger leaps down from above and advances, growling.

Do you run back through the door? Go to 9

Shoot it with your pistol (if you have one)? Go to 43

Say "Nice pussums" and head for the door opposite, marked "EXIT"? Go to 40

---

86 Z looks surprised, then a grin slowly spreads across his face. "You are right!" he exclaims. "But I canot let you pass unless you overmaster me in a contest of some kind. Mmmm . . . how about a riddle game?"

Reluctantly, you accept. It's been a long time since you read *The Hobbit*, and you never did know why that stupid chicken crossed the road.

He asks:

"Take a span of mortal life, less a score times two
Add a number equal to a witch's coven thrice
Less the year, but not the century,
of the most famous gold rush in America."

You mutter something about rhyming, but desist when he absentmindedly cuts the wings from a passing fly with his rapier. Go to the Answer.

87

You level your pistol at the door and fire point-blank. There is a deafening *crash!* Splinters fly everywhere, smoke billows out, and you curse, cough, and shriek in pain. You pick a few of the splinters out, then peek through the bullet hole in the door. There is no sign of the eunuch or the doctor, so you reload, kick the door in, and level your pistol at every corner of the room, screaming, "Hands up!" But these histrionics are wasted, as a quick glance out the window reveals the eunuch and the doctor being carried away by the swift currents of the Sleine, hotly pursued by the Slime Serpent of paragraph 82. You check out the room, but there are no other exits, or any sign of Lady Oiseaux. You go down the corridor to the door marked "Not the Auction Goods." Go to 80

88 The Windmill

In the middle of the city there is a field. In the middle of the field there is a windmill. There is no reason there should be a windmill here, except that it comes in handy for hooking people up during duels.

You may go north by northwest. Go to 59

Or grab onto one of the sails of the windmill. Go to 84

89 It's hard to get a grip on a smooth chin that curves in instead of out. You are feebly struggling for a handhold when the Montgolfier lands and a pinstripe-suited man alights. He introduces himself as an agent for "Choose Your Own Adventures," and offers you a part as the hero in a "serious" solo adventure.

Do you accept? Go to 66

Do you politely refuse? Go to 42

---

90 The eunuch carries you into a Turkish bathroom, which is currently unoccupied. He dumps you on a bench, and you hear him disappear off into the steam, lisping, "I'll jutht fetth the doctor to finith off."

You feel that waiting for the doctor would be imprudent, and you are feeling much better, so you creep back out the door. Go to 15

91

BITTERN SQUARE

You know the old saying "Once Bittern, twice as painful the next time"? That saying comes from this square, where fearsomely accurate seabirds always beak you in the same place.

You try and creep past, but . . . oh no . . . you've trod on a stick near a Bittern's nest. You hear the *snap!* of the twig, and then the fearsome *wokka wokka wokka* of a fully beaked Bittern taking off.

Do you stand there, waving your rapier over your head? Go to 46

Or run like blazes for the narrow alley on the other side of the square? Go to 56

92

Two women are playing cards around a small table. Two tigers are sleeping nearby. As you enter, the tigers leap up, growling.

Do you run back through the door? Go to 9

Or pull up a chair and say, "Deal me in. What's the game? Stud, draw, three-up two-down, écarte, vingt-et-un, snap, canasta, sudden death, gin rummy, five hundred, strip jack naked?" Go to 29

93

Smack! Crash! Thud! Wallop! Bull-like, you smash through one . . . two . . . three . . . four interior walls, leaving a trail of shrieking customers and their chosen consorts (not to mention splinters, broken furniture, embarrassment, etc.). This is fun! Smash! Crash! Splash! You fall into the Sleine and, drained by your berserk fury, dog-paddle ashore. You rest for a moment in the comfortable slime, moving on when it starts to grow on you. You head back to the main entrance of the Quay of Scented Rats. Go to 7

94

You've forgotten the door is locked. You back against it, knees knocking in fear, and mumble something about "Wrong room . . . sorry . . . I was looking for . . . ummm . . . eeerr . . ." He says, "Oh, that's all right then. Thought you were after the auction goods. I'll just get the key and let you out."

He sheathes his rapier and turns to a cabinet. You leap forward, swinging the rapier in your mouth, knock him out with the pommel, and make your smile three quarters of an inch wider. Before he has a chance to recover, you sprint across the room and open the other door. Go to 100

95

That's the last of the hulking giant. You compose yourself (bandaging appendages where necessary), and continue on your way. Soon Fishgut Alley branches into a **Y** fork.

Do you go south (that must be south . . .)? *Go to 88*

Or south, sort of west a bit? *Go to 52*

96

The dragon rears back, its rainbow-scaled head writhing in agony as your sword sinks ever deeper into its primary brain. But the secondary brain still functions, and you see the great tail swinging around, the venomous sting preparing to punch through you where you stand, precariously balanced between the creature's great yellow-centered eyes.

Do you press the stud that will explode the sword blade into a hundred heat-seeking flechettes? Go to 426

Or dive off the creature's back, trusting that your G-harness battery is not exhausted? Go to 507

97

The tank glimmers with an unearthly light—surely this is the wellspring of the changelings, the nutrient tank where the Technomancer has been growing the nervous systems of his hideous creatures. You approach closer, scanning for search webs and tracksprings. Nothing shows in the visual spectrum, but the NecroVision™ sight shows stirrings beneath the floor. Forewarned, you spring back and draw your sword, a .45 caliber emulsion sprayer springing into your left fist, just as a Mordicant emerges through the flagstones, its gravemold arms writhing!

Do you chop at its head? Go to 650

Or fire a pulse of violet emulsion at its brain stem? Go to 202

Paragraphs 96 and 97 are a blatant advertisement for "Dark Realm of the Technomancer," which is at present little more than those two paragraphs. But that's what advertising is all about. Order now!

98

Aaarghh! The pain is intense as the fat merchant rests his bulk upon you, in the mistaken belief that you are a convenient seat. Your screams of agony disconcert him—he leaps to his feet and hurries off.

You slowly clamber to your knees and crawl toward the Arc de Trihump (or the other way). Subtract one from all future combat rolls due to a severely bruised back. Go to 99 or 91

99 The Arc de Trihump

A huge monument raised to celebrate the prowess of a long-dead emperor in his personal dealings with camels, the Arc de Trihump is near the Western Wall of the city.

If you continue west (or thereabouts): Go to 6

Turn to the broad avenue that heads south: Go to 21

100

You fling open the velvet-padded door and strike a commanding pose in the doorway. Your love, the Lady Oiseaux, is sitting by the mirror, putting on her earrings. She ignores you for a moment, then says: "If you're coming in, come in. Ow! And help me with this earring. What took you so long anyway? You used to rescue me in no time at all—I guess you're getting tired of me. No, don't say you're not. I know you are, otherwise you would have been here hours ago (sob). . . ."

You stride across the room and stop her protests with a passionate kiss, sweep her into your arms, and leap out the window—onto the deck of a conveniently passing luxury wide-bodied gondola. The string quartet looks surprised, then breaks into the theme from *Love Story*. The waiter pops the champagne as you and your lady recline into the lavender-scented pillows, and the gondola gondols away into the setting sun, long life, and happiness ever after.*

---

*Hardened cynics may order the alternative, realistic, nonromantic ending (involving several hunchbacks, gruesome deeds, tragedy, and despair) by sending $2.00 to the author.

Introduction to Heart's Desire

That pesky Arthurian mythos just keeps on coming back. Every time it crosses my path, I tell myself I still dislike it, and every time, I end up writing a story set in the world of Arthurian legend.

"Heart's Desire" was written for an anthology called *The Road to Camelot*, edited by Sophie Masson. The basic premise for the anthology was to write stories about the famous characters of the Arthurian legends when they were children or teens, or just getting started on their road to . . . well . . . Camelot.

By the time I agreed to get involved, most of the better-known characters had already been snapped up by other authors. Which was just as well, really, since I didn't have any idcas about how to write a different and interesting story about Arthur, or Lancelot, or Merlin. So I started looking at some of the characters associated with the main players, like Lancelot's wife,

Elaine, or King Lot, father of the Orkney lads. But I kept coming back to the fact that the character I was most interested in was Merlin, and in turn Merlin's relationship with Nimue (sometimes called Viviane).

Basically, I never bought the standard-issue version of the Merlin-Nimue story, which stripped to its essence is that the old Merlin is besotted with Nimue and entrapped by her. Part of my problem with that story is that Merlin can actually foretell the future. Older men get besotted by younger women all the time, and, as they say, "There's no fool like an old fool." But not, I would think, if that older man could accurately tell exactly what was going to happen.

Unless there was something about that future that meant he would go along with whatever was going to happen, which he presumably wouldn't if he knew Nimue didn't really love him at all but just wanted his power. After all, not only would Merlin find himself entombed, but he would be abandoning Arthur, who is not only a kind of foster son but in many ways also Merlin's life work.

That's where "Heart's Desire" came from: a desire on my part to retell the Merlin-Nimue story in a different light, with different motivations, while still staying within the broad boundaries of the best-known versions of the original story.

Heart's Desire

"To catch a star, you must know its secret name and its place in the heavens," whispered Merlin, his mouth so close to Nimue's ear his breath tickled and made her want to laugh. Only the seriousness of the occasion stopped a giggle. Finally, after years of apprenticeship, Merlin was about to tell her what she had always wanted to know, what she had worked toward for seven long years.

"You must send the name to the sky as a white bird. You must write it in fire upon a mirror. You must wrap the falling star with your heart's desire. All this must be done in the single moment between the end of night and the dawning of the day."

"That's it?" breathed Nimue. "The final secret?"

"Yes," said Merlin slowly. "The final secret. But remember the cost. Your heart's desire will be consumed by the star. Only from its ashes will power come."

"But my heart's desire is to have the power!" exclaimed Nimue. "How can I gain it and lose it at the same time?"

"Even a magus may not know his own heart," said Merlin heavily. "And it will be the whole desire of your heart, from past, present, or future. You will be giving up something that may yet come to pass, if you choose not to take a star from the sky."

Merlin looked at her as she stared up at the sky, watching the stars. He saw a young woman, with the dark face and hair of a Pict, her eyes flashing with excitement. She was not beautiful, or even pretty, but her face was strong and lively, and every movement hinted at energy barely contained. She wore a plain white dress, sleeveless but stretching to her ankles, and bracelets of twisted gold wire and amethysts. Merlin had given her the bracelets, and they were invested with the many lesser magics that Nimue had learned from him in the last three years.

There were other things that Merlin saw, out of memory and with the gift he had taken from a falling star.

There was the past, beginning when a headstrong girl no more than fourteen years old sought him out in his simple house upon the Cornish headland. He had turned her away, but she had sat on his doorstep for weeks, living off shellfish and seaweed, until at last he had relented and taken her in. At first he had refused to teach her magic, but she had won that battle as well. He could not deny that she had the gift, and he could not deny that he enjoyed the teaching. Over the years that enjoyment in teaching her had become something else, though Merlin had never shown it. He was nearly three times her age, and he had spent many years before Nimue's arrival preparing himself for the sorrow that must come. He had not expected it to be as straightforward as simply falling in love with an impossible girl, but there it was.

There was the present, the two of them standing upon the black stone with the new sun shining down upon them.

The future, so many possible roads stretching out in all directions. If he wished, Merlin could try to steer Nimue toward one future. But he did not. The choice would be hers.

"My heart's desire is to gain full mastery of the Art," Nimue said slowly. "I can gain that mastery

only by the capture of a star, yet that ca
depends upon the sacrifice of my heart's desire
interesting conundrum."

"You should stay here and think on it," said Merlin. He stepped down from the black stone, the centerpiece of the ring of stones that he had built almost twenty years before. The black stone had been the most difficult, though it was small and flat, unlike the standing monoliths of granite. He had drawn it out of the very depths of the earth, and it had smoked and run like water before he had forced it into its current shape. "But break-fast calls me and I wish to answer."

Nimue smiled and sat cross-legged on the stone. She watched Merlin as he walked away. As he left the ring of stones, the air shimmered around him, bright shafts of light weaving and dancing around his head and arms. The light sank into his hair and skin, and when it finally settled, Merlin's hair was white and he appeared to be much older than he really was. It was a magical disguise he had long assumed, Nimue knew. Age was associated with wisdom, and Merlin had also found it useful to appear aged and infirm. Nimue expected she would probably do the same when she came into her power. A crone was always much more convincing than a maiden.

Not that she expected to be a maiden too much longer. Nimue had her own plans for that step from maiden to woman grown. Merlin was part of that plan, though he did not know it. No village boy or even one of Arthur's warriors would do for Nimue. Merlin was the only man she had ever wanted in her bed. There had been some who had tried to influence her choice over the past few years, against all her discouragement. A few were still around, croaking and sunning their warty hides down in the reedy margins of the lake. Nimue was surprised they had lived so long. Most men died from such transformations. Sometimes she fed them flies, but she never let them touch her, either as toads or men.

Nimue turned her thoughts from failed suitors back to the conundrum presented by Merlin. Her heart's desire was to have the power, yet she would lose her heart's desire to gain the power. How could this be?

She scratched her head and lay down on the rock, letting the heat from the sun fall upon her. Unconsciously, she turned her palms up to catch the rays. The sun was a source of power, one she used in many lesser magics. It was good to take in the sun's power when the sky was clear, and she no longer needed to even think about it. Nimue could draw power from many sources: the sun, the earth, the moving stream, even the spent breath of animals and men.

What had Merlin lost? Nimue wondered. What was his heart's desire? He must have wanted the power as she wanted it. He had gained it, and as far as she could see, he had lost nothing. He was the pre-eminent wizard of the age. The counsellor and maker of kings. There was no knowledge he did not have, no spell he did know.

Perhaps there was nothing to lose, Nimue thought. Or if there was, it would be something she would never miss. A heart's desire that could come to pass, but did not, was no loss. To see the future was not the same as to live it. Perhaps she would see her heart's desire in the hearth fire, and would know it could never be. How much of a loss was that?

Nothing, thought Nimue. *Nothing compared to the exhilaration of magic.*

"Tonight," she whispered, and she curled up on the black stone like a cat resting up in preparation for extensive wickedness. "Tonight, for everything."

Merlin was not asleep when she came to his chamber. He lay on his bed, his eyes open, gleaming in the thin shaft of moonlight from the tower window. Nimue hesitated at the door, suddenly shy and afraid. She had chosen to come naked, but with her long dark hair artfully arranged to both cover and suggest. She had taken a long time to get her hair exactly right, and it was held in place with charms as well as pins.

"Merlin," she whispered.

Merlin did not respond. Nimue drifted into the room. Her skin seemed to glow with an inner light, and her smile promised many pleasures. Any man would rise and take her to his bed in eager haste. But not Merlin.

"Merlin. I shall go to the black rock before the dawn. But I would go as a woman, who has known her man. Your woman."

"No," whispered Merlin. He did not move, but lay as still as the chalk carving on the green of the hill. "There are men aplenty in the village. Two of Arthur's knights are visiting tonight. They are both good men, young and unmarried."

Nimue shook her head and stepped forward. Her hair fell aside as she knelt by the bed, her magic dissolving and the pins unable to hold on their own.

"It is you I want," she said fiercely. "You! No one else. You want me too! I know it, as well as I know the ten thousand names of the beasts and the birds that you have taught me."

"I do," whispered Merlin. "But I am your teacher, and it is not meet that we should lie together now, unequal in years and power. Go back to your own place."

Nimue frowned. Then she rose and stamped her foot, and whirled away, light and shadows dancing in her wake. At the door she looked back, and her smile shone through the dark room.

"Tomorrow I shall be my own mistress and you will not be master," said Nimue. "I will catch my star and we can be as man and wife."

Merlin did not move or answer. In an instant, Nimue was gone, and the room was silent once more. The shaft of moonlight slowly crawled over Merlin's face, and darkness hid the tears that welled up out of his clear blue eyes. Young man's eyes, unclouded by age or glamour.

"Ah well," he muttered to himself. "Ah well."

They were the words Merlin's father had said upon his deathbed. Simple words, devoid of magic, greeting a fate that could not be turned aside.

Nimue did not go back to her own bed. Instead she put on her best linen dress, that she herself had dyed blue from isatis bark and stitched with silver thread that she had spun out of the deep earth.

The silver thread shone in the moonlight as she slipped out of the house and out onto the headland. There was a pool at the edge of the western cliff, a pool of soft water, fed by spring and rain. It was always placid, mirrorlike, in sharp contrast to the sea that crashed on the rocks only a few paces away, but two hundred feet below. An ancient hawthorn tree leaned over the pool, all shadows and spiky branches. It had often been mistaken in the dark for a giant, or some fell creature. Every midwinter night some hapless stranger would seek to use the power of the pool, only to flee in panic from the hawthorn. Invariably they found the cliff edge and the pounding sea that would grind their bones to dust.

Nimue stood at the edge of the pool and

hugged herself against the bite of the wind, cold in this early morning. She whispered to herself, preparing for what must be done:

"To find the secret name of a star,
Ask the moon that shares the sky.
Fix its place between the branches of the
hawthorn tree.
Send the name to the sky on the wings of
a bird.
Burn the name in fire upon the mirrored
waters of the lake.
Wrap the star with heart's desire
Between the darkness and the light.
Then you shall a magus be. . . ."

Nimue looked up to the heavens and found the great disk of the moon, yellow as ancient cheese. She let its light fall upon her face and open hands, and took in its power. But a yellow moon was not what she sought. She waited, silent, the hawthorn tree softly groaning in the wind, the surf crashing deep below.

Slowly the moon began to sink and change. The yellow faded and blue-silver began to spill across its face. Nimue felt the change and smiled.

Soon she would ask it to name her star. She had already chosen one. A bright star, but not so bright it might overpower her. Not the Evening Star, which served no one and never would. But a star as bright as Merlin's, though not as red. She would be his equal in power, if not in kind.

A bird called, the sleepy cry of something woken before its time. The wind fell and the hawthorn stilled. Nimue felt a tremor rush through her. Dawn was only minutes away. The moon was silver—she must act.

She called to the moon, a call that no human ears could hear. At first there was no answer, but she had expected that. She called again, using the power she'd drawn earlier from the sun. The moon grew a fraction brighter at the call, and through the void her silver voice came down, quiet and imbued with sadness, speaking for Nimue alone.

"Jahaliel."

As the name formed in her head, Nimue sank to one knee and looked up through the branches of the hawthorn. There, in the fork where two twisted branches met, she saw her star, bright between two strands of darkness.

Nimue splashed her hand in the pool, and the

droplets flew into the air to become a white bird, a dove whose wings made a drumroll as it rose straight up toward the sky, the name of the star held in its beak where once it would have carried an olive branch.

The pool was still before Nimue's hand had left it, still and shining, reflecting the woman, the tree, the moon, and sky. With her forefinger and all that was left of the sun's power within her, Nimue wrote in fire upon the mirrored water the three runes that spelled out the name "Ja-hal-iel."

In the heavens, a star fell. The moon sank, and the sun rose.

In the instant between night and day, Nimue caught her star and bound it forever with the promise of her heart's desire.

She felt something leave her, and tears started in her eyes. But she did not know what she had lost, and the exultation of power was upon her.

Nimue ran to the cliff top and threw herself into the air. Like a feather she drifted down, buffeted this way and that by the wind but taking no harm. Before the cold water embraced her, she became a dolphin, plunging into a wave, sliding under the water to spin out the other side, laughing as only a dolphin can.

Nimue had been a dolphin before, but it was Merlin who had made her so. It was his star's power that had given her the shapes of many things, on sea and air and land. Now she could transform herself at will. She jumped again and between two waves became a hawk, shooting up above the spray. A merlin, to be exact, and that was her joke and tribute. On bent-back wings she sped across the headland, past the pool, toward the rising sun and Merlin.

With sharp hawk eyes she saw he had already risen and was waiting for her in the ring of stones. He stood upon the black rock, without a glamour upon him, and Nimue felt love for him rise in her heart as bright and strong as the rising sun.

She flew still higher, until she was directly above him and he had to shade his eyes to look at her. Then she folded her wings and dropped straight down, down into his open arms.

They had one kiss, one brief embrace, before the stars they wore pushed them apart, the air itself wrenching them from each other's grasp. Nimue shouted and directed her will upon her newfound power, but to no avail. She was pushed completely off the black stone, to fall sprawling in the circle.

Merlin did not shout. He had fallen on his back, and was sinking into the black stone as if it were not stone at all but some peaty bog that had trapped an unwary traveler.

He did not shout, but his voice was loud and clear in Nimue's ear as she struggled to her feet.

"You were my heart's desire, Nimue, waiting in the future. You were the price I paid for the art. Love never to be fulfilled. Forgive me."

His hand stretched up from the stone. Nimue snatched at it, as if even now she might somehow pull him back. But her hand closed on empty air, and his disappeared beneath the surface of the stone.

"Forgive me, Merlin," whispered Nimue. She made no effort to stem the tears that fell upon the stone. A bright star shone in the hollow of her neck, the promise of power and wisdom beyond anything she had ever dreamed. But she was cold inside, cold with the knowledge that this power was not her heart's desire. Her true heart's desire lay entombed in dark stone, beyond her reach forever.

Or was he? Nimue clutched her star and looked up at the sky, so bright above her. If a star could be plucked from the sky, then surely it could also be made to rise again? To take its place in the firmament once more, unraveling all the threads of time that had been woven in its fall. If she could return her star, then surely Merlin would freely walk the earth, and he in turn could free his star and regain his heart's desire.

There were other powers in the world. Other places to find knowledge. Nimue stretched her slim arms above her head and in a moment was a bird, wide winged and far sailing. She rode a wind west, across the open sea, and was gone from Britain.

With her went all Merlin's wisdom and power, and all hope for the kingdom of Arthur. The kingdom that would sink into ruin as Nimue's heart's desire had sunk into the stone.

INTRODUCTION TO HANSEL'S EYES

This story was written for *A Wolf at the Door*, a collection of retold fairy tales edited by Ellen Datlow and Terri Windling. I turned to the Brothers Grimm, as one does, for a story to retell. Despite being attracted to several lesser-known stories, in the end I wrote a variation on the "Hansel and Gretel" story, probably because I had an idea about what the witch would be like, and what she would do, if transferred to a modern setting.

Because I quite like the author's note I wrote for the original anthology, I'm going to quote some of it here:

> *He first encountered Grimm's fairy tales when they were read to him at the age of five or six. He spent the next two years attempting to spin straw into gold, turn pumpkins into carriages, and find a bearskin to put on—all without success. He chose "Hansel and Gretel" for retelling as it was always a favorite,*

probably because his mother made him a fantastic gingerbread house for his eighth birthday, complete with a witch made of sweets. He chose to set the retold story in a city because he has always found being lost in cities much more terrifying than being lost in the woods—or, in his case, the bush of Australia.

All true. For those of you wracked with jealousy because my mother made me a gingerbread house complete with a witch made of sweets, prepare to become even more green-eyed. For my seventh birthday (or perhaps my ninth), she made puppets of all the characters in Tove Jansson's *Moominland Midwinter*, built a puppet theater, and performed the book as a puppet play. Needless to say, without the influence, example, and encouragement of my mother (and my father, whose collection of fantasy and science fiction books supplied me with reading matter for my most formative years), I would not be the writer I have become, or indeed, a writer at all.

Hansel's Eyes

Hansel was ten and his sister, Gretel, was eleven when their stepmother decided to get rid of them. They didn't catch on at first, because the Hagmom (their secret name for her) had always hated them. So leaving them behind at the supermarket or forgetting to pick them up after school was no big deal.

It was only when their father got in on the "disappearing the kids" act that they realized it was serious. Although he was a weak man, they thought he might still love them enough to stand up to the Hagmom.

They realized he didn't the day he took them out into the woods. Hansel wanted to do the whole Boy Scout thing and take a water bottle and a pile of other stuff, but their dad said they wouldn't need it. It'd only be a short walk.

Then he dumped them. They'd just gotten out of the car when he took off. They didn't try to chase him. They knew the signs. The Hagmom had hypnotized him again or whatever she did to make him do things.

"Guess she's going to get a nasty surprise when we get back," said Hansel, taking out the map he'd stuffed down the front of his shirt. Gretel silently handed him the compass she'd tucked into her sock.

It took them three hours to get home, first walking, then in a highway patrol cruiser, and finally in their dad's car. They were almost back when the Hagmom called on the cell phone. Hansel and Gretel could hear her screaming. But when they finally got home, she smiled and kissed the air near their cheeks.

"She's planning something," said Gretel. "Something bad."

Hansel agreed, and they both slept in their clothes, with some maps, the compass, and candy bars stuffed down their shirts.

Gretel dreamed a terrible dream. She saw the Hagmom creep into their room, quiet as a cat in her velvet slippers. She had a big yellow sponge in her hand, a sponge that smelled sweet, but too sweet to be anything but awful. She went to Hansel's bunk and pushed the sponge against his nose and face. His arms and legs thrashed for a second, then he fell back like he was dead.

Gretel tried and tried to wake from the dream, but when she finally opened her eyes, there was the yellow sponge and the Hagmom's smiling face and then the dream was gone and there was nothing but total, absolute darkness.

When Gretel did wake up, she wasn't at home. She was lying in an alley. Her head hurt, and she could hardly open her eyes because the sun seemed too bright.

"Chloroform," whispered Hansel. "The Hagmom drugged us and got Dad to dump us."

"I feel sick," said Gretel. She forced herself to stand and noticed that there was nothing tucked into her shirt, or Hansel's, either. The maps, candy bars, and compass were gone.

"This looks bad," said Hansel, shielding his eyes with his hand and taking in the piles of trash, the broken windows, and the lingering charcoal smell of past fires. "We're in the old part of the city that got fenced off after the riots."

"She must hope someone will kill us," said Gretel. She scowled and picked up a jagged piece of glass, winding an old rag around it so she could use it like a knife.

"Probably," agreed Hansel, who wasn't fooled. He knew Gretel was scared, and so was he.

"Let's look around," Gretel said. Doing something would be better than just standing still, letting the fear grow inside them.

They walked in silence, much closer together than usual, their elbows almost bumping. The alley opened into a wide street that wasn't any better. The only sign of life was a flock of pigeons.

But around the next corner, Hansel backed up so suddenly that Gretel's glass knife almost went into his side. She was so upset, she threw it away. The sound of shattering glass echoed through the empty streets and sent the pigeons flying.

"I almost stabbed you, you moron!" exclaimed Gretel. "Why did you stop?"

"There's a shop," said Hansel. "A brand-new one."

"Let me see," said Gretel. She looked around the corner for a long time, till Hansel got impatient and tugged at her collar, cutting off her breath.

"It is a shop," she said. "A Sony PlayStation shop. That's what's in the windows. Lots of games."

"Weird," said Hansel. "I mean, there's nothing

here. No one to buy anything."

Gretel frowned. Somehow the shop frightened her, but the more she tried not to think of that, the more scared she got.

"Maybe it got left by accident," added Hansel. "You know, when they just fenced the whole area off after the fires."

"Maybe . . ." said Gretel.

"Let's check it out," said Hansel. He could sense Gretel's uneasiness, but to him the shop seemed like a good sign.

"I don't want to," said Gretel, shaking her head.

"Well, I'm going," said Hansel. After he'd gone six or seven steps, Gretel caught up with him. Hansel smiled to himself. Gretel could never stay behind.

The shop was strange. The windows were so clear that you could see all the way inside to the rows of PlayStations all set up ready to go, connected to really big television screens. There was even a Coke machine and a snack machine at the back.

Hansel touched the door with one finger, a bit hesitantly. Half of him wanted it to be locked, and half of him wanted it to give a little under his hand. But it did more than that. It slid open automatically, and a cool breeze of air-conditioned air blew across his face.

He stepped inside. Gretel reluctantly followed. The door shut behind them, and instantly all the screens came on and were running games. Then the Coke machine clunked out a couple of cans of Coke, and the snack machine whirred and hummed and a whole bunch of candy bars and chocolate piled up outside the slot.

"Excellent!" exclaimed Hansel happily, and he went over and picked up a Coke. Gretel put out her hand to stop him, but it was too late.

"Hansel, I don't like this," said Gretel, moving back to the door. There was something strange about all this—the flicker of the television screens reaching out to her, beckoning her to play, trying to draw them both in. . . .

Hansel ignored her, as if she had ceased to exist. He swigged from the can and started playing a game. Gretel ran over and tugged at his arm, but his eyes never left the screen.

"Hansel!" Gretel screamed. "We have to get out of here!"

"Why?" asked a soft voice.

Gretel shivered. The voice sounded human

enough, but it instantly gave her the mental picture of a spider, welcoming flies. Flies it meant to suck dry and hang like trophies in its web.

She turned around slowly, telling herself it couldn't really be a spider, trying to blank out the image of a hideous eight-legged, fat-bellied, fanged monstrosity.

When she saw it was only a woman, she didn't feel any better. A woman in her mid-forties, maybe, in a plain black dress, showing her bare arms. Long, sinewy arms that ended in narrow hands and long, grasping fingers. Gretel couldn't look directly at her face, just glimpsing bright red lipstick, a hungry mouth, and the darkest of sunglasses.

"So you don't want to play the games like your brother, Hansel," said the woman. "But you can feel their power, can't you, Gretel?"

Gretel couldn't move. Her whole body was filled up with fear, because this woman was a spider, Gretel thought, a hunting spider in human shape, and she and Hansel were well and truly caught. Without thinking, she blurted out, "Spider!"

"A spider?" laughed the woman, her red mouth spreading wide, lips peeling back to reveal nicotine-stained teeth. "I'm not a spider, Gretel. I'm a shadow against the moon, a dark shape in the night doorway, a catch-as-catch-can . . . witch!"

"A witch," whispered Gretel. "What are you going to do with us?"

"I'm going to give you a choice that I have never given before," whispered the witch. "You have some smattering of power, Gretel. You dream true, and strong enough that my machines cannot catch you in their dreaming. The seed of a witch lies in your heart, and I will tend it and make it grow. You will be my apprentice and learn the secrets of my power, the secrets of the night and the moon, of the twilight and the dawn. Magic, Gretel, magic! Power and freedom and dominion over beasts and men!

"Or you can take the other path," she continued, leaning in close till her breath washed into Gretel's nose, foul breath that smelled of cigarettes and whiskey. "The path that ends in the end of Gretel. Pulled apart for your heart and lungs and liver and kidneys. Transplant organs are so in demand, particularly for sick little children with very rich parents! Strange—they never ask me where the organs come from."

"And Hansel?" whispered Gretel, without thinking of her own danger, or the seed in her heart that begged to be made a witch. "What about Hansel?"

"Ah, Hansel," cried the witch. She clicked her fingers, and Hansel walked over to them like a zombie, his fingers still twitching from the game.

"I have a particular plan for Hansel," crooned the witch. "Hansel with the beautiful, beautiful blue eyes."

She tilted Hansel's head back so his eyes caught the light, glimmering blue. Then she took off her sunglasses, and Gretel saw that the witch's own eyes were shriveled like raisins and thick with fat white lines like webs.

"Hansel's eyes go to a very special customer," whispered the witch. "And the rest of him? That depends on Gretel. If she's a good apprentice, the boy shall live. Better blind than dead, don't you think?" She snapped out her arm on the last word and grabbed Gretel, stopping her movement toward the door.

"You can't go without my leave, Gretel," said the witch. "Not when there's so much still for you to see. Ah, to see again, all crisp and clean, with eyes so blue and bright. Lazarus!"

An animal padded out from the rear of the shop and came up to the witch's hand. It was a cat, of sorts. It stood almost to the witch's waist, and it was multicolored, and terribly scarred, lines of bare skin running between patches of different-colored fur like a horrible jigsaw. Even its ears were different colors, and its tail seemed to be made of seven quite distinct rings of fur. Gretel felt sick as she realized it was a patchwork beast, sewn together from many different cats and given life by the witch's magic.

Then Gretel noticed that whenever the witch turned her head, so did Lazarus. If she looked up, the cat looked up. If she turned her head left, it turned left. Clearly, the witch saw the world through the cat's eyes.

With the cat at her side, the witch pushed Gretel ahead of her and whistled for Hansel to follow. They went through the back of the shop, then down a long stairway, deep into the earth. At the bottom, the witch unlocked the door with a key of polished bone.

Beyond the door was a huge cave, ill lit by seven soot-darkened lanterns. One side of the cave was lined with empty cages, each just big enough to house a standing child.

There was also an industrial cold room—a shed-size refrigerator that had a row of toothy icicles hanging from the gutters of its sloping roof—that dominated the other side of the cave. Next to the cold room was a slab of marble that served as a table. Behind it, hanging from hooks in the damp stone of the cave wall, were a dozen knives and cruel-looking instruments of steel.

"Into the cage, young Hansel," commanded the witch, and Hansel did as he was told, without a word. The patchwork cat slunk after him and shot the bolt home with a slap of its paw.

"Now, Gretel," said the witch. "Will you become a witch or be broken into bits?"

Gretel looked at Hansel in his cage, and then at the marble slab and the knives. There seemed to be no choice. At least if she chose the path of witchery, Hansel would only . . . only . . . lose his eyes. And perhaps they would get a chance to escape. "I will learn to be a witch," she said finally. "If you promise to take no more of Hansel than his eyes."

The witch laughed and took Gretel's hands in a bony grip, ignoring the girl's shudder. Then she started to dance, swinging Gretel around and around, with Lazarus leaping and screeching between them.

As she danced, the witch sang:

"Gretel's chosen the witch's way,
And Hansel will be the one to pay.
Sister sees more and brother less—
Hansel and Gretel, what a mess!"

Then she suddenly stopped and let go. Gretel spun across the cave and crashed into the door of one of the cages.

"You'll live down here," said the witch. "There's food in the cold room, and a bathroom in the last cage. I will instruct you on your duties each morning. If you try to escape, you will be punished."

Gretel nodded, but she couldn't help looking across at the knives sparkling on the wall. The witch and Lazarus looked, too, and the witch laughed again. "No steel can cut me, or rod mark my back," she said. "But if you wish to test that, it is Hansel I will punish."

Then the witch left, with Lazarus padding alongside her.

Gretel immediately went to Hansel, but he was still in the grip of the PlayStation spell, eyes and fingers locked in some phantom game.

Next she tried the door, but sparks flew up and burned her when she stuck a knife in the lock. The door to the cold room opened easily enough, though, frosted air and bright fluorescent light spilling out. It was much colder inside than a normal refrigerator. One side of the room was stacked high with chiller boxes, each labeled with a red cross and a bright sticker that said URGENT: HUMAN TRANSPLANT. Gretel tried not to look at them, or think about what they contained. The other side was stacked with all kinds of frozen food. Gretel took some spinach. She hated it, but spinach was the most opposite food to meat she could imagine. She didn't even want to think about eating meat.

The next day marked the first of many in the cave. The witch gave Gretel chores to do, mostly cleaning or packing up boxes from the cold room in special messenger bags the witch brought down. Then the witch would teach Gretel magic, such as the spell that would keep herself and Hansel warm.

Always, Gretel lived with the fear that the witch would choose that day to bring down another child to be cut up on the marble slab, or to take Hansel's eyes. But the witch always came alone, and merely looked at Hansel through Lazarus's eyes and muttered, "Not ready."

So Gretel worked and learned, fed Hansel and whispered to him. She constantly told him not to get better, to pretend that he was still under the spell. Either Hansel listened and pretended, even to her, or he really was still entranced.

Days went by, then weeks, and Gretel realized that she enjoyed learning magic too much. She looked forward to her lessons, and sometimes she would forget about Hansel for hours, forget that he would soon lose his eyes.

When she realized that she might forget Hansel altogether, Gretel decided that she had to kill the witch. She told Hansel that night, whispering her fears to him and trying to think of a plan. But nothing came to her, for now Gretel had learned enough to know the witch really couldn't be cut by metal or struck down by a blow.

The next morning, Hansel spoke in his sleep while the witch was in the cave. Gretel cried out from where she was scrubbing the floor, to try and cover it up, but it was too late. The witch came over and glared through the bars.

"So you've been shamming," she said. "But now I shall take your left eye, for the spell to graft it to my own socket must be fueled by your fear. And your sister will help me."

"No, I won't!" cried Gretel. But the witch just laughed and blew on Gretel's chest. The breath sank into her heart, and the ember of witchcraft that was there blazed up and grew, spreading through her body. Higher and higher it rose, till Gretel grew small inside her own head and could feel herself move around only at the witch's whim.

Then the witch took Hansel from the cage and bound him with red rope. She laid him on the marble slab, and Lazarus jumped up so she could see. Gretel brought her herbs, and the wand of ivory, the wand of jet, and the wand of horn. Finally, the witch chanted her spell. Gretel's mind went away completely then. When she came back to herself, Hansel was in his cage, one eye bandaged with a thick pad of cobwebs. He looked at Gretel through his other, tear-filled eye.

"She's going to take the other one tomorrow," he whispered.

"No," said Gretel, sobbing. "No."

"I know it isn't really you helping her," said Hansel. "But what can you do?"

"I don't know," said Gretel. "We have to kill her—but she'll punish you if we try and we fail."

"I wish it was a dream," said Hansel. "Dreams end, and you wake up. But I'm not asleep, am I? It's too cold, and my eye . . . it hurts."

Gretel opened the cage to hug him and cast the spell that would warm them. But she was thinking about cold—and the witch. "If we could trap the witch and Lazarus in the cold room somehow, they might freeze to death," she said slowly. "But we'd have to make it much colder, so she wouldn't have time to cast a spell."

They went to look at the cold room and found that it was set as cold as it would go. But Hansel found a barrel of liquid nitrogen at the back, and that gave him an idea.

An hour later, they'd rigged their instant witch-freezing trap. Using one of the knives, Hansel unscrewed the inside handle of the door so there was no way to get out. Then they balanced the barrel on top of a pile of boxes, just past the door. Finally, they poured water everywhere to completely ice up the floor.

Then they took turns sleeping, till Gretel heard the click of the witch's key in the door. She sprang up and went to the cold room. Leaving the door ajar, she carefully stood on the ice and took the lid off the liquid nitrogen. Then she stepped back outside, pinching her nose and gasping. "Something's wrong, Mistress!" she exclaimed. "Everything's gone rotten."

"What!" cried the witch, dashing across the cave, her one blue eye glittering. Lazarus ran at her heels from habit, though she no longer needed his sight.

Gretel stood aside as she ran past, then gave her a hefty push. The witch skidded on the ice, crashed into the boxes, and fell flat on her back just as the barrel toppled over. An instant later, her final scream was smothered in a cloud of freezing vapor.

But Lazarus, quicker than any normal cat, did a backflip in midair, even as Gretel slammed the door. Ancient stitches gave way, and the cat started coming apart, accompanied by an explosion of the magical silver dust that filled it and gave it life.

Gretel relaxed for an instant as the dust obscured the beast, then screamed as the front part of Lazarus jumped out at her, teeth snapping. She kicked at it, but the cat was too swift, its great jaws meeting around her ankle. Gretel screamed again, and then Hansel was there, shaking the strange dust out of the broken body as if he were emptying a vacuum cleaner. In a few seconds there was nothing left of Lazarus but its head and an empty skin. Even then it wouldn't let go, till Hansel forced its mouth open with a broomstick and pushed the snarling remnant across the floor and into one of the cages.

Gretel hopped across and watched it biting the bars, its green eyes still filled with magical life and hatred. "Hansel," she said, "your own eye is frozen with the witch. But I think I can remember the spell—and there is an eye for the taking here."

So it was that when they entered the cold room later to take the key of bone from the frozen, twisted body of the witch, Hansel saw the world through one eye of blue and one of green.

Later, when they found their way home, it was the sight of that green eye that gave the Hagmom a heart attack and made her die. But their father was still a weak man, and within a year he thought to marry another woman who had no love for his children. Only this time the new Hagmom faced a Gretel who was more than half a witch, and a Hansel who had gained strange powers from his magic cat's eye.

But that is all another story. . . .

INTRODUCTION TO HOPE CHEST

I love Western films. Always have, and I daresay always will. Strangely, I don't much care for Western fiction in print, with some notable exceptions, like Larry McMurtry's *Lonesome Dove*. But I love the films and regularly watch old favorites and try to catch up with the ones I've somehow missed along the way.

As I said in my original note that accompanied this story when it was first published in *Firebirds* (edited by Sharyn November), the origins of *Hope Chest* lie in watching too many Westerns, and I quoted some favorites, such as *Winchester '73*; *Red River*; *The Good, the Bad and the Ugly*; and *They Call Me Trinity*. As I have a little more space here, to that list I would add *The Wild Bunch*, *The Far Country*, and the miniseries *Lonesome Dove*.

Of course, I couldn't write a straightforward Western. I find it very difficult to write a story of any kind without introducing elements of fantasy or science fiction. I seem to have a natural tendency to divert from the straight and narrow of realism. Even writing a Western, as here, I found myself setting it in a kind of alternate United States, with a supernatural Hitler analogue, inherited magical powers, and parallel worlds. In retrospect, the latter half of the story is more Peckinpah than Hawks or Ford, but I do admire the work of all three in Westerns (and elsewhere).

hope chest

one dusty, slow morning in the summer of 1922, a passenger was left crying on the platform when the milk train pulled out of Denilburg after its five-minute stop. No one noticed at first, what with the whistle from the train and the billowing steam and smoke and the laboring of the steel wheels upon the rails. The milk carter was busy with the cans, the stationmaster with the mail. No one else was about, not when the full dawn was still half a cup of coffee away.

When the train had rounded the corner, taking its noise with it, the crying could be clearly heard. Milk carter and stationmaster both looked up from their work and saw the source of the sound.

A baby, tightly swaddled in a pink blanket, was precariously balanced on a large steamer trunk at the very edge of the platform. With every cry and wriggle the baby was moving closer to the side of the trunk. If she fell, she'd fall not only from the trunk but from the platform, down to the rails four feet below.

The carter jumped over his cans, knocking two down, his heels splashing in the spilled milk. The stationmaster dropped his sack, letters and packets cascading out to meet the milk. They each got a hand under the baby at the very second it rolled off the trunk. Both men went over the edge of the platform, and they trod on each other's feet as they landed, hard and painful—but upright. The baby was perfectly balanced between them.

That's how Alice May Susan Hopkins came to Denilburg, and that's how she got two unrelated uncles with the very same first name, Uncle Bill Carey, the stationmaster, and Uncle Bill Hoogener, the milk carter.

The first thing the two Bills noticed when they caught the baby was a note pinned to the pink blanket. It was on fine ivory paper, the words in blue-black ink that caught the sun and glinted when you held it just so. It said:

"Alice May Susan, born on the Summer Solstice, 1921. Look after her and she'll look after you."

It didn't take long for the news of Alice May Susan's arrival to get around the town, and it wasn't more than fifteen minutes later that fifty percent of the town's grown women were all down at the station, the thirty-eight of them clustering around that poor baby enough to suffocate her. Fortunately it was only a few minutes more till Eulalie Falkirk took charge, as she always did, and established a roster for hugging and kissing and gawking and fussing and worrying and gossiping over the child.

Over the next few months that roster changed to include actually looking after little Alice May Susan. She was handed from one married woman to the next, changing her surname from month to month as she went from family to family. She was a dear little girl, everyone said, and Eulalie Falkirk was hard put to decide who should adopt the child.

Her final decision came down to one simple thing. While all the womenfolk had been busy with the baby, most of the menfolk had been taking turns trying to open up that steamer trunk.

The trunk looked easy enough. It was about six feet long, three feet wide, and two feet high. It had two leather straps around it and an old brass lock, the kind with a keyhole big enough to put your whole finger in. Only no one did after Torrance Yib put his in and it came back with the tip missing, cut off clean as you please right at the joint.

The straps wouldn't come undone either, and whatever they were, it wasn't any leather anyone in Denilburg had ever seen. It wouldn't cut and it wouldn't tear, and those straps drove everyone who tried them mad with frustration.

There was some talk of devilment and foreign magic, till Bill Carey—who knew more about luggage than the rest of the town put together—pointed out the brass plate on the underside that read "Made in the U.S.A. Imp. Pat. Pend. Burglar-proof trunk." Then everyone was proud and said it was scientific progress and what a pity it was that the name of the company had been scratched off, for it'd get some good business in Denilburg if only they knew where to send their orders.

The only man in the whole town who hadn't tried to open the trunk was Jake Hopkins, the druggist, so when Stella Hopkins said they'd like to take baby Alice May Susan on, Eulalie Falkirk knew it wasn't because they wanted whatever was in the trunk.

So Alice May Susan joined the Hopkins household and grew up with Jake and Stella's born daughters, Janice, Jessie, and Jane, who at the time were ten, eight, and four. The steamer trunk was put in the attic, and Alice May Susan, to all intents and purposes, became another Hopkins girl. No one out of the ordinary, just a typical Denilburg girl, the events of her life pretty much interchangeable with the sisters who had gone before her.

Until the year she turned sixteen, in 1937.

Of her three sisters, only Jane was at home that birthday, enjoying a vacation. Janice and Jessie had married up and left, both of them now living more than twenty miles away. Jane was different. She'd won a scholarship that had taken her off to college back east, where she'd got all sorts of ideas. One of them involved criticizing everything Alice May Susan did or said, and counting the days till she could get on the train out of town and back to what she called "civilization."

"You'd better study harder so you have a chance to get away from this place," said Jane as they sat on the porch eating birthday cake and watching the world go by. None of it had gone by yet, unless you counted the Prowells' cat.

"I like it here," said Alice May. "Why would I want to leave?"

"Because there's nothing here!" protested Jane. "Nothing! No life, no color, no . . . events!

Nothing ever happens. Everyone just gets married and has children, and it starts all over again. There's no romance in anything or anyone!"

"Not everyone gets married," replied Alice May after a short pause to swallow a too-large bite of cake.

"Gwennifer Korben, you mean," said Jane. "She's a schoolmistress. Everyone knows they're always spinsters. You don't want to be a schoolmistress."

"Maybe I do," answered Alice May. She spun her cake fork into a silver blur and snatched it handle first out of the air.

"Do you really?" asked Jane, momentarily shocked. "A schoolmistress!"

Alice May frowned and threw the cake fork into the wall. It stuck, quivering, next to the tiny holes in the wood that showed several years of practice in the gentle art of cake-fork throwing.

"I don't know," she said. "I do feel . . . I do feel that I want to be something. I just don't know what it is."

"Study," said Jane firmly. "Work hard. Go to college. Education is the only way for a woman to have her own life."

Alice May nodded, to avoid further discussion.

It was her birthday, and she felt hot and bothered rather than happy. The cake was delicious, and they'd had a very pleasant lunch with her family and some friends from school. But her birthday somehow felt unfinished and incomplete. There was something that she had to do, but she didn't know what it was. Something more immediate than deciding her future life.

It didn't take more than two hours in the rocking chair on the porch to work out what it was she needed to do, and wait for the right moment to do it.

The steamer trunk. It had been a long time since she'd even looked at it. Over the years she'd tried it many times, alone and in company. There had been times when she'd gone up to the attic every day to test if by some chance it had come undone. There'd been times when she'd forgotten about it for months. But no matter what, she always found herself making an attempt to open it on her birthday.

Even when she forgot about opening it, the trunk's brooding presence stayed with her. It was a reminder that she was not exactly like the other Hopkins girls. Sometimes that was pleasant, but more often not, particularly as she had got older.

Alice May sighed and decided to give it yet another try. It was evening by then, and somewhat cooler. She picked up her lantern, trimmed the wick down a little, and went inside.

"Trunk?" asked her foster father, Jake, as she went through the kitchen. He was preserving lemons, the careful practice of his drugstore carried over to the culinary arts. No one else in Denilburg preserved lemons, or would know what to do with them once they were preserved.

"Trunk?" asked Stella, who was sewing in the drawing room.

"Trunk?" asked Jane on the stairs, as Alice May passed her. "Trunk?"

"Of course the trunk!" snapped Alice May. She pulled down the attic ladder angrily and climbed up.

It was a very clean attic, in a very clean house. There was only the trunk in it, up against the small window that was letting in the last of the hot summer sun. A red glow shone on the brass lock and the lustrous leather straps.

Alice May was still angry. She set the lantern down, grabbed a strap, and pulled. When it came loose, she fell over backward and hit her head on the floor. The sound it made echoed through the house. There was a noticeable pause, then three voices carried up in chorus.

"Are you all right?"

"Yes!" shouted Alice May, angrier still. She wrenched at the other strap and it came loose too, though this time she was ready for it. At the same time, the brass lock went *click*. It wasn't the sort of click that was so soft, you could think you might have imagined it. This was a slow, drawn-out click, as if mighty metal gears were slowly turning over.

The lid of the trunk eased up half an inch.

Alice May whispered, "It's open."

She reached forward and lifted the lid a little farther. It moved easily, the hinges free, as if they'd just been oiled.

"It's open!" screeched Alice May. "The trunk is open!"

The sound of a mad scramble below assured her that everyone had heard her this time. Before they could get there, Alice May pushed the lid completely back. Her brow furrowed as she looked at what lay within. All her life she had been waiting to open this trunk, both dreading and hoping that she would find some clue to the mystery of her birth and arrival in Denilburg. Papers, letters, perhaps a family Bible.

Nothing of that kind was obvious. Instead, clipped into the back wall of the trunk there was a lever-action rifle, an old one, with a deeply polished stock of dark wood and an octagonal barrel of dark blue steel chased with silver flowers.

Underneath it were two holstered revolvers. Big weapons, their barrels were also engraved in silver with the flower motif, which was repeated on the holsters, though not in silver but black thread, somber on the leather. A belt with bullet loops was folded up and pinned between the holsters. More dark leather, more flowers in black thread.

On the left side of the trunk there was a teak box with the word AMMUNITION burned into the lid in slim pokerwork.

On the right side there was a jewelry case of deep purple velvet plush.

Underneath the ammunition box and the jewelry case, along the bottom of the trunk, there was a white dress laid out flat. Alice May stared at the strange combination of cowgirl outfit and bridal gown, cut from the finest, whitest shot silk, with the arms and waistcoat—it had a waistcoat—sewn with lines of tiny pearls. It looked a little big for

Alice May, particularly in the region of the bust. It was also indecently short, for either wedding dress or cowgirl outfit. It probably wouldn't go much below her knees.

"A Winchester 'seventy three," said Jake behind her, pointing at the rifle. He didn't make any attempt to reach forward and touch them. "And two Colt forty-fives. Peacemakers, I think. Like the one my grandfather had above the mantelpiece in the old house."

"Weird," said Jane, pushing her father, so he moved to allow her and Stella up.

"What's in the jewelry box?" asked Stella. She spoke in a hushed tone, as if she were in a temple. Alice May looked around and saw that Jake, Stella, and Jane were all clustered around the top of the ladder, as if they didn't want to come any closer.

Alice May reached into the trunk and picked up the jewelry case. As she touched the velvet, she felt a strange, electric thrill pass through her. It wasn't unpleasant, and she felt it again as she opened the case: a frisson of excitement that raced through her whole body, from top to toe.

The case held a metal star. A sheriff's badge, or something in the shape of one, anyway, though there was nothing engraved upon it. The star was shinier than any lawman's badge Alice May had ever seen, a bright silver that picked up the last glow of red sunlight and intensified and purified it, till it seemed that she held an acetylene light in her hand, a blinding light that forced her to look away and flip it over.

The light faded, leaving black spots dancing in front of her eyes. Alice May saw there was a pin on the back of the star, but again there was nothing engraved where she had hoped to see a name.

Alice May put the star back in the case and closed it, letting out the breath she didn't know she'd held. A loud exhalation from behind told her that the rest of her family had been holding their breaths as well.

Next she slid the rifle from the straps that held it in place. It felt strangely right in her hands, and without conscious thought she worked the action, checked the chamber was empty, and dry fired it. A second later she realized that she didn't know what she'd done and, at the same time, that she could do it again, and more. She could load and fire the weapon, and strip and clean it too. It was all in her head, even though she'd only ever fired one firearm in her life before, and that was just her uncle Bill's single-shot squirrel gun.

She put the rifle back and took down the twin revolvers. They were heavy, but again she instinctively knew their weight and heft, loaded or unloaded. She put the revolvers, still holstered, across her lap. The flower pattern on the barrels seemed to move and flow as she stared at them, and the herringbone cut on the grips swung from one angle to another. The grips were some sort of bone, Alice May realized, stained dark. Or perhaps they were ebony and had never been stained.

She drew one of the revolvers, and once again her hands moved without conscious thought. She swung the cylinder out, spun it, checked it was empty, slapped it back again, cocked and released the hammer under control, and had it back in the holster almost before her foster family could blink.

Alice May put the revolvers back. She didn't even look at the box with the pokerwork AMMUNITION on it. She closed the trunk firmly. The lock clicked again, and she rapidly did up the straps. Then she turned to her family.

"Best if we don't mention this around . . ." she started to say. Then she saw the way they were looking at her. A look that was part confusion, part awe, and part fear.

"That star . . ." said Jake.

"So bright," said Stella.

"Your hands . . . a blur . . ." said Jane.

"I don't want it!" burst out Alice May. "I'm not . . . it's not me! I'm Alice May Susan *Hopkins*!"

She pushed past Jane and almost fell down the ladder in her haste to get away. The others followed more slowly. Alice May had already run to her room, and they all could hear her sobbing.

Jake went back to the kitchen and his preserved lemons. Stella went back to her sewing. Jane went to Alice May's door, but turned aside at the last second and went downstairs to write a letter to a friend about how nothing ever, ever happened in Denilburg.

When Alice May came down to breakfast the next morning, after a night of no sleep, the others were bright and cheerful. When she tentatively tried to talk about what had happened, it became clear that the others had either no memory of what they had seen or were actively denying it.

Alice May did not forget. She saw the silver star shining in her dreams, and often woke with the feel of the rifle's stock against her cheek, or the harsh weight of the holstered revolvers on her thighs.

With the dreams came a deep sense of dread.

Alice May knew that the weapons and the star were some sort of birthright, and with them came the knowledge that someday they were to be used. She feared that day, and could not imagine who . . . or what . . . she was supposed to shoot. Sometimes the notion that she might have to kill a fellow human being scared her more than anything. At other times she was more terrified by a strange notion that whatever she would ultimately face would not be human.

A year passed, and summer came again, hotter and drier than ever before. The spring planting died in the fields, and with the small seedlings went the hopes of both the farmers of Denilburg and the townsfolk who depended on the farmers' making money.

At the same time, a large number of apparently solid banks went under. It came as a surprise, particularly since they'd weathered the credit famine of '30 and the bursting of the tantalum bubble two years previously. The bank crash was accompanied by a crisis of confidence in the currency, as the country shifted from gold and silver to aluminum and copper-nickel coins that had no intrinsic value.

One of the banks that failed was the Third

National Faith, the bank that held most of the meager savings of Denilburg residents. Alice May found out about it when she came home from school, to discover Stella weeping and Jake white-faced in the kitchen, mechanically chopping what might have once been a pumpkin.

For a while it looked like they'd lose the drug-store, but Janice's husband had kept a highly illegal cache of double eagles, the ones with the Dowager Empress's head on them. Selling them to a "licensed coin collector" brought in just enough to pay the Hopkinses' debts and keep the store a going concern.

Jane had to leave college, though. Her scholarship was adversely affected by inflation, and Jake and Stella couldn't afford to give her anything. Everyone expected her to come home, but she didn't. Instead she wrote to say that she had a job, a good job with a great future.

It took a few more months and a few letters before it turned out that Jane's job was with a political organization called the Servants of the State. She sent a tonatype of herself in the black uniform with the firebrand badges and armband. Jake and Stella didn't put it up on the mantelpiece with the shots from her sisters' lives.

The arrival of Jane's tonatype coincided with Alice May—and everyone else—spending a lot more time thinking about the Servants. They'd seemed a harmless enough group for many years. Just another right-wing, bigoted, reactionary, pseudomilitary political organization with a few seats in Congress and a couple of very minor advisory positions at the Palace.

But by the time Jane joined the party, things had changed. The Servants had found a new leader somewhere, a man they called the Master. He looked ordinary enough in the newspapers, a short man with a peculiar beard, a long forelock, and staring eyes. He had some resemblance to the kinetocomedian Harry Hopalong, who favored the same sort of overtrimmed goatee—but the Master wasn't funny.

The Master clearly had some charisma that could not be captured by the tonatype process or reproduced in print. He toured the country constantly, and wherever he appeared, he swayed local politicians, the important businesspeople, and most of the ordinary population. Mayors left their political parties and joined the Servants. Oil and tantalum barons gave large donations. Professors wrote essays supporting the economic theories of the Master. Crowds thronged to cheer and worship at the Master's progress.

Everywhere the Servants grew in popularity, there were murders and arson. Opponents of the Servants died. Minorities of every kind were persecuted, particularly the First People and followers of the major heresies. Even orthodox temples whose haruspices did not agree that fortune favored the Servants were burned to the ground.

Neither harassment, beatings, murder, arson, or rape was properly investigated when done by, or in the name of, the Servants. Or if they were, matters never successfully came to trial, in either State or Imperial courts. Local police left the Servants to their own devices.

The Emperor, now a very old man roosting in the palace at Washington, did nothing. People wistfully spoke of his glory days leading hilltop charges and shooting bears. But that was long ago and he was senile, or close to it, and the Crown Prince was almost terminally lazy, a genial buffoon who could not be stirred into any sort of action.

Off in Denilburg, Alice May was largely insulated from what was going on elsewhere. But even in that small, sleepy town, she saw the rise of the

Servants. The two shops belonging to what the Servants called Others—pretty much anyone who wasn't white and a regular worshiper—had red firebrands painted across their windows and lost most of their customers. In other towns their owners would have been beaten or tarred and feathered, but it hadn't yet come to that in Denilburg.

People Alice May had known all her life talked about the International Other Conspiracy and how it was to blame for the bank failures, the crop failures, and all other failures—particularly their own failures in the everyday business of life.

The fact that something really serious was happening came home to Alice May the day that her uncle Bill Carey walked past dressed not in his stationmaster's green and blue, but the Servants' black and red. Alice May went out into the street to ask him what on earth he thought he was doing. But when she stopped in front of him, she saw a strange vacancy in his eyes. This was not the Bill Carey she had known all her life. Instinctively she knew that something had happened to him, that the adopted uncle she knew and loved had been changed, his natural humanity driven deep inside him and overlaid by something horrible and poisonous.

"Praise the Master," snapped Bill as Alice May looked at him. His hand crawled up to his shoulder and then snapped across his chest in the Servants' knife-chop salute.

He didn't say anything else. His strange eyes stared into the distance until Alice May stepped aside. He strode off as she rushed inside to be sick.

Later she learned that he had been to Jarawak City, the state capital, the day before. He had seen the Master speak, out of curiosity, as had a number of other people from Denilburg. All of them had come back as committed Servants.

Alice May tried to talk to Jake and Stella about Bill, but they wouldn't listen. They were afraid to discuss the Servants, and they would not accept that anything had been done to Bill. As far as they were concerned, he'd simply decided to ride with the tide.

"When times are tough, people'll believe anything that puts the blame somewhere," said Jake. "Bill Carey's a good man, but his paycheck hasn't kept up with inflation. I guess he's only just been holding on for some time, and that Master gave him hope, somehow."

"Hope laced with hatred," snapped Alice May. She still felt sick to the very bottom of her stomach at seeing Bill in his Servants' uniform. It was even worse than the tonatype of Jane. More real, more immediate. It was wrong, wrong, wrong.

A knock at the door stopped the conversation. Jake and Stella exchanged frightened looks. Alice May frowned, angry that her foster parents could be made afraid by such a simple thing as a knock at the door. They would never have flinched before. She went to open it like a whirlwind, rushing down the hall so fast, she knocked the portrait of Stella's grandsire onto the floor. Glass shattered and the frame broke in two.

There was no one outside, but a notice had been pushed half under the door. Alice May picked it up, saw the black and red and the flaming torch, and stormed back inside, slamming the door behind her.

"The Master's coming here! This afternoon!" she exclaimed, waving the paper in front of her. "On a special train. He's going to speak from it."

She put her finger against the bottom line.

"It says, 'Everyone must attend,' she said grimly. "As if we don't have a choice who we listen to."

"We'd better go," muttered Stella. Jake nodded.

"What!" screamed Alice May. "He's only a politician! Stay at home."

Jake shook his head. "No. No. I've heard about what happens if you don't go. There's the store to think about."

"And my grandsire was a Cheveril—an accommodator," Stella said quietly. She looked down at the splintered glass and the smashed painting. "We mustn't give them a reason to look into the family. We must be there."

"I'm not going," announced Alice May.

"You are while you live in this house," snapped Jake, in a rare display of temper. "I'll not have all our lives and livelihood risked for some silly girl's fancies."

"I am not going," repeated Alice May. She felt strangely calm, obviously much calmer than Jake, whose face was flushed with sudden heat, or Stella, who had gone deathly pale.

"Then you'd better get out altogether," said Jake fiercely. "Go and find your real parents."

Stella cried out as he spoke, and clutched at his arm, but she didn't speak.

Alice May looked at the only parents she had ever known. She felt as if she was in a kinetoplay, with all of them trapped by the script. There was an inevitability in Jake's words, but he seemed as surprised to say them as she was to hear them. She saw a terror deep in his eyes, and shame. He was already afraid of what he was becoming, afraid of the place his fears were driving him toward.

"I'll go and pack," she said, her voice dull to her own ears. It was not the real Jake who had spoken, she knew. He was a timid man. He did not know how to be brave, and anger was his only escape from acknowledging his cowardice.

Alice May didn't pack. She stopped by her room to pick up a pair of riding boots and then went up to the attic. She opened the trunk, breathing a sigh of relief as the straps and lock gave no resistance. She took out the box marked AMMUNITION and set it on the floor, and placed the holstered revolvers and the belt next to the box.

Then she stripped down to her underclothes and put on the white dress. It fitted her perfectly, as she had known it would. She had grown in the year since her first sight of the dress, enough that two undone shirt buttons could derail the trains of thought and conversation of most of the boys she knew—and some of the men.

This dress was not low cut, but it hugged her breasts and waist before flaring out, and it was daringly short at an inch below her knees. The waistcoat that went over it was also tailored to show off her figure. Strangely, it appeared to be lined with woven strands of hair. Blond hair that was a shade identical to her own.

The dress, even with the waistcoat, was cold to the touch, as if it had come out of an ice chest. The temperature outside had forced the mercury out the top of the old thermometer by the kitchen door, and it was stifling in the attic. Alice May wasn't even warm.

She strapped on the revolvers next. The gun belt rested on her hips, with the holsters lower, against her thighs. She found that the silk was double-lined there, to guard against wear, and there were small ties to fix the snout of each holster to her dress.

The ammunition box opened easily. It held a dozen smaller boxes of blue tin. Alice May was somehow not surprised by the descriptions, which were handwritten on pasted labels. Six of the boxes were labeled "Colt .45 Fourway Silver Cross" and six "Winchester .44-40 Silvercutter."

She opened a tin of the .45 Fourway Silver Cross. The squat brass cartridges were topped with lead bullets, but each had four fat lines of silver across the top. Alice May knew it was real silver. The .44-40 cartridges looked similar, but the bullets were either solid silver or silver over a core of lead.

Alice May quickly loaded both revolvers and then the rifle and filled the loops on her belt with a mixture of both cartridges. Instinctively she knew which ammunition to use in each weapon, and she put the .45 Silver Cross cartridges only on the left of the eagle buckle and the .44-40 only on the right.

Even with the rifle temporarily laid on the floor, the revolvers and the laden bullet belt came to quite a load, heavy on her hips and thighs.

There was still one thing left in the trunk. Alice May picked up the jewelry case and opened it. The star was dull till she touched it, but it began to shine as she pinned it on. It was heavy, too, heavier than it should have been, and her knees buckled a little as the pin snapped in.

Alice May stood absolutely still for a moment, breathing slowly, taking the weight that was as much imagined as real. The light of her star slowly faded with each breath, till it was no more than a bright piece of metal reflecting the sun. Everything felt lighter then. Revolvers, belt, star—and her own spirits.

She closed the trunk, sat on it, and pulled on her boots. Then she picked up the rifle and climbed down the ladder.

No one was downstairs. The broken glass and picture frame were still on the floor, in total contradiction of Stella's nature and habit. The painting itself was gone.

Alice May let herself out the back way and quickly crossed the street to her Uncle Bill's house. The other Uncle Bill, Bill Hoogener. The milk carter. She wanted to talk to him before she did . . . whatever she was going to do.

It was unusually quiet on the street. A hot breeze blew, throwing up dust devils that whirled on the fringes of the graveled road. No one was outside. There were no children playing. No one was out walking, driving, or riding. There was only the hot wind and Alice May's boots crunching gravel as she walked the hundred yards diagonally down the street to the Hoogener house.

She stopped at the picket fence. There was a red firebrand splashed across the partly open door, the paint still wet and dripping. Alice May's hands worked the lever of her rifle without conscious thought, and she pushed the door open with the toe of her boot.

The coolness of her dress was spreading across her skin, only it was colder now, a definite chill. Bill, as his surname gave away, was a descendent of Oncers, even if he wasn't practicing himself. The Servants reserved a special hatred for the monotheistic Oncers.

Everything in the hall had been broken. All of Bill's paintings of the town and its people, a lifetime of work, were smashed upon the floor. The wire umbrella stand had been wrenched apart, and the canes and umbrellas it had contained used as clubs to pummel the plasterboard. It was full of gaping holes, the wallpaper flapping around them like torn skin.

There was blood on the floor. Lots of blood, a great dark ocean of it close by the door, and then smaller pools leading back into the house. A bloody handprint by the kitchen door showed where someone—no, not someone, Alice May thought, but Bill, her uncle Bill—had leaned for support.

She stepped through the wreckage, colder still, colder than she had ever been. Her eyes moved slowly from side to side, the rifle barrel with its silver flowers following her gaze. Her finger was flat and straight against the trigger guard, an instant away from the trigger, a shot, a death.

Uncle Bill was in the kitchen. He was sitting with his back against the stove, his skin pale, almost translucent against the yellow enamel of the oven door. His eyes were open and impossibly clear, the white whiter than any milk he had ever carted, but his once-bright blue pupils were dulling into black, black as the undersize bow tie that hung on his chest, the elastic broken.

His mouth was open, a gaping, formless hole. It took Alice May a moment to realize that his tongue had been cut out.

From his waist down, Bill's usually immaculate whites were black, sodden, totally saturated with blood. It still dripped from him slowly, into the patch under his legs. Someone had used that same blood to paint a clumsy firebrand symbol on the floor, and two words. But the blood had spread and joined in the letters, so it was impossible to read whatever Bill's murderers had intended. The firebrand was enough, in any case, for the death to be claimed by the Servants.

Alice May stared at her dead uncle, thinking terrible thoughts. There were no strangers in town. She would know the murderers. She could see it so easily. The men dressed up in their black and red, drinking whiskey to make themselves brave. They would have passed the house a dozen times before they finally knocked on Bill's door. Perhaps they'd spoken normally for a minute to him, before they pushed him back inside. Then they'd cut and cut at him as he reeled back down his own hallway, unable to believe what was happening and unable to resist.

Bill Hoogener had died at the hands of neighbors, without having any idea of what was going on.

Alice May knew what was going on. She knew it deep inside. The Master was a messenger of evil, a corrupter of souls. The Servants were not Servants of the State, but slaves to some awful and insidious poison that changed their very natures and made them capable of committing such dreadful crimes as the murder of her uncle Bill.

She stepped toward him, toward the pool of blood. An echo answered her, another footfall, in the yard beyond the kitchen door.

Alice May stopped where she was, silent, waiting. The footsteps continued, then the screen door swung open. A man came in, not really looking where he was going. He wore a Servant's black coat over his blue bib-and-brace overalls. There was blood splashed above his knees. There was blood on his hands. His name was Everett Kale, assistant butcher. He had once walked out with Jane Hopkins and had given a much younger Alice May a single marigold from the bunch he'd brought for Jane.

Alice May's star flashed bright, and Everett looked up. He saw Alice May, the star, the leveled rifle. His hand flashed to the bone-handled skinning knife that rattled in the broad butcher's scabbard at his side.

The shot was very loud in the confined space, but Alice May didn't flinch. She worked the lever, the action so fast the sound seemed to fall behind it, and then she put another round into the man who had fallen back through the door. He was already dead, but she wanted to be sure.

Noise greeted her as she stepped outside. Shouts and surprised cries. There were three men in the yard, looking at the dead butcher on the ground. They had got into Bill's home brew, and they were all holding bottles of thick, dark beer. They dropped the bottles as Alice May came out shooting.

They were armed with slim, new automatic pistols that fit snugly into clipped holsters at the nipped-in waists of their black tunics. None of them managed to get a pistol out. They were all dead on the ground within seconds, their blood mixing with black, foaming beer, their death throes acted out upon a bed of broken glass.

Alice May looked at them from a weird and forbidding place inside her own head. She knew them but felt no remorse. Butcher, baker, ne'er-do-well, and ore washer. All men of the town.

Her hands had done the killing. Her hands and the rifle. Even now those same hands were reloading, taking bullets from her belt and slipping them with a satisfying click into the tubular magazine.

Alice May realized she had had no conscious control over her hands at all. Somewhere between opening the front door of Bill's house and entering the kitchen, she had become an observer within her own body. But she didn't feel terrified by this. It felt right, and she realized she was still in charge of her actions. She wasn't a zombie or anything. She would decide where to go next, but her body—and the weapons—would help her do whatever had to be done when she got there.

She walked around the still-twitching bodies and out the back gate. Onto another empty street with the unforgiving, hot wind and the dust and the complete absence of people.

There should have been a crowd, come to see what the shooting was about. The town's two lawmen should be riding up on their matching grays. But there was only Alice May.

She turned down the street, toward the railway station. Her boot heels crunched on the gravel. She felt she had never really heard that particular sound before, not so clear, so loud.

The wind changed direction and blew against her, stronger and hotter than ever. Dust blew up, heavy dust that carried chunks of grit. But none hit Alice May, none got in her eyes. Her white dress repelled it, the wind seeming to divide as it hit her, great currents of dust and grit flying around on either side.

A door opened to her left, and she was facing it, her finger on the trigger. A man half stepped out. Old Mr. Lacker, in his best suit, a Servants of the State flag in his trembling hand. His left hand.

"Stay home!" ordered Alice May. Her voice was louder than she expected. It boomed in her ears, easily cutting through the wind.

Lacker took another step and raised his flag.

"Stay home!"

Another step. Another wave of the flag. Then

he reached inside his jacket and pulled out a tiny pocket pistol, a single-shot Derringer, all ancient, tarnished brass.

Alice May pulled the trigger and walked on, as Old Man Lacker's best suit suddenly fountained blood from the lapel, a vivid buttonhole of arterial scarlet.

She reloaded as she walked. Inside she was screaming, but nothing came out. She hadn't wanted to kill Mr. Lacker. He was old, harmless, no danger. He couldn't have hit her even if she was standing next to him.

But her hands and the rifle had disagreed.

Alice May knew where she had to go. The railway station. Where the Master was to arrive in under an hour. She had to go there and kill him.

It didn't seem sensible to walk down the main street, so Alice May cut through the field behind the schoolhouse. From the top of the cutting beyond the field, she looked both ways, toward the station and out along the line.

The special train was already at the platform. One engine, a tender, and a single private car, all painted in black and red. The engine had a shield placed on the front of the boiler above the cowcatcher. A shield with the blazing torch of the

Servants. The train must have backed up all the way from Jarawak City, Alice May thought, just so the balcony at the rear of the private car faced the turning circle at the end of the main street.

There were a lot of people gathered in that turning circle. All the people whom Alice May had expected to see in the streets. They'd come down early, to make sure they weren't marked as tardies or reluctant supporters. The whole population of the town had to be there, many of them in Servants' uniforms, and all of them waving red-and-black flags.

Alice May slid down the cutting and walked between the rails. This was the way she'd come as a baby, all those years ago. But somehow she didn't think she'd come from Jarawak City.

All the attention was at the rear of the train, though it was clear the Master hadn't yet appeared. It was too noisy for that, with the crowd cheering and the town band playing something unrecognizable. The newspapers all made a big thing about the total silence that fell in any audience as the Master spoke.

Alice May crossed the line and crept down the far side of the engine. Just as she came to the tender, an engineer stepped down. He wore denim overalls, topped with a black Servants' cap, complete with the badge of the flaming brand.

Alice May's hands moved. The butt of the rifle snapped out and the engineer went down to the rails. He crawled around there for a moment, trying to get up, as Alice May calmly waited for the crowd to cheer again and the band to crescendo with drums and brass. As they did, she fired a single shot into the engineer's head and stepped over him.

I'm a murderer, she thought. *Many times over. I wish they'd stay out of my way.*

Alice May stepped up to the private car's forward balcony. She tried to look inside, but the window was smoked glass.

Alice May tried the door. It wasn't locked. She opened it left-handed, the rifle ready.

She had expected a small sitting room of some kind, perhaps opulently furnished. What she saw was an impossibly long corridor, stretching off into the distance, the end out of sight.

The crowd suddenly went silent at the other end of the train.

Alice May stepped into the corridor and shut the door behind her.

It was dark with the door closed, but her star

shone more brightly, lighting the way. Apart from its length, and the fact that the far end was shrouded in mist or smoke, the corridor seemed pretty much like any other train corridor Alice May had ever seen. Polished wood and metal fittings, and every few steps a compartment door. The only strange thing was that the compartment doors all had smoked glass windows so you couldn't see in.

Alice May was tempted to open a door, but she held out against the temptation. Her business was with the Master, and he was speaking down at the far end of the train. Who knew what she would get herself into by opening a door?

She continued to walk as quietly as she could down the corridor. Every few steps she would hear a sound and would freeze for a moment, her finger on the trigger. But the sounds were not of people, or weapons, or danger. They came from behind the compartment doors and were of the sea, or wind, or falling rain.

Still the corridor continued, and Alice May seemed no closer to the end. She started to walk faster, and then began to run. She had to get there before the Master finished talking, before his poison took her foster parents and everyone she knew.

Faster and faster, boot heels drumming, breath rasping, but still cold, cold as ice. She felt like she was pushing against a barrier, that at any moment it would break and she would be free of the endless corridor.

It did break. Alice May burst out into a smoking room, one full of Servants, a long room packed with black-and-red uniforms.

Alice May's hands and eyes started shooting before she even knew where she was. The rifle was empty in what seemed like only seconds, but each bullet had struck home. Servants slumped in their chairs, writhed on the ground, dived for cover, clutched at weapons.

Alice May flung the rifle aside and drew a revolver, a movement so fast that to the shocked Servants, the rifle appeared to transform in her hands. Six more Servants died as their nemesis fanned the hammer with her left hand, the shots sounding together in one terrible instant.

Alice May holstered one revolver and drew the other, right hand and left hand in perfect, opposite motion. But there was no one left to shoot. Gun smoke mixed with cigar and pipe smoke, swirling up into the ceiling fans. Servants coughed out their final bloody breaths, and the last screams died away.

So this is what they mean by a charnel house, thought Alice May as she surveyed the room, calmly watching from somewhere deep inside herself as some other part of her watched the final shudders and convulsions of dying men and women, amidst the blood and brains and urine that spread and soaked into the once-blue carpet.

Her hands—but not her hands, because surely hers would be shaking—reloaded her revolvers as she watched. Then they picked up the rifle and reloaded that.

The door opened at the far end of the smoking room. Alice May caught a brief glimpse of the Master's back, caught a few of his shouted words, all of them tinged with the hint of a scream.

Her rifle came up as a young woman in black and red entered the room.

It was Jane. Alice May knew it was Jane, and still her finger tightened around the trigger.

"Hello, Alice May," said Jane. She didn't look at the newly dead around her, or bother to step back from the spreading pool of blood. "The Master said you would come. I'm to stop you, he said, because you won't shoot your own sister."

She smiled and picked up a pistol from the table. Its previous owner had slid underneath, leaving a wet trail of blood and skin and guts against the back of his chair.

Alice May's finger pulled the trigger and she shot Jane. Only a last desperate exertion of will twitched her aim away from her sister's chest to her right arm.

"The Master is always right," said Jane. Her right arm hung at her side, her black sleeve torn apart, chips of white bone strewn along it.

"No," said Alice May, as Jane stepped across the room and picked up another pistol with her left hand. "The Master's wrong, Jane. I have shot you. I will shoot you again. I . . . I can't help it. Don't—"

"The Master is always right," repeated Jane, with serene confidence. She started to raise the pistol.

This time, Alice May wasn't strong enough to resist the inexorable pull of the rifle. It swung steadily to point at Jane's chest, and it could not be turned aside.

The shot sounded louder than any of the others, and its effect was more terrible. Jane was knocked off her feet. She was dead before she even joined the piled-up bodies on the floor.

Alice May stepped over the corpses and knelt by Jane. Tears slid from her dress like rain from glass. The white cloth could not be stained. It turned the blood and broken flesh aside, just as it had the dust.

But her hands were different, thought Alice May. Her hands would never be clean.

"Nothing ever happens in Denilburg," whispered Alice May.

She stood up and opened the door to the rear balcony. To the gathered town, and the Master.

He was shouting as she came out, his arms high above his head, coming down to pound the railing so hard that it shivered under his fists.

Alice May didn't listen to what he said. She pointed her rifle at the back of his head and pulled the trigger.

A dry, pathetic click was the only result. Alice May worked the lever. A round ejected, brass tinkling and rolling off the balcony onto the rails below. She pulled the trigger again, still with no result.

The Master stopped speaking and turned to face her.

Alice May's star burst into light. She had to shield her eyes with the rifle so she could see.

The Master didn't look like much, up close. He was shorter than Alice May, and his goatee was ridiculous. He was just a funny little man.

Till you looked into his eyes.

Alice May wished she hadn't. His eyes were like the endless corridor, stretching back to some nameless place, a void where nothing human could possibly exist.

"So you killed your sister," said the Master. His voice was almost a purr, the screaming and shouting gone. There was no doubt that everyone outside the train could still hear him. He had a voice that carried when he wanted it to, without effort. "You killed Jane Elizabeth Suky Hopkins. Just like you killed Everett Kale, Jim Bushby, Rosco O'Faln, Hubert Jenks, and Old Man Lacker. Not to mention my people inside. You'd kill the whole town to get to me, wouldn't you?"

Alice May didn't answer, though she heard the crowd shuffle and gasp. She dropped the rifle and drew a revolver. Or tried to. It stayed stuck fast in its holster. She tried the left-hand gun, but it was stuck too.

"Not that easy, is it?" whispered the Master, leaning across to speak to her alone. His breath smelled like the room she had left behind. Of blood and shit and terror. "There are rules, you know, between your kind and mine. You can't draw until I do. And fast as you are, you can't be as fast as me. It'll all be for nothing. All the deaths. All the blood on your hands."

Alice May stepped back to give him room. She didn't dare look at the crowd, or at the Master's eyes again. She looked at his hands instead.

"You can give in, you know," whispered the Master. "Take your sister's place, in my service. Even in my bed. She enjoyed that, you know. You would too."

The Master licked his lips. Alice May didn't look at his long, pointed, leathery tongue. She watched his hands.

He edged back a little, still whispering.

"No? This is your last chance, Alice May. Join me, and everything will turn out for the best. No one will blame you for killing Jane or the others. Why, I'll give you a—"

His hand flickered. Alice May drew.

Both of them fired at the same time. Alice May didn't even know where his gun had come from. She felt something strike her chest a savage blow and she was rammed back into the balcony rail. But she kept her revolver trained dead-center on the Master, and her left hand fanned the hammer as she pulled the trigger one . . . two . . . three . . . four . . . five times.

Then the revolver was empty. Alice May let it fall, and she fell herself, clutching her chest. She couldn't breathe. Her heart hammered with the knowledge that she'd been shot, that these were her last few seconds of life.

Something fell into her hand. It was hot, scorching hot. She gazed at it stupidly as it burned into her palm. Eventually she saw it was a bullet, a misshapen projectile that was not lead but some sort of white and pallid stone.

Alice May dropped it, though not quickly enough to avoid a burn deep enough to scar. She tried to breathe again, and could, though there was a sharp, stabbing pain in her lungs.

She looked at her chest, expecting to see blood. But her waistcoat was as clean as ever, save for a small round hole on the right-hand side, exactly parallel with the dimming silver star on the left. Gingerly, Alice May reached in. But her hands felt only the woven hair. There was no hole in her undershirt, and no blood.

Alice May sat up. The Master was lying on his back on the far side of the balcony. He looked just like a small, dead man now. The dread that Alice May had felt before was gone.

She crawled over, but before she could touch

him, his flesh began to quiver and move. It crawled and shivered, his face changing color from a reddish pink to a dull silver. Then the Master's flesh began to liquefy, to become quicksilver in fact as well as color. The liquid splashed out of his clothes and dribbled across the floor into a six-spoked bronze drain hole in the corner. Soon there was nothing left of him but a small automatic pistol, a pile of clothing, and a pair of empty boots.

Alice May looked out on the crowd. It was already breaking up. People were taking off their Servants' uniforms, even down to their underwear. Others were simply walking away. All had their heads downcast, and no one was talking.

Alice May stood up, her hands pressed against her ribs to ease the pain. She looked out on the crowd for her foster parents, for her surviving uncle Bill.

She saw them, but like everybody else, they would not look toward her. Their backs were turned, and they had their eyes set firmly toward the town.

Jake and Stella held each other tightly and walked down the main street. They did not look back. Uncle Bill sidled toward the platform. For a moment Alice May thought he was going to look at her. But he didn't.

Alice May watched them walk away and felt them take whoever she had been with them.

The fourth Hopkins girl, like the third, was dead to Denilburg.

Listlessly, she picked up her rifle and revolver and reloaded them. Her bullet belt was almost empty now.

She was surprised when the engine whistled, but only for a moment. She had entered this life on a train. It seemed only fitting to leave it the same way.

The train gave a stuttering lurch. Smoke billowed overhead, and the wheels screeched for a grip. Alice May opened the balcony door and went inside. The smoking room had disappeared, taking Jane and all the other bodies with it. There was the endless corridor again, and at her feet the steamer trunk.

Alice May picked up one end of the trunk, opened the first compartment door she came to, and dragged it in.

From the platform Uncle Bill the stationmaster watched the train slowly pull away. Before it got to the cutting, it veered off to a branch line that wasn't there and disappeared into the mouth of a tunnel that faded away as the private car passed into its darkness.

Bill wiped a tear from his eye, for a friend who had borne the same name, for a town that had lost its innocence, and for his almost-daughter, who had paid the price for saving them all.

INTRODUCTION TO MY NEW REALLY EPIC FANTASY SERIES

This began life as a spoken-word piece that I wrote for a panel session at the 1999 Worldcon in Melbourne, Australia. I learned long ago that if possible, it's best to read something short and funny to an audience, rather than parts of longer, serious works. It's usually best to avoid pieces with lots of dialogue as well, unless you're gifted at doing different voices or are a trained actor.

So I wrote this piece, notionally about the new epic fantasy series I'm going to write. Given that it would be delivered to extremely well-read fantasy readers, I thought they would appreciate some gentle fun being poked at some of the stereotypes and peculiarities of the genre. I took the added precaution of apologizing in advance to some of the authors whose titles I had playfully manipulated, just in case any rabid fans took exception. Or the authors themselves, as at least one was there.

The piece went over well at Worldcon, so I

have repeated it a few times here and there and eventually put it up on my website. I never expected that this would prompt a few readers to e-mail me, one suggesting that I shouldn't write such a long series of books because it would take too long and I should be writing more stories set in the Old Kingdom; and another wanting to know when the first of the forty-seven novels would be coming out as they wanted to know what happened to the boy with eyes the color of mud who swam with dolphins.

Somehow, e-mailing to explain that the article is a joke took some of the fun out of it. I trust I will not need to do so again. . . .

My New Really Epic Fantasy Series

I'M GOING TO READ the prologue from my new forty-seven-book epic fantasy series, which is currently titled *The Garbeliad*. The titles of the individual books include:

Book One: *A Time of Wheels*
Book Two: *A Throne of Games*
Book Three: *The Dragon Who Died Young*
Book Four: *The Sorcerer's Thirty-seven Apprentices*
Book Five: *The Witch Wardrobe of Lyon*
Book Six: *The Dark Is Falling*
Book Seven: *The Seventh Book*
Book Eight: *The Return of the Mistakenly Purchased King*

To tell the truth, I'm not entirely sure about the other thirty-nine books yet, though I'm toying with *The Book Whose Title Must Not Be Spoken* for Book Twenty-six. You know, to keep the series sort of atmospheric and spooky.

Anyway, I decided that before I wrote this series, I'd analyze the components of successful epic fantasy. Like when to have the ultimate evil first be mentioned and so on—should it be page forty-two or page sixty-seven? And one thing I discovered pretty early on is that you need to have a prologue and preferably a prophecy as well. A bird's-eye view of something is a bonus, and you can add that in if you like, but it's not essential.

So this is the prologue and prophecy from the first book of my new fifty-eight-book series—I just decided I'd need another eleven books to do it properly; forty-seven isn't enough.

PROLOGUE: FROM THE SECRET LEDGER OF THE ACCOUNTANT

HIGH ABOVE THE DUSTY plains, an eagle whose wings stretched from side to side soared and soared and . . . soared. Its eagle eyes focused on the ground below, seeking out tasty vihar-vihar rabbits.

Then a glitter caught its eye. Not the glitter of dull vihar-vihar rabbits. No, this was metal, not fur.

The eagle folded the wings that went from side to side and dropped like an eagle that has stopped flying. Down and down and down it plummeted, until two hundred three feet and seven inches above the ground its wings snapped out. The eagle stopped in midair.

When it recovered from the shock of stopping so suddenly, the great bird of prey, the raptor of the skies, the lord of the birds, saw that the glitter came from a metal badge. A metal badge that was fastened to a brim. The brim of a hat. A hat that was on a head. A head that was connected to a body. The body of a man who was a traveler. This was not a vihar-vihar rabbit. This was not food. Still, the eagle circled in a soaring sort of way, watching and listening. For this eagle had not always been an eagle. It had once been an egg. But even so, it had the gift of tongues and could understand human speech. It could speak it too, though badly. It had a stutter because its beak was bent.

This is what the eagle heard when the man with the metal badge on the brim of his hat began to speak to the other men who didn't have metal badges and thus didn't glitter in a way that attracted the attention of eagles that soar.

What the Man with the Metal Badge on the Brim of His Hat Said:

Gather round, unpleasant acquaintances, and partly listen to a tale of our knuckle-dragging forebears and the battles they ran away from. Our recorded history goes back some three weeks to the time that Sogren the Extremely Drunk burned down the museum. But I remember tales older still . . . going back almost ten years, to the time when Amoss the Stupidly Generous gave the Midwinter Party with the ice-skating accident.

Know that this is a story before even that—back to the almost legendary but still quite believable times of twenty years ago. The time when rumor reached the Lower Kingdoms of a new, dark power growing without aid of fertilizer in the north. The name of the "Overlord" was spoken softly for the first time in secret and troubled councils. In many dark corners lips whispered it, and then trembled with the effort of not laughing.

For the Overlord's name was Cecil and he was

known to have a lisp. Naturally enough, he preferred to be referred to as "Overlord," and whenever his agents heard his true name spoken, dire retribution would swiftly follow. No one was safe. The merest innocent mention of the word *Cecil* would result in hideous and usually magical destruction of everyone within hearing distance.

Within days of the first outbreak, the town of Cecil was completely vaporized, and poor unfortunates who had been baptized Cecil were forced to change their names to Ardraven or Belochnazar or other wimpish monikers lacking the macho virility of their own true names.

How is it that I dare to mention the word *Cecil* to you now? I have this amulet, which magically erases the word *Cecil* from the minds of listeners after ten minutes have passed. Instead, you will remember a conversation littered with small chiming sounds where the word *Cecil* has been erased.

But I digress. Where was I? Yes. Frantic messages from the Dwarves went unanswered, as their messenger service took so long to walk over the mountains that they weren't actually received until three years after the dire warnings they contained were sent. In any case, Falanor and Eminholme were unprepared to send men to war. Instead, they offered a troop of armored monkeys and the entire population of a reform school for small children.

This elite force went into the mountains and never returned alive. However, they did come back dead, even more horrible than before and in the service of Cecil . . . I mean the Overlord.

Shocked, the kingdoms ordered a massive mobilization, and the kings had extra horses harnessed to their personal escape chariots. Yet even as they extracted the most valuable items from their treasuries, many feared it would be too late.

The forces of Cecil were on the march. Slowly, it is true, for dead Dwarves march even slower than live ones. Yet it became clear to the minds of the Wise that within the next seventeen years something must be done.

But it seemed that there was no power in the south that could resist the Overlord. For he was the mightiest sorcerer in his age bracket, the winner of all the gold medals in the Games of the Seventeenth Magiad. He was also a champion shotputter, who practiced with the skulls of his enemies filled with lead. And his teams of goblin synchronized swimmers could cross any moat, could emerge at any time in private swimming pools, or even infiltrate via the drains, dressed in clown suits. No one was safe.

It was then that the Wise remembered the words written on the silver salad bowl they had been using for official luncheons the last hundred years. It was brought from the kitchens, and despite the scratches and dents from serving utensils, the Wise could still make out the runes that said "Sibyl Prophecy Plate. Made in Swychborgen-orgen-sorgen-lorgen exclusively for aeki."

The other side appeared completely blank. But when olive oil was drizzled upon it, strange runes appeared around the rim. Slowly, letter by letter, the Wise began to spell it out.

"A s-a-i-l-o-r w-e-n-t t-o s-e-a s-e-a s-e-a t-o s-e-e w-h-a-t h-e c-o-u-l-d s-e-e s-e-e s-e-e."

Days went by, then weeks, then months, as you would expect. If it was the other way around, it would be a sign that the Overlord had already triumphed. Finally the Wise puzzled out the entire prophecy.

A sailor went to sea sea sea to see what
he could see see see
But all that he could see see see

Was the bottom of the deep blue
sea sea sea

The meaning of this prophecy was immediately clear to the Wise. They knew that somewhere in the Lower Kingdoms a boy would be born, a sailor who would use the power of the sea to defeat the Overlord. A boy with eyes as black as the bottom of the deep blue sea. A boy who might even have vestigial gills and some scales or maybe a sort of fin along his back.

But the Wise also knew that the Overlord would know the prophecy too, for his spies were everywhere, particularly among the waiters at the Wise Club. They knew that he knew that they knew that he knew.

They all knew that the Wise must find the boy with the power of the sea at his command first, and take him somewhere where he could grow up with no knowledge of his powers or his destiny. They must find him before the Overlord did, for he would try to turn the boy to the powers of darkness.

But who was the boy? Where was the boy? Was there a second salad bowl, a second verse to the prophecy, long lost to the Wise but known to an aged crone in the forest of Haz-chyllen-boken-woken, close by the sea, where a small boy with eyes the color of dark mud swam with the dolphins?

Yes, there was.

INTRODUCTION TO THREE ROSES

I wrote this story the day before I needed to read something at an event in Melbourne in late 1997. The occasion was the annual celebration organized by Australian children's literature champion Agnes Nieuwenhuizen for librarians, teachers, and book aficionados, and this one was entitled "An Enchanted Evening." Half a dozen authors were to speak, each reading or telling a story about love or in some way related to love.

I don't know why I wrote a story about a dead wife, since at that time I was single, I had never been married, nor had I ever had a significant partner die. I also don't know why it came out as a fable or fairy tale. Part of it was written on a plane, and part in a hotel room. It wasn't even typed when I read it for the first time at "An Enchanted Evening."

But it surely was a tale of love, and the evening was indeed enchanted, as I met my future wife, Anna, there. So perhaps it is the most important story I have ever written, for the greatest reward.

THREE ROSES

THIS IS THE STORY of a gardener who grew the most beautiful single rose the world had ever seen. It was a black rose, which was unlikely, and it bloomed the whole year round, which was impossible.

Hearing of this rose, the King decided to see it for himself. With his entourage, he rode for seven days to the gardener's simple cottage. On the morning of the seventh day, he arrived and saw the rose. It was even more beautiful than the King had imagined, and he wanted it.

"How did you come to grow such a beautiful rose?" the King asked the gardener, who was standing silently by.

"I planted that rose on the day my wife died," replied the gardener, looking only at the flower. "It is a true, deep black, the very color of her hair. The rose grew from my love of her."

The King turned to his servants and said,

"Uproot this rosebush and take it to the palace. It is too beautiful for anyone but me."

But when the rosebush was transplanted to the palace, it lasted only a year before it withered and died. The King, who had gazed upon it every day, angrily decided that it was the gardener's fault, and he set out at once to punish him.

But when he arrived at the gardener's cottage, he was amazed to see a new rosebush growing there, with a single rose. But this rose was green, and even more beautiful than the black rose.

The King once again asked the gardener how he came to grow such a beautiful rose.

"I planted this rose on the anniversary of my wife's death," said the gardener, his eyes only on the rose. "It is the color of her eyes, which I looked into every morning. The rose grew from my love of her."

"Take it!" commanded the King, and he turned away to ride the seven days back to his palace. Such a beautiful flower was not fit for a common man.

The green rose bloomed for two years, and the King looked upon it every day, for it brought him great contentment. Then, one morning, it was dead, the bush withered, the petals fallen to the ground. The King picked up the petals and spoke to no one for two days. Then he said, as if to convince himself, "The gardener will have another rose."

So once again he rode off with his entourage. This time, they took a spade and the palace jardinier.

Such was the King's impatience that they rode for half the nights as well as days, but there were wrong turns and flooded bridges, and it still took seven days before he once again rode up to the gardener's cottage. And there was a new rosebush, with a single rose. A red rose, so beautiful that the King's men were struck silent and the King himself could only stare and gesture to the palace jardinier to take it away.

Even though the King didn't ask, the gardener spoke before the spade broke the earth around the bush.

"I planted this rose three years after the death of my wife," he said. "It is the color of her lips, which I first kissed under a harvest moon on the hottest of summer nights. This rose grew from my love of her."

The King seemed not to hear but kept staring at the rose. Finally, he tore his gaze away and turned his horse for home.

The jardinier watched him go and stopped digging for a moment.

"Your roses are the most beautiful I have ever seen," he said. "They could only grow from a great love. But why grow them only to have these memories taken from you?"

The gardener smiled and said, "I need nothing to remind me of my wife. When I walk alone under the night sky, I see the blackness of her hair. When the light catches the green glass of a bottle, I see her eyes. When the sun is setting all red against the hills and the wind touches my cheek, I feel her kiss.

"I grew the first rose because I was afraid I might forget. When it was gone, I knew that I had lost nothing. No one can take the memory of my love."

The jardinier frowned, and he began to cut again with his spade. Then he asked, "But why do you keep growing the roses?"

"I grow them for the King," said the gardener. "He has no memories of his own, no love. And after all, they are only flowers."

INTRODUCTION TO ENDINGS

This is one of those odd stories that come out of nowhere. It was written in one sitting and then revisited numerous times over several years as I tried to make it work. Finally, when I thought it did work, I wasn't sure what I could do with it, as it was very short. Fortunately, a year or so after I felt it was done, an opportunity arose for it to be the final story in the anthology *Gothic!*, edited by Deborah Noyes. As a kind of coda for the whole collection, it found its place in the world.

I was particularly pleased (and surprised) that this story also then went on to be selected for the inaugural volume of *The Year's Best Science Fiction & Fantasy for Teens*, edited by Jane Yolen and Patrick Nielsen Hayden. It'll be interesting to see if they put it at the end, as at the time of this writing I haven't seen that book.

If they do put it at the end, as it is in this book, I can draw all the wrong conclusions (like a Hollywood studio looking at last summer's hits) and will immediately begin work on a story called "Beginnings" and another one called "Middlings," in order to maximize my chances of inclusion in future collections.

ENDINGS

I HAVE TWO SWORDS. One is named Sorrow and the other Joy. These are not their real names. I do not think there is anyone alive who knows even the letters that are etched into the blue-black blades.

I know, but then I am not alive. Yet not dead. Something in between, hovering in the twilight, betwixt wakefulness and sleep, caught on the boundary, pinned to the board, unable to go back, unable to go forward.

I do rest, but it is not sleep and I do not dream. I simply remember, the memories tumbling over one another, mixing and joining and mingling till I do not know when or where or how or why, and by nightfall it is unbearable and I rise from my troubled bed to howl at the moon or pace the corridors. . . .

Or sit beneath the swords in the old cane chair, waiting for the chance of a visitor, the chance of change, the chance . . .

I have two daughters. One is named Sorrow and the other Joy.

These are not their real names. I do not think even they remember what they were called in the far-distant days of their youth. Neither they nor I can recall their mother's name, though sometimes in my daytime reveries I catch a glimpse of her face, the feel of her skin, the taste of her mouth, the swish of a sleeve as she leaves the room and my memory.

They are hungrier than I, my daughters, and still have the thirst for blood.

This story has two endings. One is named Sorrow and the other Joy.

This is the first ending:

A great hero comes to my house without caution, as the sun falls. He is in the prime of life, tall and strong and arrogant. He meets my daughters in the garden, where they stand in the shade of the great oak. Two steps away lies the last sunlight, and he is clever enough to make use of that, and strong. There is pretended *amour* on both sides, and fangs strike true. Yet the hero is swifter with his silvered knife, and the sun is too close.

Silver poisons, and fire burns, and that is the finish of Sorrow and the end of Joy.

Weakened, the hero staggers on, intent on finishing the epic that will be written about him. He finds me in the cane chair, and above me Sorrow and Joy.

I give him the choice and tell him the names.

He chooses Sorrow, not realizing that this is what he chooses for himself, and the blades are aptly named.

I do not feel sorrow for him, or for my daughters, but only for myself.

I do drink his blood. It has been a long time . . . and he was a hero.

This is the second ending:

A young man not yet old enough to be a hero, great or small, comes to my garden with the dawn. He watches me through the window, and though I delay, at last I must shuffle out of the cane chair, toward my bed.

There are bones at my feet, and a skull, the flesh long gone. I do not know whose bones they are. There are many skulls and bones about this house.

The boy enters through the window, borne on a shaft of sunlight. I pause in the shadowed doorway to watch as he examines the swords. His lips move, puzzling out what is written there, or so I must suppose. Perhaps no alphabet or language is ever really lost, as long as some of it survives.

He will get no help from that ancient script, from that ancient life.

I call out the names I have given the swords, but he does not answer.

I do not see which weapon he chooses. Already memories rush at me, push at me, buffet and surround me. I do not know what has happened or will happen or might happen.

I am in my bed. The youth stands over me, the point of a sword pricking at my chest.

It is Joy and, I think, chosen through wisdom, not by luck. Who would have thought it of a boy not yet old enough to shave?

The steel is cold. Final. Yet only dust bubbles from the wound.

Then comes the second blow, to the dry bones of the neck.

I have been waiting a long time for this ending.

Waiting for someone to choose for me.

To give me Joy instead of Sorrow.

ENTER THE WORLDS OF

GARTH NIX

THE ABHORSEN TRILOGY

SABRIEL
Hc 0-06-027322-4
Pb 0-06-447183-7
Pb rack 0-06-057581-6

LIRAEL
Hc 0-06-027823-4
Pb 0-06-000542-4
Pb rack 0-06-059016-5

ABHORSEN
Hc 0-06-027825-0
Pb 0-06-052873-7
Pb rack 0-06-059498-5

THE RAGWITCH
Pb rack 0-06-050807-8

SHADE'S CHILDREN
Hc 0-06-027324-0
Pb rack 0-06-447196-9

An Imprint of HarperCollins*Publishers*
www.harperteen.com